CARNEGIE'S MAID

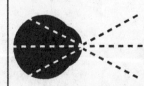

CARNEGIE'S MAID

MARIE BENEDICT

THORNDIKE PRESS
A part of Gale, a Cengage Company

GALE
A Cengage Company

Farmington Hills, Mich • San Francisco • New York • Waterville, Maine
Meriden, Conn • Mason, Ohio • Chicago

Copyright © 2018 by Marie Benedict.
Andrew Carnegie's memo used as published in *Autobiography of Andrew Carnegie,* published in 1920 by Houghton Mifflin Company.
Text is in the public domain.
Thorndike Press, a part of Gale, a Cengage Company.

LIBRARY OF CONGRESS CIP DATA ON FILE.
CATALOGUING IN PUBLICATION FOR THIS BOOK
IS AVAILABLE FROM THE LIBRARY OF CONGRESS.

ISBN-13: 978-1-4328-4703-6 (hardcover)

Published in 2018 by arrangement with Sourcebooks, Inc.

Printed in Mexico
1 2 3 4 5 6 7 22 21 20 19 18

CARNEGIE'S MAID

PROLOGUE

December 23, 1868
New York, New York

The gentle melody of a Christmas song lifted into the air of his study from the street below. The music did nothing to change his mood or his actions. Ensconced behind the black walnut desk in his luxuriously appointed St. Nicholas Hotel suite, fountain pen in hand, Andrew Carnegie wrote like a madman.

He paused, searching for the correct word. Glancing around the study lit by the very latest in gaslights, he saw it as if anew. The walls were hung with a heavy, yellow brocade wallpaper, and dark-green velvet curtains framed the windows, tied back by heavy, gold cords, affording him a fine view of Broadway. He knew this suite was superior to any found in America or even Europe. Yet this fact, which had so pleased him

7

during his earlier visits to New York, now repulsed him. The curtain's gold cords seemed like binding ropes, and he felt trapped inside a rarefied prison.

He had argued with his mother that they should stay elsewhere, somewhere less ostentatious. He longed to reside somewhere that was not haunted by memories of Clara, although he did not say that aloud. It no longer seemed right to stay at the St. Nicholas, not without her. He had spent the better part of a year searching for her, with no success. Not even the detectives, his top security men, or bounty hunters — the best in the business — could locate a hint of her trail.

But his mother would have none of it. *Andra,* she called him in her inimitable brogue, *the trappings of wealth are the Carnegies' right and due, and by God, we will secure our place.* He acquiesced, depleted of the energy to argue. But on their arrival at the St. Nicholas Hotel earlier that day, Andrew had taken the extraordinary step of banishing his mother to her adjoining suite of rooms and ignoring her pleas that they attend a holiday dinner at the Vanderbilts, an invitation to the near-highest echelon of New York City society that had been hard-won. He needed to be alone with his thoughts of Clara.

Clara. He whispered her name, letting it roll over his tongue like a fine cordial. In the privacy of his study, he let his very first memory of her wash over him. Clara had trailed behind his mother into the parlor of Fairfield, their Pittsburgh home, with a step so light that he barely noticed the tap of her shoes or the swish of her skirts as she crossed the room. Her demure manner and averted gaze did nothing to draw his attention until his mother had barked out some order in Clara's direction. Only then, when Clara lifted her eyes and met his square on, did her presence register. In that fleeting moment, before she quickly lowered her eyes again, he witnessed the sharp intelligence that lay beneath the placid demeanor required for a lady's maid.

Other, more intimate memories of Clara began to take hold, along with a longing so intense, it caused him physical pain. But then a roar of laughter and the clink of crystal glasses from the Grand Dining Room below his study interrupted his reverie. He wondered who might be celebrating in that gilded room. Could it be one of his business colleagues visiting from out of town, or perhaps one of the elusive "upper ten" families deigning to leave their cosseted, insular world of brownstone dinners to peer into the latest in sumptuous New York City dining establishments? Should he go downstairs to see?

Stop, he chastised himself. *This is precisely the sort of status-seeking, greedy thinking that Clara would have loathed.* He had vowed to her that he would carve out a different path from those materialistic industrialists and society folk, and he would keep that vow, even though she was gone. He returned to his mission of honoring her, one he'd attempted countless times as he drafted and redrafted this document. Pressing the tip of the fountain pen so hard that the ink bled through the fragile paper, he wrote:

Thirty-three and an income of $50,000 per annum! By this time two years I can so arrange all my business as to secure at least $50,000 per annum. Beyond this never earn — make no effort to increase fortune, but spend the surplus each year for benevolent purposes. Cast aside business forever, except for others.

Settle in Oxford and get a thorough education, making the acquaintance of literary men — this will take three years' active work — pay especial attention to speaking in public. Settle then in London and purchase a controlling interest in some newspaper or live review and give the general management of it attention, taking a part in public matters, especially those connected with education and improvement of the poorer classes.

Man must have an idol — the amassing of wealth is one of the worst species of idolatry — no idol more debasing than the worship of money. Whatever I engage in I must push inordinately; therefore should I be careful to choose that life which will be the most elevating in its character. To continue much longer overwhelmed by business cares and with most of my thoughts wholly upon the way to make more money in the shortest time, must degrade me beyond hope of permanent recovery. I will resign business at thirty-five, but during the ensuing two years I wish to spend the afternoons in receiving instruction and in reading systematically.

Lifting the pen from the paper, Andrew read. The words were rough and imperfectly formed, but he was satisfied. Although God had willed that he could not have Clara, he would brandish her beliefs like a sword. He

11

would worship the idols of status and money — for their own sake — no longer. Instead, he would amass and utilize reputation and money for one higher purpose only: the betterment of others, particularly the creation of ladders for the immigrants of his adopted land to climb. Through the heavy fog of his despair, Andrew permitted himself the smallest of smiles, the tiniest of appeasements. The letter would have pleased his Clara.

CHAPTER ONE

November 4, 1863
Philadelphia, Pennsylvania

I shouldn't be here. Cecelia or Eliza could have been swaying on this stinking vessel instead of me. It was their right — Eliza's duty anyway, as the eldest daughter — to make the voyage and take the chance on a new land. But Mum and Dad offered a litany of excuses for my sisters — the twenty-one-year-old Eliza was on the brink of a marriage that would allow the family to keep our farm tenancy intact, a status that had eluded me due to my overcleverness, Dad said, and Cecelia was too young for the voyage at fifteen and too weak-spirited in any event — and so, knowing my parents were right, I boarded the *Envoy* in their place. Forty-two days later, I regretted the preening and arrogance to which I subjected my sisters when I'd learned of my parents' decision. I knew now that being considered my parents' *síofra* — their changeling capable of transmuting into whatever America required — was no prize. And I desperately missed my sisters.

Light snuck through the hatch into the steerage cabin, blinding me for a moment. My eyes closed spontaneously. Even as the light faded a bit, I chose to keep my eyes shut, surrendering to the remnants of the sun's heat. I wanted the fading rays to burn me clean. I wanted them to burn away the sour smell of the long Atlantic passage and the recurrent tears of leave-taking.

The steward clanged the ship's bell to signal our disembarking. I opened my eyes and reluctantly glanced around the cabin. Mothers with listless infants in their arms pushed themselves to standing, while their older, hollow-eyed children clung to their skirts, scared by the relentless ringing of the bell. Fathers and old men struggled to smooth their filthy, rumpled suits into some sad approximation of dignity. Only the few young men, the *fir òga,* were strong enough — and eager enough — to readily form a queue.

The journey had been rough, taking its toll on even the *fir òga.* Nearly three weeks prior, after an already tumultuous crossing,

14

a storm hit the *Envoy*, tumbling those of us in steerage out of our beds into a hold with two feet of water. As the crew and my fellow passengers began working the pump in the pitch-dark of the moonless night, the ship began rolling from side to side like the heavy log it was, causing one Dublin girl of about sixteen, traveling alone like myself, to crash into one of the wooden posts keeping the ceiling firm above our heads. Moaning as she fell with a splash onto the still-flooded floor, she never regained consciousness. When she died the next morning, the captain sent the first mate and a sailor to steerage to sew her up in a sheet, with some rocks at her feet to weigh her down, and throw her overboard without a single word or prayer. This loss and her treatment bore heavily upon me, upon all of us really, as it seemed a portent of the treatment we might expect in the new land.

Footsteps clapped on the wooden deck above our heads, followed by the thud and drag of trunks. My cabinmates rushed to assemble their meager belongings: rucksacks, wicker baskets, tools, treasured pictures, and Bibles, even the odd battered trunk. But I knew we needn't hurry. We would bide our time until all the other classes had left the ship. Steerage always waited: for the dry biscuits, putrid water, and rancid oatmeal that serve as sustenance; for sleep uninterrupted by hacking coughs and crying babies; for air uncontaminated with the stink of vomit and full chamber pots; for storms to break and the hatch to be unlocked to grant us a few blissful moments above deck; for privacy that never came.

I was tired of waiting, but we had no choice but to stand in the queue, immobile but for the rocking of the ship in the harbor. I glanced at the young mother beside me, her tattered brown dress stained with the evidence of her baby's constant seasickness. At seventeen or so, she was a couple of years younger than my nineteen years, but her eyes looked older. There, lines had given way to furrows. All alone throughout this terrible voyage, she bore the weight not only of her own worries and suffering, but also those of her child. I felt ashamed at wallowing in my own discomfort and longing for home.

"*Ádh mór,*" I said, having nothing to offer her and her baby but luck. No worries here that we'd receive tallies on our *bata scóir* for speaking Irish instead of English and then receive the corresponding punishment, as teachers at the hedge schools for the Irish were instructed to do. Not that this poor mother had ever been beaten for speaking Irish in school, as it wasn't likely that she'd attended school of any sort.

She looked surprised at my words. I'd maintained my distance from fellow passengers, at Mum's request, and this young mother and I had never spoken. This separation kept me healthy if unpopular among my gregarious countrymen, who resented my standoffishness. Too weary to speak, she nodded her thanks.

The hatch flew open, and crisp, salty air filled the cabin. I inhaled deeply, and for a long minute, the fresh breeze was enough. The air smelled of home, and I gulped it down hungrily.

"Line up, people!" The steward yelled at us. His pinched, sallow face had terrorized steerage for forty-two days, withholding food, water, and deck time if he deemed us not compliant enough. If he didn't hold the power to deny us admission to our new land, I would have shared with him my thoughts on his cruelty. I'd refuse to still my tongue as Mum and Dad often chided me to do.

We tidied the queue and waited again. Some silent signal finally reached the steward, and he motioned for us to climb the stairs and mount the deck. Single file, we left the stinking pit of steerage for the last time and walked into the muted light of the Philadelphia harbor.

The gangway leading to shore felt unsteady underfoot, as did the rocky ground once I reached land. It felt almost as if the earth was rocking rather than the ship. My legs seemed to have grown more accustomed to the swaying of sea than the constancy of land.

Black-uniformed officials guided us into a building labeled *Lazaretto.* In the long, dark nights, my shipmates had spoken with fear of Lazaretto, a quarantine station. From relatives' earlier crossings, they had learned that any sign of illness in the ship's passengers could mean weeks or months at Lazaretto, a place where people often entered well and left sick. Or worse.

I didn't worry that I harbored some disease. Mum's instructions kept me safe. Even so, I'd heard too much coughing to think the rest of the passengers were brimming with health, and our fates rose and fell with one another. If the inspector found one contagion in one steerage passenger, it was in his discretion to hold all of us at Lazaretto until every last person in steerage recovered.

One by one, we moved up in line toward the health inspectors. I winced as the officials inspected my cabinmates like they were Dad's farm animals, lifting up their gums and eyelids for signs of disease, sifting through their hair for evidence of lice or other vermin, examining their skin and fingernails for yellow fever or cholera, and pawing through their belongings. Any infraction could be enough to condemn us all to Lazaretto, and I said a silent Hail Mary that the toddler prone to coughing all night managed to keep quiet.

The line shifted forward, and it was my turn. I took off my crumpled bonnet and heather-gray outer coat, extended my arms, and submitted my body for examination.

"You look well enough," a heavily bearded inspector said in my ear as he unpinned my heavy, dark-red hair. The gesture and the whisper felt strangely intimate and wholly inappropriate. But I couldn't object. It could ruin everything for which Mum and Dad sent me here. It could render useless all the sacrifices made to pay for my ticket.

I nodded in acknowledgment, as if his remark were perfectly fine. Just a simple statement on my health. But my hands shook as I repinned my hair, and he continued his review of my skin. Only when he

19

turned his attention to my rucksack did my shallow, fast breathing slow.

With the shadow of a smile, he waved me forward. It seemed I'd passed the test, but what of my shipmates?

With the rest of steerage, I was herded into a large, dingy waiting room that reeked of unwashed bodies and urine. Once again, we waited. I promised myself that, if I ever made it through Lazaretto and onto American soil, I would not wait anymore.

After another long hour, during which passengers trickled in and anxiety mounted, a bell rang. Old men and tired mothers and young children looked at one another quizzically. Should we know what it meant?

Finally, a door slammed open, and a thick shaft of light entered the room. "Welcome to America," a bespectacled official announced.

Even though no one spoke, the relief in the room was audible, like a collective exhalation. We assembled into the last line we would ever form together and walked outside into the American daylight.

I breathed in hope.

All around me, I heard cries of reunion as my fellow passengers fell into the arms of their waiting relatives. But I walked on. No one was waiting for me.

CHAPTER TWO

November 4, 1863
Philadelphia, Pennsylvania

I walked with purpose. I hadn't a clue where I was headed, but I couldn't afford any hesitation that marked me as weak. Even in our small Galway village outside of Tuam, we heard rumors of immigrants who, upon landing in America, had been victimized by sharpers, unscrupulous men engaged in all manner of trials, plots, and chicanery. I'd talked a brash game to my family and friends when Mum and Dad decided I'd be the one to emigrate, but now, I wondered how I would fare in this strange land.

Except for the cry of seagulls and the clop of horses, this harbor didn't sound anything like the harbors in Galway. The fishmongers called out their wares in a language I knew was English but sounded like gibberish, and news peddlers cried out the day's news with the same inflection. Except for the salty air and scent of horse droppings and fish, the smell was unlike home as well. Arriving passengers stumbled around me as they regained their land legs, and the air was thick with the stench of their bodies. Unwashed for weeks in turbulent seas, even the sea air couldn't freshen them. Even the beggars recoiled from the stink of my fellow passengers.

For the first time, in this mass of humanity, I really understood how alone I was in the vast land.

A voice drifted through the din. "Clara Kelley?"

The name was unmistakable. It was my own.

I listened hard, but I didn't hear it again. I wondered if, in my loneliness, I had imagined it. I decided that I must have. No one expected me here.

"Clara Kelley? I'm looking for a Miss Clara Kelley from Galway," the voice bellowed louder.

I followed the voice. It belonged to a tall, clean-shaven man wearing a bowler hat and a houndstooth topcoat finer than I'd seen in some time. Before I got too close, before I identified myself, I stopped and watched him. Was he one of those runners we had heard about from our farming neighbors, the O'Donnells? A fellow Irishman had approached their nephew Anthony at the New York City docks, promising him a pleasant room at a reasonable rate, only to settle him in a rat-infested tenement room in the Lower East Side of the city that was already inhabited by nine other immigrants, at a rate many times more than what he had been told. When Anthony couldn't meet the exorbitant payment, the runner tossed Anthony out onto the street, keeping his stored trunk — his only belonging in the New World — as final payment. The O'Donnells and Anthony's poor parents had not heard from him since his last letter describing the machinations of this evil runner. This terrible fate wasn't the worst an immigrant could expect. I overheard the O'Donnells whispering to my parents about a girl from a neighboring village traveling alone to Boston who encountered a runner who exacted a far worse penance from her than the confiscation of her luggage.

This man didn't look the part. In fact, my little sister, Cecelia, would have called him posh, especially as he was leaning against a highly polished black livery coach with two dappled gray horses attached. And anyway, how would a runner know my name?

The man caught me watching him and asked, "You wouldn't be Miss Clara Kelley, would you?" His American accent was thick and flat, but I made sense of him.

"Yes, sir."

He stared long and hard at my face, clothes, and rucksack. "A Miss Clara Kelley who was on board the *Envoy*?"

"Yes, sir," I answered with a half curtsy.

He looked surprised. "You're not what I expected," he said with a shake of his head. "But Mrs. Seeley knows her business. It's not my job to judge."

I was about to ask him why he was looking for me and who was this Mrs. Seeley when he said, "Come on, miss. Climb into the carriage. We've been waiting for you for well over an hour. Long after the rest of second class exited from Lazaretto. God alone knows what sort of dawdling you were up to. Now we're well behind schedule to Pittsburgh. And Mrs. Seeley does not like us to be late, particularly since she's paying extra fare to get you to Pittsburgh safely by coach."

I knew there were confusing assertions imbedded in the man's words, but all I heard was "Pittsburgh." Was he truly offering to take me to Pittsburgh? The industrial city over three hundred miles from Philadelphia was my planned destination. Back home, we'd heard the city had work aplenty, and it was the one place in this boundless country where my family had relatives. Not close kin, mind, but a second cousin close enough to reach out to once I found employment in a textile mill or in one of the big homes that needed domestics.

I'd squirreled away the rest of the pounds and pence Mum and Dad had given me to secure the passage to Pittsburgh. I'd assumed I would have to cobble together the cheapest route I could find, some combination of rail and canal rides and wagon, since the train route didn't extend all the way from Philadelphia to Pittsburgh. But now a complete stranger was offering me a continuous horse-drawn carriage ride across the Allegheny Mountains and seemingly not asking for payment. Would I be a fool to decline? Or would I be a fool to accept?

I had a choice. I could tell this man the truth. That I was not the Clara Kelley for whom he was looking. That Clara Kelley was a common enough name. That the second-class passenger Clara Kelley for whom he was waiting probably never made it off the ship ferrying her here from Ireland if he had not yet come across her. Cholera and typhoid took many of us from all classes of travel. Illness did not discriminate. It was perhaps the one thing that did not.

Or I could become that other Clara Kelley. At least until I got to Pittsburgh.

I stared at the black carriage, trying to decide. On board the *Envoy,* I had promised myself that I wouldn't wait any longer, that I would take my future in my own hands when I could.

The man opened the door to the carriage for me. "Come on, miss."

I glanced up at him and said, "My apologies for the delay, sir. It won't happen again." And then I climbed up the steps into the carriage.

CHAPTER THREE

November 4, 1863
Philadelphia, Pennsylvania

The carriage was not empty. Once my eyes adjusted to the dim interior, I saw that there were two other girls inside. Both were near my age, with the reddish hair of my people, but there, the similarities stopped. Wearing dresses with crinoline underskirts peeking out at the hem, thick silk sashes, high necklines with lace collars, and wide pagoda sleeves, the girls had clothes finer and more fashionable than anything I'd ever owned. Finer than anything I'd ever seen, in fact, except the two occasions I served as a temporary kitchen maid for a holiday meal at Castle Martyn, the medieval citadel owned by the Martyn family, who served as landlord to all the farmers in our region.

Who in the name of Mary was this Clara Kelley I'd become?

From their gawking, I saw that the girls found me as alien as I found them. But I could not let on, or I risked losing my place in the carriage. How could I best ensure that I stepped into the mysterious shoes that the other Clara left me to fill?

Not by speaking in my usual manner, that was for certain. These girls didn't look as though their accents would match my farmer's daughter's West Ireland lilt, no matter how posh our fellow neighbors found it compared to their own, thanks to Dad's education of us girls. And I guessed the other Clara Kelley spoke like them. Not me.

Mrs. Seeley's man poked his head into the carriage. "Miss Kelley, I need to load your trunk onto the carriage. Where is it?"

How could I answer that the rucksack slung over my shoulder contained the entirety of my worldly possessions? The real Clara Kelley undoubtedly had traveled with trunks large enough to carry the kind of dresses these girls wore, and my bag was so small that it wouldn't hold even a single one of my treasured volumes of history and poetry, only my necessaries. No matter my efforts, Dad's battered copy of Alexis de Tocqueville's *Democracy in America,* which he had used as inspiration for his earlier political involvement with the Fenians and I used as a primer to understand American life before my departure, would not fit. Leaving behind those books, from which Dad had educated all his daughters (much to the outcry of our farming neighbors), was nearly as hard as leaving behind my family.

I answered, "My apologies, sir. I should have told you that my trunk was lost en route." I prayed that these words bore a good approximation of an Anglo-Irish accent, with which I assumed my carriage-mates spoke. My model was the Martyn family.

The Martyns. It pained me to conjure them up in any form, even as a reference point. Their actions were the cause of my departure. When rumors surfaced again about Dad's years-earlier alignment with the Fenians — an Irish-led movement that maintained Ireland should be its own state, that farmers should have fair rent and fixity of tenure, and that all people should have rights and the ability to better themselves, it had arisen from the near nonexistent assistance offered by English leaders to the sufferers of the Irish famine — the Anglo-Irish Martyns retaliated. Bit by bit, the Martyns took away land from the twenty-acre tenant farm Dad had amassed, a size permitting the crop diversity that allowed our family to survive the famine, unlike so many with the standard one-acre tenancies that could grow one crop only, the decimated potato. Our family needed another source of income to bank against the reduction in the family's earnings, and I was to be that other source. Lord Marytn, his wife, and their daughter might as well have placed me on the *Envoy* themselves and steered the ship through the rough Atlantic waters to America.

"Lost?" the driver asked.

Did he not understand my feigned accent, or was it skepticism I saw in his eyes? Either way, he was questioning my explanation, and I had to stay firm.

"Yes, sir. Lost in a squall." As soon as the lie spilled from my lips, I regretted it.

The girls, who had been surreptitiously watching this exchange behind the slow wave of their fans, openly stared. They too were on board the *Envoy,* and while the boat regularly cut through rough chop and suffered through the storm that had flooded steerage, no squall had pummeled the old whaling ship. Would the girls reveal my lie?

He tilted his head in clear disbelief. "A squall? These girls said nothing of it. Nor have I heard any talk of a squall among the sailing folk."

"Yes, sir." I nodded emphatically. The girls' askance expression or no, I had to adhere to my claim and convince this man.

Shaking his head, in disbelief or frustration, I could not tell, the man slammed shut the carriage door. I was left alone with the two girls, who had curiously chosen to keep my secret. For now.

The crack of a whip broke the awkward silence, and the carriage lurched forward. The careening took us off guard, and at first, we were all preoccupied with restoring our belongings and ourselves to order. Once the carriage began rumbling along with only the odd jerk when the wheels hit a rock or rut, the uncomfortable quiet and scrutiny began again.

I stared out the window, pretending to be engrossed in the passing sights. It started as a ruse to avoid the girls' gaze, but as the minutes passed, my astonishment was genuine. As the carriage left the harbor and progressed into the grid of Philadelphia streets, I saw no gray stone buildings climbing with moss and ivy. None of the verdancy and history of Galway existed in this new city. Instead, the streets were wide and straight, intersecting at right angles, and abounded with redbrick buildings trimmed with bright-white columns and window sashes as well as freshly painted signs proclaiming the name of the purveyors and their wares. Everything here looked tidy and freshly hewn, though not as elegantly designed as the Dublin and London buildings and squares of which I had seen engravings in Dad's books.

"Miss Kelley?"

I looked away from the window. "Yes, Miss —" I realized that I had not been properly introduced to the girls.

"I am Miss Coyne, and this is Miss Quinn. You told the driver that you were on board the *Envoy*?"

Now I understood. Even though the girls chose to keep my secret from Mrs. Seeley's man for reasons known only to them, they weren't going to let me off so easily in the privacy of the carriage. I would have to maintain my confidence, no matter our shared, unspoken understanding that my story was, at least in part, fabrication. "Yes, I was."

"In the second-class cabin?"

"Yes." I hoped I sound convincing. I needed to tread carefully, or they might reveal my lie to Mrs. Seeley's man and ruin this opportunity.

"Curious. Neither Miss Quinn nor I saw

you during the long days of travel."

"Nor I you. Although from my vantage point, I did not see much of anything or anyone during the voyage." My words, spoken slowly and deliberately to maintain the accent, sounded false to my ears.

"Your vantage point?"

"The floor of a laundress's cabin. My seasickness was so profound, no one would bunk with me." I gestured to my dress. "It also explains the dowdiness of my attire. None of my own gowns survived my illness. I was forced to buy clothing from a shipmate."

The girls recoiled in unison at the very word *seasickness*. Although they might have suffered from the same affliction, it was not considered polite to discuss the reality of the common sailing condition. It shut down the conversation, as I'd hoped.

I returned to my window and tried to keep my attention fixed on the world of curiosities unfolding before me. But the whispering of the girls distracted me, and I used the opportunity to try and glean a few words and phrases from their hushed mutterings. "Seeley," "service," and "Mrs. Carnegie" were only a few that stood out from their murmurs.

"Did I hear the driver say that you were

headed to Mrs. Seeley in Pittsburgh?" The other girl, Miss Quinn, spoke this time.

"I am. Are you as well?"

"We are indeed. Do you know to whom you will be posted?"

What did she mean by "posted"? Wracking my mind for a response, I thought on the whispers I had overheard and pieced together an understanding of her question. Perhaps she was asking to whom I would be placed in service. Was that the role Mrs. Seeley played, matching employers with servants? If so, she must be asking what family I would be serving.

After an uncomfortably long pause during which my fear of giving the wrong answer paralyzed me, Miss Quinn asked, "You aren't going to serve Mrs. Carnegie, are you?"

I grasped at her suggestion. "Yes. Yes I am."

The girls shot a glance at one another. I interpreted nothing of its meaning. "You are to be the new lady's maid to Mrs. Margaret Carnegie? We were considered for that role, but then Mrs. Seeley realized that our educations qualified us for the more important positions of tutors." This time, their meaning was unmistakable. Clearly, they deemed me unsuitable for the role. Most mistresses would agree. I looked like a farmer's daughter — which I was — and such girls were rarely permitted above the station of scullery maid, if they were ever permitted into service at all.

"Yes," I answered, steeling my voice. If the girls wished to challenge this role I was playing, then better the battle commence here than in front of Mrs. Seeley. Whoever she was. At least then I would already be in Pittsburgh.

Miss Quinn was cowed by the steadiness of my stare, and her eyes shifted to the floor. But Miss Coyne held my gaze and finally spoke the thoughts that had been brewing. "Well, you certainly don't look the part. A servant's appearance conveys not only her standing but the standing of her mistress, as a lady's maid should well know. As tutors to the daughters of the Oliver and Standish families, I can assure you we would be rejected out of hand if we were to appear for our positions dressed like you, Miss Kelley. Seasickness or not." She crinkled her tiny nose as if the very thought of nausea conjured up its smell. "But then you will be serving the Carnegie family, and I understand that they are new in their rise. Perhaps they don't yet know the difference in servants." The girls giggled at Miss Coyne's boldness.

If Miss Coyne hoped to discourage me by her words, she was wrong. In fact, her words had the opposite effect. They only wedded me to this new role I played, firing the stubborn determination Mum and Dad often accused me of having in droves. It was that determination they hoped would serve me well in America and perhaps pave the rest of the family's way here, if the Martyns exacted the worst upon the family.

Reminding myself of my parents' *síofra* label, I thought about how this new Clara Kelley would respond. I smiled sweetly and folded my hands in my lap. "Doesn't Proverbs say that 'strength and honor are her clothing'? I think I'll let my character — character of which Mrs. Seeley is undoubtedly aware — speak for me in lieu of my clothes."

CHAPTER FOUR

November 11, 1863
Pittsburgh, Pennsylvania

Mrs. Seeley stared at me as though she could see beneath the tattered dress I wore, straight through the story I'd started to tell, and deep into the identity of the Clara Kelley I truly was. My false confidence started to slip away. Fear began to replace it, and I knew that if I didn't right myself and stare straight into Mrs. Seeley's eyes as the Clara Kelley I pretended to be, this opportunity would be lost. The prize that Mrs. Seeley held, a coveted job, so recently unimaginable but now in my sights, would be gone forever.

Did I dare continue to spin my confection for Mrs. Seeley like a feast-day treat from the market? But what other offering did I have? I could not lose this chance.

I breathed deeply and said, "My deepest

apologies, Mrs. Seeley, for arriving at your door in such a deplorable state. I know that I've already explained the arduousness of my voyage and its impact on my wardrobe, but I know that is no excuse for my condition. Here of all places." I gestured around Mrs. Seeley's sitting room, a place surprisingly immaculate given the blackness of the city in which it lodged.

In the short walk from the carriage to Mrs. Seeley's establishment, I saw filth the likes of which I'd never imagined. Black clouds billowing in plumes from tall stacks. Buildings turned ashen from sooty air, outlines of posters in white, like ghosts on their walls. Why didn't anyone tell me that industrialization would look like biblical hell?

I quickly lowered my eyes in an approximation of modesty and shame and awaited her verdict.

Mrs. Seeley didn't respond, and I daren't look up. Was she judging the state of my dress — already filthy, blackened further by airborne soot in the few short hours I'd been in Pittsburgh — against the relative poshness of my speech? Was she weighing her reputation as an upscale servants' registry against the toll she might suffer from taking a gamble on me? From snippets and wisps of overheard — nay, stolen — conversation between Misses Quinn and Coyne during our eight days of travel, I'd learned that my guess was correct. Mrs. Seeley owned the preeminent servants' registry in town, the place where society ladies wanting specially trained servants — not your run-of-the-mill laundress, mind — would find them for a fee. Mrs. Seeley prided herself on the impeccable written references, called "characters," and work of her servants. The other Clara Kelley must have had a first-class character, one challenged mightily now by my attire.

Patience was a virtue hard-won for me, but this opportunity rested on my ability to become the person Mrs. Seeley sought. Without breaking my penitent stance or silence, I watched as her gaze traveled from the dirty folds of my dress to my face. We locked eyes. I could see that she doubted me. Doubted my story, my accent, my modesty. But she wanted to believe me. Maybe she needed to.

So she took a chance too.

"Well, we will have to clean you up. To make your appearance match your character. Mrs. Carnegie knows precisely the qualities she seeks in a lady's maid, and even if you have them in droves, she will never be able to see them beneath that filthy dress. Or your stench."

My stench? I'd spent so long in these clothes, inhabiting this smell, that I couldn't sense it anymore. Mrs. Seeley was gambling with my stink as well as my clothes.

"Of course, Mrs. Seeley," I answered with a grateful curtsy.

"I have a reputation to uphold if I'm to continue placing servants in the finest homes." She paused, scanning me up and down once again and shaking her head, as if she couldn't believe that she was actually going to let me walk through a client's door. "Not to mention that I've already invested in you and need to recoup my money. The ride from Philadelphia cost nearly two months of your wages."

With the sharp staccato of a sigh, she marched past me to a wardrobe on the far wall, past a list posted next to her desk. Girls' names scribed larger than was necessary were enumerated there, along with a corresponding offense. I could make out "lazy" and "slovenly" several times. It seemed to serve as a warning for the girls who passed through Mrs. Seeley's doors. I vowed to *never* be on that list.

Mrs. Seeley pulled a plain, charcoal dress from the wardrobe and walked toward me.

The worsted wool gown, adorned with none of the sashes and fanciful sleeves of Misses Quinn's and Coyne's frocks, which were perhaps suitable only for the loftier role of tutors, was akin to the serviceable uniform of a servant. She held it next to me, assessing size and fit, and said, as if quoting, "A neat and modest servant should wear nothing too dirty or fine."

Then, with a quick nod, she pronounced, "It will suffice. I will add its cost to the amount you owe me for the carriage ride and deduct it from your first wages. Assuming the mistress takes you on, of course, which is no sure matter."

"Yes, Mrs. Seeley." I curtsied again. Anything to prevent her from rethinking her decision.

"You'll find water for washing up those stairs to the right. Once you've cleaned and changed, bring your awful gown downstairs and put it in the fire." She picked up a fire iron and stoked the flames dwindling in the fireplace. "Nothing for it now but to burn."

CHAPTER FIVE

November 11, 1863
Pittsburgh, Pennsylvania

The dreary day gave way to sunlight as the carriage left the city. After Mrs. Seeley and I made our way past tall office buildings arched toward the sky and around mills spewing black clouds into the air and black water into the river, I realized that the day wasn't dismal at all but was actually bright and clear. The poison of the city had obscured the sun.

The farther we went, the more bucolic and green the scenery became. I hadn't expected farms and homes and rolling hills — not unlike home — to abut the city. The carriage ride became more unsteady as the cobblestone pavers disappeared, but I clung to my seat with the most ladylike posture I could muster, determined not to raise another eyebrow on Mrs. Seeley's stony face.

The carriage stopped in front of an enclave of miniature castles. Well, not quite miniature, but more human sized. Castles designed not for a medieval siege but for life. A privileged life, that was.

As we stepped out of the carriage in an area that Mrs. Seeley called Homewood, I realized that the corsets to which I was accustomed were loose enough to allow for house chores and farm work. The corsets required of me now were very tight, requiring me to sashay when I walked. I realized that the distinctive coy flounce with which most upper-class women moved was less artifice than necessity.

I followed Mrs. Seeley's lead toward a gabled mansion with so many turrets I lost count at six. As we approached the ornate oak main door, with the name "Fairfield" scripted on a brass plate, I started toward the steps. Before I could place my foot on a single one, Mrs. Seeley yanked my arm. "What do you think you're doing? You're a servant, not a guest."

Instead, we rounded the house, past a laundry line with flapping sheets that was hidden between a carriage house and the main home. There, we found a simple pine door upon which Mrs. Seeley knocked. The door was opened by a young girl, younger than me, who was wiping her hands on a stained apron.

"Yes?" she asked with a blank face.

"We are here for an appointment with Mrs. Carnegie."

The girl said nothing, but the blank look changed to one of confusion. I gathered that few callers for Mrs. Carnegie arrived at the servants' door.

"Can you please let the butler know that Mrs. Seeley is here for her appointment?" Mrs. Seeley said, less a request than a command.

"Mrs. Seeley, you said?" The girl's eyes went wide. Even servants as low-ranking as this girl knew of Mrs. Seeley, it seemed.

"Yes," Mrs. Seeley answered, her voice irritable.

"What is your name?"

"Hilda, ma'am."

"Please fetch your butler, girl."

The girl nodded and moved back to allow our entrance. We stepped into a back hallway onto a diamond-shape-tiled floor of tan and white that peered directly into the scullery. From the state of the scullery, I saw that we had interrupted Hilda at the hard work of peeling a mountain of potatoes. But for the waiting grandeur of the rest of the house, I could have been home. And I could have been the girl.

"Please wait in the kitchen, ma'am. I'll fetch the butler." She gestured for us to walk down a short hallway.

Following her gesture, Mrs. Seeley and I turned left into a vast, white-tiled kitchen. There, next to a black cast-iron stove so large, Mum could have fit an entire cow into it, was an equally enormous man stirring something in a huge copper pot underneath a massive metal hood. The smell emanating from the pot was intoxicating — a savory mix of stewed meat, onions, and herbs, I guessed — and it reminded me that a long time had passed since I'd had a proper meal.

The man looked up at the sound of our footsteps, and I stared into the darkest face and eyes I'd ever seen. He was the first man of color I'd ever encountered. This was who the Americans were fighting their Civil War over.

"Afternoon, Mrs. Seeley." He greeted us with a smile in his voice. "You are back again, I see."

"Good afternoon, Mr. Ford. I hope to have more success on this visit."

"Do you think you've finally brought a winner for the mistress?" His voice rumbled

45

low and steady. The tone was almost sooth-ing.

"I do indeed. Although I don't think the blame for my earlier failures lay with the girls I brought over. While I don't like to speak ill of others, your mistress has high standards."

"I'm all too familiar with those high standards," he said with a chuckle. "Tell me about this girl here."

They began talking about me as if I weren't there. Talking about the other Clara Kelley, in truth, not really me. I listened hard, absorbing the history of the other Clara Kelley. Born in Dublin, but of English heritage, Clara hailed from a family of fallen tradespeople. Well-educated for a girl, particularly in the ways of the home, Clara had been slated for a life as the wife of a prosperous shopkeeper until the family's fortune turned. Without a dowry, a life as a lady's maid became Clara's life instead, and as the positions evaporated in post-famine Ireland, she sailed for fresh opportunities in America.

This was the Clara Kelley I was meant to be. The knowledge made me feel dishonor-able in her skin, for as of this moment, I was the only one who knew that the real Clara never finished the journey across the

Atlantic.

As their chatter devolved into neighborhood gossip about people I didn't yet know, I stared around the kitchen, with its chest-high, white-tiled walls topped by butter-yellow-painted panels. Newfangled devices hung on the walls and sat on the tables. A contraption that looked like a whisk attached to some form of crank sat on the butcher's block in the room's center, alongside an elaborate miniature scale and several sifters. A device hung on the wall with thirty buttons labeled with names like "parlor" and "blue guest bedroom."

A shrill buzz sounded from the wall device, and a light flashed above the word *parlor*. I jumped and, without thinking, cried out, "What in the name of God is that?"

Mrs. Seeley stared at me. "It is just the enunciator. Surely, you have those in Ireland."

My heart pounding, I gathered my wits, praying to Mary that my accent hadn't slipped in my outburst. "Sorry, ma'am. None of the other homes in which I worked had that sort of device."

Mr. Ford said, "I'm not surprised, miss. The master of the house, the elder son of Mrs. Carnegie, always secures the latest inventions for his home, as you can probably see from all these contraptions. Not every house has an enunciator."

I tried to remember what sort of calling system Castle Martyn used. "Most of the homes I'm familiar with had the more traditional system with bells."

Mrs. Seeley's eyes were still narrowed, but she seemed willing to accept my explanation. For now. "Mr. Ford, our appointment with Mrs. Carnegie was set for two o'clock. It is now ten minutes past that time, and I would hate for her to think that we arrived late. You know how she values punctuality. Do you think we might wait in the front hallway so she knows we are here? Even if she isn't ready to see us?"

"I prepared tea and cakes for Mrs. Carnegie and her guests and had them delivered over an hour ago, so I'm guessing the afternoon calling hour is coming to a close. I don't see the harm in waiting in the front hall, but you should check with Mr. Holyrod. My domain only extends so far as these kitchen walls."

A man with a meticulously groomed beard and gray-streaked hair strode into the kitchen. He was dressed in a black suit with knife-edge pressed pants and looked so officious, I assumed he was the gentleman of

48

the house. I curtsied to him, but he continued walking toward Mrs. Seeley as if he could not see me.

"Ah, Mrs. Seeley. You've arrived. Mrs. Carnegie is still in the parlor. The guests are gone, but she is speaking with her elder son. You and your candidate may wait in the main entryway for her to finish."

From his words, I knew he wasn't the master of the house but the butler, Mr. Holyrod.

Without waiting for our response, he pivoted, leading us from the kitchen through a back hallway with a small sink and wall of hooks into a grand entryway. As the decor grew more elaborate — the molding changing from simple blond pine to intricately carved mahogany and the window glass shifting from clear to stained glass in vivid patterns of cobalt blue, persimmon, and citrine — the air grew colder. It was as if all the warmth of the house abided in the kitchen.

We stood underneath a gleaming crystal chandelier hung from the high ceiling, which was painted with fanciful swirls of gold. Portraits of ladies and gentlemen in gilt frames hung on the red-damask-covered walls. Turkish carpets in carmine and a marble fireplace completed the scene, ensuring that the Carnegies' guests would wait for their hosts in the utmost comfort. I'd never seen anything like this cocoon of luxury, in which everything was so new, I could almost smell the paint on the walls.

Voices rumbled from a room so red in decor that it smoldered like a fire even from my limited vantage point in the entryway. Mrs. Seeley took note of the noise and moved closer to the room. Loud laughter punctuated the silence in the entryway.

"Ah, Mother," a man said. His voice had a lilt that I couldn't quite place. "No one makes me laugh the way you do. The blunt way in which you assess my business colleagues never fails to surprise."

"Andra, someone must take the frank measure of the men with whom you enter into ventures. After all, it is on behalf of all three Carnegies that you operate. Tom Miller, those Kloman brothers, young Harry Phipps, and that iron business you are thinking of forming together need a proper vetting." A clock chimed the quarter hour. "Oh dear, look at the time. That overbearing Mrs. Seeley will be here with her latest chattel — another lady's maid. Let's hope she doesn't think she can pass off another lump of coal as a diamond."

The man laughed again, a good-natured

chuckle. "Now, Mother, be kind. It isn't Mrs. Seeley's fault that no one can meet your standards."

She chortled back. "Andra, you think all ducks are swans."

A bell rang out, and Mr. Holyrod invited us to enter the parlor. As we passed into its ruby opulence, I saw the shadow of a man leaving the room.

CHAPTER SIX

November 11, 1863
Pittsburgh, Pennsylvania

Paintings crowded the crimson parlor walls: scene after scene of rolling farm hills, herds of lamb, cows in their pastures, images of home, all. The artwork covered nearly every inch of the etched cerise velvet wallpaper. It was almost as if the Carnegies were afraid of empty space. What did they fear might creep through a break in their sumptuous barrier? Dad used to always say that the Martyns' thick castle walls were designed to keep out poverty as much as invaders.

"So this is your latest candidate, Mrs. Seeley?" a small, squat woman with a pug nose said from the depths of an armchair tufted in more red damask. I had almost missed her amid the suffocating layers of ruby that swathed the parlor. From the laughter spilling out from her while we waited in the front hall, I assumed she would be at least a touch merry, but the dark eyes peering up at me from the armchair were suspicious and stern.

Unlike her son, the woman's accent was thick, like a slab of butter on Mum's brown bread. It was thick enough to recognize as Scottish.

Was this the woman I was meant to serve?

"Yes, Mrs. Carnegie." Mrs. Seeley's voice suddenly sounded meek. Perhaps she was presenting a softer version of herself to counter Mrs. Carnegie's remark about her despotic nature. Or perhaps Mrs. Carnegie intimidated the prepossessing Mrs. Seeley.

"She looks the part, but can she play it?" Mrs. Carnegie asked with a cock of her head and a sip of her tea.

"All her references attest to her excellent work."

"Then she has served in the finer homes?"

"Yes, Mrs. Carnegie."

The woman's eyes squinted, taking the measure of me. "If she's accustomed to the leading homes in Ireland, why has she been gawking at my parlor?"

Mrs. Seeley recovered a bit of her natural confidence and said, "Perhaps yours is even finer than those."

Mrs. Carnegie chuffed a bit at this, and I

could see that flattery had an effect on the prickly matron. I stored this information and then curtsied to her as if I were a daughter of Castle Martyn paying respects to the visiting king of England.

She waved her hand, signaling me to get up, but I saw that she enjoyed the gesture. "No need for such airs, girl. We are just ordinary folk around here."

"Yes, Mrs. Carnegie." Still, I did not overstep by raising my eyes to hers.

"She's polite enough," Mrs. Carnegie said to Mrs. Seeley. "But is she a worker?"

"By all accounts, yes. You do understand I would bring only my finest to you."

"The last girl you sent me did not meet anyone's definition of finest, Mrs. Seeley. Or anyone's definition of average for that matter. I caught the girl napping midday when it was time to help me change my clothes for luncheon. Slovenly is what I'd call her."

I thought about that blacklist on Mrs. Seeley's wall and watched as a cowed expression appeared on Mrs. Seeley's face. She said nothing in defense of her candidate. Or herself.

"Does she understand the routines?" Mrs. Carnegie moved onto another topic.

"She's just arrived, ma'am, but I've been

told she's a fast learner."

"You haven't yet explained to her how I like things done? The routines of this home?" Mrs. Carnegie sounded incredulous.

"There has been no opportunity, Mrs. Carnegie. She only arrived from Philadelphia a few hours ago. I can take a moment now if you like, but she is described as knowledgeable and highly adaptable."

"I suppose that if she is experienced and adaptable as you claim and as her character maintains, then it shouldn't be a problem. After all, our house keeps to the same schedules as the finest in Europe."

"Of course, Mrs. Carnegie."

"I'm fine with her being Irish, but I must be certain she's not Catholic. These Catholic Irish running from the havoc wreaked by their famine and pouring onto American shores are not like the hardworking Protestant Irish who immigrated in earlier years. This new Catholic crop is rough and uneducated, and they'll destroy the fabric of this country's shaky democracy if we let them, especially in these days of Civil War unrest, just like they did back home in Scotland when they stole factory jobs away from Scottish men and women. An Irish Catholic servant might suffice as a scullery maid but not as my personal maid."

Mrs. Seeley was long in replying, giving me time to wonder. Were the whispers by Misses Coyne and Quinn true? Had the Carnegies immigrated recently themselves, making Mrs. Carnegie keenly aware of the hierarchy among immigrants and giving rise to her comment? Certainly, Mrs. Carnegie's accent suggested as much, as did Mrs. Seeley's hesitation in responding.

"Of course she isn't Catholic, Mrs. Seeley. She comes from a fine Anglo-Irish Protestant household that found itself down on its luck. So Miss Kelley entered service."

I waited as Mrs. Carnegie looked at me for a long moment, saying nothing. In my silence, I felt terribly disloyal to my family. My people were fiercely Catholic, and so staunch were my parents in their faith that in my final moments with Dad, on the dock before I set sail, he exacted a commitment from me: "Promise me you will keep to the one true Catholic faith while you are in that heathen land." Not proclaiming my faith when faced with such disparaging pronouncements about Catholicism felt like treachery, but I could not stop thinking about the benefits I could deliver my family if I kept quiet and procured this position.

Finally, she said, "I will take her for a

thirty-day trial period. Neither you nor she will receive payment unless I'm satisfied."

"I understand, Mrs. Carnegie."

"We are in agreement then." She stretched her foot out and pressed a button that was on the floor. "I've sent for Holyrod. He will arrange for her bags to be carried to her room on the third floor, and she can begin immediately after she has unpacked her belongings."

"Ah, her bags. That's another issue altogether, ma'am. Her belongings were lost in a storm at sea."

"She has nothing?"

"Nothing but what she's wearing." Mrs. Seeley was careful not to mention the unsuitable dress in which I actually arrived and that the dress I was wearing didn't even belong to me. This information would not speak well of my propriety.

"There was a time when one dress would be enough," Mrs. Carnegie muttered under her breath. "We can see to it that she has an alternate dress for service and a chemise for nighttime. Although it will come from her wages."

"That is understood, Mrs. Carnegie," Mrs. Seeley answered quickly.

Mrs. Carnegie hoisted herself from her chair with an unsteady step. Instinctively, I

57

rushed to her side to help — I hadn't suspected from the strength of her voice and opinions that she might be infirm — but she brushed my hand away. Then she looked straight into my eyes.

In her gaze, in such close proximity, I saw something familiar. Intelligence. Determination. Even grit perhaps. Something I didn't expect in a lady. But something I knew very well from the eyes of my father. It was the quality that procured us a much larger farm than most one-acre tenancies. It was the grit that gave our family land enough for varied crops, which had been the key to our survival of the famine. A survival that now depended on me.

I admired that grit. But it didn't mean I wasn't scared of it. And it didn't mean that I wasn't scared of her.

CHAPTER SEVEN

November 11, 1863
Pittsburgh, Pennsylvania

Mrs. Carnegie and I didn't face each other again until after dinner.

After forty-two days rocking on board the *Envoy* on the relentless Atlantic in a mix of boredom and anxiety and another eight days spent lurching in the horse-drawn carriage over the Allegheny Mountains, once my life as the new Clara Kelley started, it began immediately. While I had not expected a lengthy reprieve in my new quarters with time to wash away the residual grime from the city and the road, I had thought I might receive a full introduction to the staff and a brief tour of the Carnegie mansion to acquaint myself with the building's layout. Instead, Mrs. Seeley took her immediate leave of me and Mrs. Carnegie, Mrs. Carnegie passed me into the hands of the cold Mr. Holyrod, and Mr. Holyrod put me to work for my new mistress.

Mr. Holyrod instructed me that I was to begin to prepare Mrs. Carnegie and her bedchamber for the evening. What in the name of Mary did this entail? Why would someone's bedchamber need preparing if all they were planning on doing there was sleeping? While I had always toiled hard at my family farm, that work was limited to tending the animals, keeping the house tidy, cultivating and harvesting the crops, and helping with the wash and the family meals — never the finer service. What the work of a lady's maid involved, I had no idea, other than old remembrances from Mum of her days as a scullery maid. I had been so fixated on securing the position, I had forgotten that I would actually have to perform the job.

But Mrs. Carnegie would expect me to know, and I endeavored to glean information from Mr. Holyrod as he led me through an incomprehensible series of hallways and back staircases into her bedchamber. Interjecting a note of respectful meekness into my tone, I asked, "I want to make certain that I serve Mrs. Carnegie well. Would you mind sharing with me her evening routine? Each lady has her own particular desires."

Mr. Holyrod sniffed. "I imagine her habits are similar to those of other ladies you've served. She'll want help with her dressing; her clothes will need cleaning and mending; her hair will need styling; her person will need cleaning and tending; and she will need accompaniment to her various social activities."

As we reached the top of a curved mahogany staircase, he paused, turning to me. "But please do not presume that I will be giving your instructions, Miss Kelley. I'm not certain how it works in European households, but in American homes, neither the housekeeper nor the butler oversees the lady's maid. That is the province of the mistress alone. The lady's maid role is singular and separate from the rest of the staff in that respect."

I wondered why he was loathe to assist me. Was he so inundated with his own duties that taking on the tutelage of the new lady's maid, who was not technically his responsibility as he was quick to point out, seemed overwhelming? I would think a happier mistress would yield a happier household. But I spoke aloud none of these thoughts. Instead, I said, "Of course, Mr. Holyrod. I thank you for your insights."

Unlatching the door at the top of the

stairs, he stepped back to allow my entrance. I crossed the threshold into a bedroom suite nearly as opulent as the parlor. Lined in ultramarine silk wallpaper hand-painted with alabaster roses and decorated with curtains and bed coverings in fabric of the same lush pattern, the bedroom felt like the inside of a private garden with actual blooms wrapping around and dangling from a trellis border. A matching chaise longue, for a lady's afternoon rest while still confined by a corset I presumed, sat at the foot of a wide bed bordered by wooden head and footboards carved with roses, and a marble dressing table faced it. A wide fireplace presided over it all, topped by a mahogany mantel with a painted cherubic statue at its center.

Rendered speechless by the sumptuous bedchamber interior, I stared around the room for a long moment, imagining the luxury of sleeping in the silken space. By the time I regained my composure and turned to thank Mr. Holyrod, he was gone. He must have padded away, closing the door behind him with a silence that no doubt served him well in his profession. Left to myself, I felt unmoored, as if I no longer knew how to behave without someone for whom to perform.

What to do? I decided to familiarize myself with Mrs. Carnegie's bedroom suite so I would at least appear skilled in the handling of her belongings. I opened drawers and trunks and wardrobes, locating her under and outer garments. But instead of lingering among the exquisite fabrics and delicate embroidery as I would've liked, I explored the inside of her dressing table, learning the sorts of brushes and creams and perfumes she preferred, and memorized its marble surface with its very particular array of four ivory-backed brushes, a matching comb and mirror, a small leather case, and four ivory-topped jars containing flower-scented oils. I studied the dark-colored dresses in the small room off her bedroom, which contained her gowns, trying to understand the manner in which the various flounces and bustles affixed to the dress itself. I marveled at her bathroom, a wonder of running water that poured into a porcelain sink topped with marble, claw-foot tub, and flushable toilet.

Yet nothing impressed me — or astonished me — more than Mrs. Carnegie's study. At its center stood an escritoire covered with papers. Peering over the sheaves, I expected to see invitations to social engagements, menus for the housekeeper and cook, and letters to and from acquaintances. Instead, the rose-colored stone desktop was nearly obscured by papers containing rows of figures next to the names Piper and Schiffer and contracts for an iron company. What was the mistress of the house doing with such papers in her possession? Did Mrs. Carnegie undertake the role of consulting on these ventures? Was it common for a woman of the higher classes to engage in business? Certainly, married or widowed Irish women of my acquaintance worked, but only in the home, unless their circumstances were desperate and factory jobs were necessary.

The little clock on the fireplace mantel chimed, and I realized the dinner hour would soon be concluding. Remembering a pile of mending I spotted in the closet, I sat in a simple chair along the wall and busied myself with it. I figured that when Mrs. Carnegie arrived, I should at least look the part of lady's maid.

I began to darn a pair of plain, black silk stockings, trying to keep my stitches invisible as Mum had taught me. In the safe refuge of Mrs. Carnegie's bedchamber, made warm by the fire roaring in her fireplace, freshly lit for her comfort, I started to drift into sleep. Just as the needle and thread dropped, along with my lids, footsteps thudded down the hallway, jolting me awake. I scrambled for the fallen needle and thread and resumed sewing before Mrs. Carnegie entered the room.

The door swung open wide, and I stood at attention. Without a word or a glance to me, she strode into her bedchamber. Settling into the upholstered chair at her dressing table, she began unpinning her hair without even a look into her mirror or in my direction. It was as if she begrudged my presence instead of viewing me as a necessary part of her daily routine. Or perhaps she was testing me.

I rushed to her side. Even though I knew almost nothing about the precise duties of a lady's maid, I imagined it was poor form to not attend your mistress's evening disrobing. "Please allow me to help you, ma'am."

Narrowing her already small eyes, she glanced at my reflection in her mirror. Her expression was inscrutable, but she lowered her hands and allowed me to proceed with the business of readying her for bed. As I unpinned the rest of her hair and undid her old-fashioned hairstyle — hair drawn into a high bun with a smooth loop meeting over each ear — her body stiffened. I saw that this ritual, presumably second nature to most ladies, made her uncomfortable. Why would a woman of her stature be made uncomfortable by a maid's ministrations? Was she indeed newly wealthy, as Misses Quinn and Coyne had intimated?

When I finished her hair, she rose to allow me to tend to her attire. While I knew other ladies might find her gown plain and somber, with its black, patternless fabric and sole adornment the vertical pleats running down the sides, its design was far more intricate than anything we wore at home. I made a quick study of her dress, searching for the easiest way to remove it. Once I located a row of hooks hidden beneath a decorative seam down the back, I began to unlatch them. My already shaking fingers fumbled on the minuscule hooks, and I despaired of ever reaching the vast layers of clothing that I knew lay underneath. I expected barbs from her sharp tongue, but she was oddly quiet as she watched my efforts through the mirror. The damnable mantel clock ticked out the long minutes as I slowly unearthed and undid the horsehair crinoline that gave her dress its voluminous shape, the corset cover and vest that covered the crinoline, and the petticoats, corsets, and silk stockings that hid underneath.

Finally, I reached her chemise. There my

mistress stood, in a plain, white cotton chemise with her arms and lower legs exposed and her white hair spread out over her shoulders like a maiden. She looked petite and oddly vulnerable, and for that moment, I no longer felt in awe of her but simply uncomfortable. I shifted my gaze to the ground.

Mrs. Carnegie must have sensed my discomfort, because in an effort to reassert her power, she said, "Haven't you forgotten something?"

I had no idea to what she referred. Mentally, I ran through the possible ministrations a society lady might want before retiring to bed but came up wanting. "My apologies. I am yours to educate, ma'am."

"You haven't tended to my hands, girl," she said, gesturing to what must have been a nail kit that sat upon her dresser.

The expression on my face must have been one of stupefaction, because she pointed to a crystal bowl and a few silver instruments lying beside it and yelled out, "Get the water and then start trimming and buffing."

"Of course, ma'am. I will not forget again," I answered with a curtsy, and then I raced into the bathroom to fill the little crystal bowl with water.

Mum often regaled us with stories of the Castle Martyn ladies' demands, but as I watched the water run, I didn't recall a single tale about shaping the ladies' nails. Potatoes, not the toiletry, had been her purview. What in the name of Mary was I meant to do?

When I returned to the bedroom, Mrs. Carnegie had sat back down upon her ultramarine, tufted dresser chair. After setting the crystal bowl down on the dresser, I kneeled before her and asked, "May I inquire in what order you would like me to proceed, ma'am?"

She paused for a moment, searching my face. "In what order would your prior mistresses have proceeded?" From her expression, I could not tell if this was a test or a quest for information.

Glancing over at the array of instruments — two tiny pairs of scissors, a leather buffer, and several jars of oil — I improvised. "Typically, my ladies would begin by soaking their hands, after which I would trim the nails. I would then buff their nails and finish by massaging cream or oil into their skin. But of course, if your habits are different, I will follow your instructions, ma'am."

"Your usual practice will suffice. Assuming they buffed the nails for a full five minutes," she said and stretched out her fingers.

As I dried Mrs. Carnegie's hands and began to trim her cuticles, I noticed that her hands were deeply stained and chapped and her joints were swollen beyond what age would suggest. In fact, her hands resembled Mum's. These were the hands of a woman who'd worked hard for decades, not the delicate hands of a lady.

As I rubbed the rosewater cream into her hands, we shared an uncomfortable moment of locking eyes. A cold breeze drifted across the room, and I realized that the windows were cracked open slightly. Into the quiet, I stammered, "Would you like me to have the fire lit for you first thing in the morning, ma'am? Your room will be quite chilly."

She stared at me as if I'd asked if I could murder her in her sleep. "I hope you don't think this is a home where wanton luxury is practiced, girl."

I stopped rubbing. "Of course not, ma'am."

"I hope not. Mrs. Seeley's last girl thought that my sons minted American dollars. I assure you that our success is due to hard work and thrift."

"Of course, ma'am."

"Even if we were spendthrifts, the doctor recommends that we keep the windows open at night to allow air to circulate in the bedrooms and foster a sanitary home environment." She stood and pulled herself up to her full height, tiny though that was, and asked, "I assume you undertook this practice in the other homes in which you worked?"

An accusatory tone tinged her question, and I paused, uncertain what the correct answer should be. Would the masters and mistresses of the Anglo-Irish homes in which the true Clara Kelley worked have slept with open windows? It seemed unlikely in the constant dampness and cold of the Irish weather, but perhaps this open-window business was a foible common to all upper-class folk.

In my moment of vacillation, fear flickered across her face, and her eyes searched my face for traces of judgment. I was confused. It seemed she cared about *my* judgment of *her* almost as I much as I cared about hers.

I understood something about Mrs. Carnegie. This world was indeed new to my mistress as well. And the only thing that saved me in my first hours as lady's maid was my mistress's own ignorance.

CHAPTER EIGHT

November 18, 1863
Pittsburgh, Pennsylvania

I rejoiced in my mistress's ignorance. It allowed me the latitude of time to gain my bearings in this house and in this role. But I knew that in order to survive in this role, in order to convince the other society ladies whom we would encounter in the afternoon of tea and whist that Mrs. Carnegie would be hosting on that eighth day that I belonged, I needed every advantage I could glean for myself. Not only did I have to make myself indispensable to my mistress, but I also had to become a necessary shield for those moments when she was unsure of herself and her behavior didn't precisely match the dictates of the social rules.

From the moment a rap on my window woke me at five o'clock in the morning — the Carnegies employed a "knocker upper" armed with a long cane and a lantern to tap us servants awake — I memorized my mistress's preferences on those matters in her particular control. I studied precisely how she wanted her hairstyle, the manner in which she liked her bustle arranged, whether she preferred lavender or rosewater scent, the temperature she wished for her morning washing water, the exact brush she mandated for cleaning her dresses, the sorts of thread she preferred for the mending of her stockings and undergarments, and especially the number of steps she liked me to walk behind her. She never liked me too close to her in public. I closely monitored her facial expressions to understand which of my behaviors pleased her and which were not up to snuff.

My attempts at indispensability, however, did not stem solely from this ability to please. When Mrs. Carnegie seemed unsure about a habit governed by society's whim, when she searched my face for approval about the proper place setting for tea or the most suitable way to perch her bonnet upon her head, I broke out of the silent servitude she liked best and quietly filled in the gaps in her social graces with the practices of my fictional Anglo-Irish mistresses. I knew that the conventions of the European elite trumped any tradition of the provincial Pittsburgh upper classes, and my suggestions would provide her with the comfort to proceed in society.

My task was made easier by the fact that we spent the seven days in relative isolation. Her sons Andrew and Tom, the elder and younger Messrs. Carnegie respectively, who, as unmarried gentlemen, also resided in the family home, were away. At first, I assumed that they were soldiers in the American Civil War about which I'd read and that my fleeting glimpse of one son reflected a brief visit home from the front. But Mr. Ford, the sole member of the staff who showed me any kindness, told me that the Messrs. Carnegie had been deemed critical railroad employees by the elder Mr. Carnegie's former boss, Mr. Thomas Scott, who was now the assistant secretary of war. As such, the brothers were exempt from actual fighting, and their absence was explained by the business of war rather than its bloodshed. I found this curious, as I assumed they would not want the exemption but would want to fight for the country where they'd had such success, even though they were immigrants.

The day before the tea and whist party, it occurred to me that the one thing I couldn't fabricate was an understanding of whist, which I might well need to know when I attended Mrs. Carnegie at her event. The game had been played by the highborn for over a hundred years, and I doubted that my lack of understanding could be explained away by European variances in the game.

After I settled Mrs. Carnegie in her room for her usual afternoon rest before dinner, I asked her leave to tend to some mending in the housekeeper's room, the often empty room where I took my breakfast, tea, and supper separate from the rest of the staff. The protocol referenced by Mr. Holyrod, in which the lady's maid fell under the control of neither the butler nor the housekeeper, Mrs. Stewart, a prickly woman who was short of stature and temper, dictated my detachment from the rest of the servants, another reason they kept their distance.

Instead of turning toward the housekeeper's room as I'd told Mrs. Carnegie, where I had the option of doing my mending in the event that I did not feel like working in my bedroom, I turned down a long hallway. I tiptoed past the parlor where the household maids were dusting and skirted into the library. The day before, while tending to Mrs. Carnegie in the library as she selected a volume to read during her rest period, I had spied a copy of *Mrs. Perkins's Guide to Managing House*. Perhaps an explanation of whist was contained within its pages.

Gleaming mahogany bookshelves stretched from floor to ceiling in the library, necessitating a sliding ladder for access. The only interruption in the vast expanse of books was a marble fireplace faced by two leather, wing-backed chairs, each with a book rest clamped to an arm for ease of reading, and a frieze of green-and-gold-embossed leather that ran above the bookshelves. My fingers itched to touch the spines and crack open volumes in the history section, such as Edwards Gibbon's *The History of the Decline and Fall of the Roman Empire* or Herodotus's *The Histories*. I had always lost myself in Dad's history lectures — tirades, more like — and his beloved texts. But I stilled my itchy fingers. I was here for a purpose.

Sliding *Mrs. Perkins* from its place on the crowded bookshelf, I crept into the darkest corner of the library, hoping to stay invisible if I inhabited the shadows. I turned to the table of contents, and while I saw no mention of whist or any game specifically, certain categories did describe social engagements. Yet even sections entitled "Morning Calls," "Afternoon Visits," or

"The Dinner Party" — which could prove helpful for future social occasions I might have to attend as Mrs. Carnegie's maid — offered no guidance for an afternoon of tea and whist.

As I hunted through *Mrs. Perkins*, I stumbled across a description of the role of lady's maid.

The Lady's Maid: Daily Duties

Before the Mistress awakens, you must return her clothes from the evening before to her armoire and prepare her clothes for the morning.

No later than eight o'clock, you must wake the Mistress by bringing her tea and bread, a newspaper, and any correspondence. Depending on her desires, you must light the fire, run her bath, help her to dress, tend to her person, and style her hair.

At half past nine, while the Mistress takes her Breakfast, you must tidy and clean her Bedroom and arrange outdoor clothes should she choose to go walking after the Family's Breakfast.

After the Family's Breakfast, if the Mistress intends to go out, you must assist her in changing into her outdoor attire. You must accompany the Mistress if she is going out.

After Luncheon, assuming that the Mistress does not require your particular service, you must brush her dresses, undertake needlework or repairs to her clothing, or wash her underwear and personal articles. The Mistress will rest until it is time to ready for Afternoon Tea.

You must dress the Mistress for Afternoon Tea, which will be taken at five o'clock.

While the Mistress takes her Afternoon Tea, you must tidy her bedroom once again and begin to prepare her attire for Dinner.

From half past six onward, you must assist the Mistress to dress for Dinner.

After eight o'clock, you must tidy the Mistress's Bedroom, ensuring that her flowers are fresh, her linens are ironed, her chamber pot is emptied, her bottles are filled, and her hairbrushes and combs are cleaned.

You may spend the remainder of the evening at your leisure, until the Mistress retires to bed when you will need to assist her undressing and tend to her hair, nails, and grooming.

"Captivating reading, is that?" A man's voice boomed across the library.

I jumped up and turned to see a man leaning against the doorframe, legs crossed and a merry grin on his lips. His bushy, red beard and sweep of darker red hair across his high forehead added to his blithe appearance. His stance was comfortable and his smile broad and unwavering, as if he'd been enjoying his vantage point for some time. His humorous mien, pierced by his square chin and distinct cheekbones, only heightened my unease.

"I do beg your pardon, sir." I curtsied deeply, careful to keep the book behind my back. A true lady's maid would have no need of *Mrs. Perkins.* She would already know all the details of her position. This man had caught me in a much more compromising situation than the mere prohibited act of reading books in the family library would suggest. My very selection of books could be my demise.

"Please do not apologize, miss. We enjoy our reading here in the Carnegie household. No shame in that," he said, the smile never leaving his lips. I detected a hint of a Scottish brogue in his voice, albeit much softer than that of Mrs. Carnegie. Was this one of her sons? The one I overheard joking with her in the library? It was the only laughter I'd heard from her in the seven days since I arrived.

How should I respond? I took the safer — but harder — road. "I do not think my mistress would be well pleased to discover that I was reading in the family library, sir, when I was supposed to be mending. I must excuse myself to report my malfeasance to her and take what punishment she decides is merited."

He began walking toward me, and as he grew nearer, I realized he was small in stature, a shortness that did nothing to diminish the largeness of his presence. His smile softened, and his brow knotted in sympathy. "Ah, miss, there is no need to fall on your sword. I won't tell if you don't."

Was his proffered lifeline a trap of some sort? A test arranged by Mrs. Carnegie? Would he expect something untoward in exchange for his silence? Even in my small village in Galway, I had heard rumors of various masters' improper demands from their maids.

I didn't know how to answer.

Into the silence, he asked, "You're the new lady's maid, aren't you?"

I nodded and choked out, "Yes, sir."

"My mother is notoriously hard to please, and by all accounts, you've achieved the impossible task of making her happy. I wouldn't disrupt that for the world." His broad smile returned. "Anyway, I've heard a bit about your background, and I'm guessing a highborn lass such as yourself must be accustomed to regular use of the library. I'll keep your secret . . . as long as you tell me what you're reading."

I stepped back, burying *Mrs. Perkins* even deeper in the folds of my gown. His voice sounded kindly enough, but was his offer truly innocent? Either way, I couldn't take the chance. Mrs. Carnegie might forgive me if I confessed to her directly but not if my crime was reported by another. Especially one of her beloved sons. "I do not think that secrets are the proper course, sir."

The smile faded, and his brow raised in alarm. "I've upset you, miss. My apologies. I truly meant to set you at ease. May I legitimize your visit to the library by reading aloud to you a passage from my favorite poet, Robert Burns? In that way, your time here will have been at my request and not your own idea. There would be no need to share it with my mother."

I nodded in relief, although the thought of remaining in the library while the master read poetry aloud to me was most peculiar, even inappropriate.

He strode over to a table piled high with brown, leather-bound volumes. Glancing at their spines, he slid out one particular book. Without even consulting the table of contents, he opened it to a poem he called "Is There for Honest Poverty." As he read the poem aloud to me, his brogue deepening with each word, it sounded familiar. But from where? Politics, not poetry, were the usual language of my upbringing. Poetry was something I enjoyed alone, on blustery nights at our farmhouse near Tuam.

What though on hamely fare we dine,
Wear hoddin grey, an' a that;
Gie fools their silks, and knaves their wine;
A Man's a Man for a' that:
For a' that, and a' that
Their tinsel show, an' a' that;
The honest man, tho' e'er sae poor,
Is king o' men for a' that.

With that verse, I realized why the words sounded familiar. Years ago, Dad and his political mates sung this poem aloud at their meetings, a sort of rallying cry for egalitarianism, one of the Fenians' core views, and even now, he occasionally sang this tune. This reminder of Dad's beliefs and the threat to my family's well-being because of the Martyns' reactions to old rumors of those same politics — the very reason I was standing in this odd land listening to a stranger read poetry — brought tears to my eyes.

Mr. Carnegie finished his elegant recitation and glanced over at me. I wiped the tear from my cheek in the hopes he wouldn't see it, but from the softening in his expression, I could see that it was too late.

In the stillness that sat between us, I heard the soft sound of a bell ringing in the background. With a curtsy but without another word, I dashed away. I knew Mrs. Carnegie was ringing that bell for me.

CHAPTER NINE

January 21, 1864
Pittsburgh, Pennsylvania

"Letter for you," Mrs. Stewart said as I passed her in the kitchen, arms laden with a tray from Mrs. Carnegie's afternoon tea.

"For me?" I asked, incredulous. I had waited months for a reply from the letter I sent my family upon securing my position with the Carnegies, and now that one had arrived, I could not quite believe it. Day after day, letters arrived for other staff members, but nothing for me. My feelings had swung like a pendulum between worry over my family's well-being and relief that no one from the real Clara Kelley's family had written, looking for her.

"Two actually," she answered, her doleful expression unchanged by my excitement. The nature of our few exchanges, usually limited to discussions over Mrs. Carnegie's meal requests, petitions for fresh sewing supplies, and comments delivered on behalf of my mistress about various cleaning inadequacies, meant that our relationship was practical at best. Mrs. Stewart, like the rest of the staff, viewed me as aligned with my mistress, not as one of them. They kept a cautious distance.

Could Eliza and Dad each have sent letters? It was unlikely that they'd waste the expense of posting two separate letters. Perhaps they were family letters sent at two different times.

Mrs. Stewart pulled the travel-tattered letters from the deep pocket in front of her apron and held them up to a nearby wall sconce. Squinting, she read, "One from someplace called Tuam and the other from Dublin."

My exhilaration at the prospect of reading my dear sister Eliza's words plummeted when I heard "Dublin." I knew no one in Dublin. But the other Clara Kelley certainly did. That letter could only be for her.

After delivering the tea tray to the scullery, I glanced at the two letters, one with script so familiar, it could nearly be my own and one with utterly foreign lettering, and slipped them into my skirt pocket. My steps felt leaden as I trudged up the back staircase

84

to tend to my mistress. As I settled Mrs. Carnegie for her late-afternoon rest — loosening her dress a bit, propping pillows behind her back, and fetching her copy of a railroad contract that sat on her escritoire — I felt the letters burning in my pocket. Had I been discovered as a fraud? Would this be my last day of service in the Carnegie household? The news from home — for which I'd been waiting impatiently since I landed — now hardly seemed to matter in light of the other missive that had arrived.

Mrs. Carnegie pointed to a pile of laddered stockings near her armoire and said, "Tend to those while I take my rest, won't you, Clara? I'll ring when I'm ready to dress for dinner."

"Yes, ma'am," I answered with a quick curtsy. Grabbing the pile and closing the bedchamber door behind me, I raced up the servants' stairs to my room.

My hands shook as I sat on the heavily patched blanket covering my bed and pulled the letters from my pocket. I ran my fingertip along my sister's elegant rendering of my name, a script Dad had made us practice over and over, and decided to put aside my fear and open it first. Whatever fate lay in store for me with the letter addressed to the other Clara Kelley could wait a few more minutes, and if the situation on the family farm had improved, then the sting of the other letter would be lessened.

With the edge of my sewing shears, I slit the letter open. There, in cramped writing that spoke to the scarcity and expense of both paper and postage, were my beloved sister's words. I imagined her auburn hair falling over her shoulder as she hunched over the paper to write. Although the perfectly formed letters were as exquisite as ever, the tightness of the script made the words hard to decipher until I settled into a rhythm.

Dearest Clara,
We feared the worst when no letter came for over two months. We had felt certain that you would send word of your safe landing the moment your foot touched upon American soil. When nothing arrived for us at the parish church, well, you can imagine the state in which we found ourselves. We wondered that a terrible fate had befallen you or that, in the land of plenty, you had forgotten us. We very nearly bore the expense of another letter and wrote our cousin in Pittsburgh to see if he had word of you. But now, with your first missive firmly in our grip,

86

we see that communication will not be easy, that it will be subjected to the vagaries of the sailing packets and hand-to-hand deliveries, and we will not fret so. We will trust in your stalwart nature and constancy while we await your next words, confident that they will come.

How I long for you, Sister. The house is quiet and mournful without your quips and your bustle and your high-minded notions. To be sure, the house remains busy. Mother continues with her constant mending, cooking, and drying of herbs. Dad tills the soil until not a single leaf dare abandon its assigned post whilst he laments our shrinking acreage. And even sunny, young Cecelia diligently tends to her chores without a single complaint. But the mirth is gone. We are as deflated as an empty sack of wine without you. My longing for you is selfish, I know. You are the one who has taken the great risks of ocean crossing and made the tremendous sacrifice of leave-taking all that is familiar for the benefit of us, your family. The very least I should do is suffer your absence quietly. But I cannot.

I find solace in the sort of domestic service into which you have landed. The

Carnegie family sound a fair if demanding lot. If the stories that the Mullowneys shared with us about the perils of service are true, then you have sidestepped the worst of American masters and found a steady haven, no matter the uneven disposition of your mistress. You will manage her mercurial disposition better than most — after all, you have managed Dad's temperaments well enough — and they are lucky to have you.

I know that you are meant for grander places than the scullery of the Carnegie household, my dearest Clara, and more than anything, I am sorry that Dad decided to send you instead of me. I have had to accept his explanation that I should stay because my anticipated union with Daniel gives him the best opportunity to pass on the farm intact, well able to survive the crop changes necessitated by the famine, yet it does not seem fair. You are the brightest of us Kelley girls, Clara, the most deserving of an ambitious destiny exceeding the tenant farmer status into which we were born. If I had been stronger, that destiny would not have been stolen from you, and you would not have been pressed into service across the sea, a service that grows more important as Lord Martyn's veiled threats about the tenancy increase. I pray nightly that you forgive me my weakness.

Write, please write.

I remain, ever, your devoted,
Eliza

Her words brought tears to my eyes. How could Eliza blame herself for Dad's decision to send me to America? No one had ever thought me suitable for marriage to a local Irish farm boy who might help take over the tenancy. The family was fortunate that Eliza had made such a well-timed, appropriate match. As I brushed my tears away, intending to write her back straightaway to assuage her guilt, I noticed a tiny postscript in the unmistakable, rough handwriting of Mum.

We miss you something awful but do not fret. Do nothing to forfeit your soul. Pray to the one and only true Roman Catholic Church.

Mum would be devastated by the Protestant role I'd had to play in the Carnegie household and even more so by my weekly attendance at the local Presbyterian church with the rest of the staff, even though the Carnegies themselves did not attend any church. No domestic's wage could be high enough to risk one's soul in such a way, Mum would undoubtedly think. But my duplicity would be revealed to the Carnegies and my position terminated if I insisted on attending Catholic mass.

Fishing my tiny, silver Agnus Dei medallion necklace out from the folds of my chemise where I kept it hidden from Mrs. Carnegie's searching eyes, I fingered the little lamb symbol on its surface, a symbol only a Catholic would wear, and thought on Mum's words. Was I risking my soul by pretending to be someone I was not? If what Eliza said was true and Lord Martyn's wrath over Dad's long-forgotten Fenian ways still simmered, then the farm could be lost, and my family along with it. I could be their sole hope. I would have to take that risk and pray for forgiveness.

I resolved to write Eliza back before the five o'clock post, to send her the reassuring words she needed as soon as I could. Picking up the ink, pen, and paper I had squirreled away in my chamber, I began to write:

My dear Eliza,

How could you have feared that I had forgotten you? I think of nothing but you, Dad, Mother, Cecelia, and our land many times every day. Memories of home, even those more recent recollections of farm days filled with worry as Lord Martyn chipped away at Dad's hard-won acreage, sustain me. As I lie awake in my bed in this strange house in this strange land, I pretend that you lie beside me in our shared bed at home, exchanging a late-night laugh or worry. And I am consoled. But then the moment fades, and I must be buoyed by the knowledge that my work here will assist our family should Father's worse concerns manifest: that Lord Martyn will rescind the farm tenancy altogether on rumors of Dad's past Fenian allegiances.

Eliza, dare not chastise yourself for Dad's decision to send me to America instead of you. Father believes that, if he passes the tenancy to you and your future husband, Lord Martyn will stop his persecution of our family's right to the full twenty-acre tenancy. Your marriage to Daniel and your assumption of the farm are our family's future; surely, you see this. After the famine, small, one-acre farms no longer survive since potato crops no longer grow, and thus Dad cannot resort to the traditional gavelkind to divide the farm equally among us. He must keep the farm intact, and your marriage is the only way. How could Dad have possibly designated me as the one to marry instead of you? Who in the name of Mary would have agreed to wed the odd, intellectual daughter instead of the kindly one? I am not viewed as good stock for a farmer's wife. No, you have long favored Daniel and he you, and thus your marriage will secure our family's legacy in the land.

This domestic work of mine in America is meant only to tide us until the time of your union when Lord Martyn's ire abates. Then I can return home. But until those events transpire, it is my duty. Have Dad and Mum not instilled in us the gravity and centrality of duty? It is my privilege to fulfill it, and I cannot think of a nobler destiny, as you so grandly called it.

I will write you as often as this schedule of mine allows. While not as physically grueling as the work that the poor Irish men must face in the mines and the mills, it is relentless in its demands on my time. Until then, you will be in my thoughts.

Your loving sister,
Clara

After I sealed the letter to Eliza, I stood up, eager that it make the five o'clock post even though I knew the letter would not reach Ireland's shores for weeks. I had very nearly left the room when I realized I had momentarily forgotten about the letter from Dublin. It poked out from beneath the bedding under which it had slipped, and I reached for it. My stomach churning with dread, I sat down again and slit it open.

The words were few and spare. They took no more than half the page, requiring none of the cramping of Eliza's lettering. The script was rougher than the formal style Dad taught me, Eliza, and Cecelia. But the letters were well formed.

Dearest Clara,
You have every right to leave Dublin and start a new life in America, where I have no doubt your skills would be valued highly. I should have told you that I had a child living in the country with his grandmother. No matter the gossip you

heard, the child is no bastard. I was married to the child's mother when I was but a child myself, but she died during childbirth, and the grandmother took the child in so I could enter service. I send the child most of my wages. But still, I lied to you and in the same breath asked you to be my wife. I know I do not deserve you, but if there was a glimmer of hope that you'd forgive me, I would take the first ship to America. Forgive me, Clara, and allow me to join you so that you will no longer be alone in this world.

I am still your,

Thomas

The tears I had brushed away moments before returned. Not because fear of my fraud being discovered had mounted — I assumed this Thomas would need a letter of encouragement before setting sail to Pittsburgh, one he would never receive — but because, for the first time, the other Clara Kelley felt real. And her death seemed real as well.

CHAPTER TEN

February 12, 1864
Pittsburgh, Pennsylvania

I fastened the gold watch and chain upon the bosom of Mrs. Carnegie's gown, always the final step in the morning's grooming ritual. Stepping back, I studied her gown. A stray silver hair on her dress drew my attention, and I fetched the brush designed specifically for silk gowns to give the fabric a thorough, final cleaning before I left. I wanted every detail to be correct. This was my first day off in the three months since my arrival in the Carnegie household, and I couldn't risk any rogue thoughts about my competency sneaking into my mistress's judgmental head in my absence.

In that time, not only had I developed a deft hand at Mrs. Carnegie's personal routines, but I had also become adept at the regular tasks that occupied my time outside Mrs. Carnegie's company — the endless cycle of washing hair combs and brushes; removing stains from soiled garments; starching muslins; washing the basins, glasses, and water jugs used in Mrs. Carnegie's personal chambers; maintaining a strict schedule of fresh water, flowers, towels, and ironed linens in her bath and bedchamber; assessing the state of Mrs. Carnegie's garments, darning stockings, mending linens, and brushing out her gowns. I had even become competent at serving as Mrs. Carnegie's companion in the formal social occasions that peppered her days, accompanying her on the daily round of morning calls to female acquaintances and the teas that occurred in the late afternoons. Moreover, after I paid Mrs. Seeley the wages I owed her for the dress and the transportation from Philadelphia, I had managed to send home a few pennies to my family. Mum and Dad would be proud of their *síofra,* and I felt content that I was fulfilling my duty.

What began as a solid determination to please Mrs. Carnegie solely to secure my position developed into a fervent desire to succeed for its own sake. Born of my innate desire to undertake the impossible — that *síofra* quality — I wanted to infuse my mistress with delight. Not that I always succeeded with the mercurial, persnickety Mrs. Carnegie. And not that I didn't worry about being called out as a fraud every step of the way. But I tried.

I watched and waited as she examined herself in the mirror.

"I look tidy, Clara," Mrs. Carnegie said to me as she studied her reflection. I almost smiled at this rare compliment but willed my mouth toward modesty. She loathed any display of emotion tending toward self-indulgence.

"May I take your leave then, ma'am?"

"Yes, Clara. Please make certain to be back to the house in time to assist me at bedtime."

"Of course, ma'am."

After a respectful curtsy, I backed out of Mrs. Carnegie's bedchamber and padded up the back staircase to my bedchamber, happy that I didn't run into the elder Mr. Carnegie in the process. Since our encounter in the library, I'd only seen him occasionally, as he had been traveling. Mercifully, this meant that my exposure to him was minimal, consisting of brief curtsies as I dropped Mrs. Carnegie off at the dining room for dinner or the parlor for a business conversation with her sons. My discomfort in his presence had not abated since our library encounter, and I was relieved that our exchanges were few.

Surveying my little room — a steel-framed single bed, three-drawer dresser, and washstand with a pitcher — I was tempted to lie down under the coverlet and sleep the day away. Nearly one hundred and fifty days had passed since I had indulged in rest uninterrupted by shipmates' noises or my maid's duties. But Eliza's letter had reminded me to make contact with my mother's distant relatives — those same relatives who had lured me to Pittsburgh in the first place — and I had already committed to them for an afternoon meal.

Yawning at the tantalizing notion of sleep, I belted my gray tweed coat over my servant's dress of black wool. I wondered whether I should change into a nicer gown for the family visit. But into what would I change? The only dress I owned besides my uniform was Mrs. Seeley's castoff, and it resembled a uniform in any event. Not to mention I'd still have to serve Mrs. Carnegie in my uniform as soon as I returned. No, the black wool would have to suffice.

I landed on the final step of the back staircase with an unexpected thud. Mary and Hilda, the scullery maids, glanced up and, seeing it was me, quickly returned to their chopping of vegetables for the luncheon stew without so much as a smile. The divide between the lady's maid and the rest of the staff was a chasm I'd yet to bridge, although in truth, I'd been too busy to make much of an effort. Only Mr. Ford acknowledged me with a grin. Like me, he seemed to exist in a world separate from the two realms dominated by Mr. Holyrod and Mrs. Stewart. Was it because of his color or his station? I did not know, but I was grateful for his small kindnesses in a domain where I was either ignored or obliquely derided, by Hilda in particular.

"It must be your day off, Miss Kelley," he called over.

"It is indeed, Mr. Ford," I answered with a smile. I actually felt like skipping.

"Enjoy, but hurry back to us. We can't have the mistress wanting you too long."

Stepping onto the sidewalk, the first time unencumbered by Mrs. Carnegie or a list of errands, I began the long walk down the cobblestones of Reynolds Street to the streetcar stop that would take me to Allegheny City, the town abutting Pittsburgh to the west. The air nipped at my fingers and cheeks — warm gloves and a scarf were too dear to purchase — but I didn't care. I felt free and light.

At my leisure, I stared at the homes bordering the Carnegie house. Although I'd accompanied Mrs. Carnegie into certain of them several times as she made morning calls or took afternoon tea, the homes looked grander from my vantage point now than on the heels of my mistress. I could hardly believe that I was allowed entrance into them. It never ceased to astonish me that my ruse as Clara Kelley was working.

Thinking for a moment of the real Clara Kelley, I wondered how her Thomas was faring. I had heard nothing from him since the letter, but I often imagined him at home in Dublin, waiting for a response from his beloved, much like I waited for word from my family. But Thomas's reply would never come. He would forever believe that Clara had rejected him, not that she had died at sea. He would never be able to mourn her.

Thinking of Thomas made me feel guilty for the luck I had in landing this position and the lies I'd told. The money was far more plentiful than I'd earn in a mill or as a low-level domestic like Hilda. Yet in my determination to insinuate myself into the graces of Mrs. Carnegie, I'd had little time to consider the source of my luck. Sometimes, I almost forgot that my gain had been at the expense of another's sacrifice.

My lighthearted mood turned dark with these thoughts of the other Clara Kelley as I stepped from the streetcar platform into a passenger car. The streetcar was almost empty at this off-hour, and I claimed a wooden bench for my own. As the streetcar rumbled to life, I stared out the window at the landscape made white by a blanket of fresh-fallen snow. Although the churches and stores and houses grew steadily less grand the farther we traveled from Homewood, the snow made the city glisten, a sight that would normally have inspired delight.

The horse-drawn streetcar from Homewood station to Allegheny City passed by Pittsburgh, quite close to its three rivers lined with mills and factories. More snow began to fall, but the nearer the streetcar drew to the city, the more fleeting the snow's cleansing powers became. The snow washed white the black skies for mere moments before the spewing soot blackened it again. By the time the streetcar crossed a suspension bridge from Pittsburgh into Allegheny City, the snow lost the battle with the soot, and black smuts sailed down like a new species of snow, settling on everything with an inky, sticky layer.

The streetcar stopped at Rebecca Street,

and I left the relative order of the station and joined the human stream bobbing along the road. I walked down crowded, filthy streets, and the acidic air, made acrid by the nearby tanneries, burned the inside of my mouth and nose. I could see not a single street sign amid the chaos. Had I gotten off at the wrong stop? Before venturing too far, I retreated back to the station, searching for a conductor or engineer who could be trusted to help me.

I implored a uniformed ticket agent, harried by a long queue. "I'm looking for 354 Rebecca Street, sir. Do you happen to know where it is?"

"Ah, that's in Slab Town, a bit of a walk from here."

I was confused. I would have sworn the engineer had called out Rebecca Street just before we pulled into the station. "I thought this was the Rebecca Street stop."

"It is. But this is Slab Town, miss — it's no Ridge Avenue neighborhood. It's like a rabbit's warren in there. I can give you general directions, but you'll be at the mercy of the locals once you get there to find the exact house."

"Perhaps I should hire a cab to take me there."

"No cab will go into Slab Town, miss."

He turned away to answer the call of a clamoring customer.

Following the ticket agent's direction to the letter, I made my way down Rebecca Street, dodging piles of steaming horse dung and mucking up my shoes in a muddy street that had never seen a cobblestone lining. Gangs of grubby street urchins scampering down the thoroughfare nearly toppled me into a group of men playing dice on the curb and a woman hanging laundry, a futile task in such a place. After begging their pardon, I finally reached the 330 section of Rebecca Street. The houses there were silhouetted against the bloodred flames from the factories just behind. Incredible how industry spilled onto the streets right next to homes without any border between the two.

Try as I might, I could not locate my cousin's house number. The passersby looked inhospitable at best, and I was reluctant to approach anyone for help. Finally, a kindly looking older gentleman, in ragged but scrupulously clean clothes, hobbled past, and I dared to ask his assistance.

With a thick German accent, he answered my question. "You can't find the number because 354 doesn't have a number painted on it. It's squeezed between those two houses there."

Feeling like a trespasser, I skulked down the road to where the elderly man pointed. He was right. Here, squeezed between the dilapidated homes of Rebecca Street, stood a house made from salvaged wood and scrap metal, even more decrepit than the others and even closer to the sparks flying out from the factory behind the houses.

Whether from its position on the slope of a hill or from the shoddy construction of the home itself, my cousin's house slanted into the house next door, almost like a lean-to. No paint adorned the ragged wood exterior, and the two upstairs windows were covered in paper instead of glass. This poor house would have been my home but for the death of the other Clara Kelley.

I hesitated before knocking. Only the fact that these poor people would have prepared for my visit — possibly spending what little they might have on a meal in my honor — stopped me from turning away. Only that commitment prevented me from running from what would have been my fate.

The door opened before my knuckles could rap. "We thought you'd never get here," a bearded man in his late thirties called out. He could only be Patrick Lamb, my mother's second cousin.

Patrick clapped his arms around me. "You must be Alice's girl. You've got your mother's eyes. Come in out of the cold."

Squinting into the dim candlelight, I walked into the single room that made up the ground floor of Patrick's house. When my eyes adjusted, I could make out a pregnant woman with a baby on her hip and a toddler clutching her ankles. Two other children, one boy and one girl of perhaps five and six years of age, hid behind her dun-colored skirts. They stood in front of a rectangular wooden table set for supper in a room so covered in the grimy residue from the nearby factories and mills that cinereous was the only way I could think of to describe it.

"Welcome, Cousin. It's good to see a friendly Irish face in this sea of Germans," Patrick's wife, Maeve, said. Petite but for her burgeoning belly, she was quietly pretty, an attractiveness marred only by the dark circles under her eyes. Looking at their many young children, I could well understand her exhaustion.

Patrick gestured to the table. "Come sit. Tell us of your journey from Ireland. We expected you here some time ago."

Children flanking me, I settled at the

table, which, as I suspected, was heaped high with the best food they could afford. Stewed rabbit, boiled potatoes, and a loaf of bread spread out over the table, paltry compared to the Carnegies' dining table but simple, hearty fare nonetheless. And from the state of the family and their home, it looked hard-earned.

I struggled to return to my natural brogue after so many days of feigning an Anglo-Irish accent. "You shouldn't have done all this."

"Nonsense. I've had solid work here in the mills, as I wrote your mother. We've been able to afford our own home. No sharing rooms with others." He glanced over at his wife with pride. "Our children have hard-soled shoes on their feet and full bellies. No hunger like we had in Galway."

"And I take in some needlework at night for the extras," Maeve chimed in, eager to share her contribution. "Like tonight."

My fork, full of stewed rabbit, froze midair. The thought of this young, pregnant mother, tending to four small children while undertaking needlework by dim candlelight to feed me, turned my stomach. How could I take food from the mouths of these children?

But refusing to eat would insult the

Lambs, something I would never do to this proud family. As I chewed on my rabbit, I explained that I worked in the Carnegie home, although I described myself as a scullery maid, as I had to my own family. No one from our sort of background would be permitted to serve as a lady's maid, and I wanted no one to know the deceptive means by which I had procured the position. My face burning with shame over my lies, I turned the conversation away from myself and toward Patrick and Maeve's life in Pittsburgh — the dangerous work Patrick undertook in the mills, the constant fighting among groups of immigrants for a higher rung in the hierarchy, Maeve's Sisyphean battle with the grime, waged with vigor but without success, the threat of cholera due to the lack of a sewage system. I instinctively winced at their recounting but reminded myself that they wouldn't want me to pity them. No matter the soot permeating every pore on their skin and every surface of their home in Slab Town, no matter the precariousness of Patrick's work, their life was inestimably better than what they would have faced in Galway, where the famine ravaged entire families and left those without larger farms like the one maintained by my family with no means to support themselves.

What had I done to deserve a better chance than them? Perhaps more importantly, what would I do with my good fortune beyond ensuring the well-being of my family at home?

CHAPTER ELEVEN

February 12, 1864
Pittsburgh, Pennsylvania

In a gloom as thick as the black clouds billowing from the riverbank mills, I returned to the Rebecca Street Station. My mind swirled with conflicting emotions, distracting me such that I almost slipped on a pool of waste on the stairs to the platform. I couldn't wait to crawl into the anonymity of the streetcar and shed the many masks I wore, if only for an instant.

When the streetcar arrived, I sought out the most remote, isolated corner and curled into it. There, amid the invisibility of the nameless, faceless passengers that surrounded me and in complete contravention of a culture that admonished women for expressing any public emotion, I allowed myself to cry.

Rationally, I knew I had no right to these

tears. I had a good job, better than my background would allow, far better than if I had lived with the Lambs as I'd planned. I sent money home to my family. I missed them, but I knew I served them best from here. For whom was I crying? For all the immigrants like the Lambs, who came to America seeking a better life but settled instead for a soot-infested home and dangerous work in the mills and gave thanks for it? For the education Dad bestowed on me that held no purpose other than to sharpen my wits to become the perfect servant? What did it say about society that the best a lowborn, educated girl could hope for was respectable servitude? It was as if all of Dad's teaching gave me a glimpse into a world for which I longed but had no means of entering.

A few stops into the journey, at Grant Street, in the heart of downtown Pittsburgh, a man slid next to me on my otherwise empty bench. Mindful of his proximity, I pulled my handkerchief out from my coat pocket and dabbed at my eyes, as if the pollution alone had irritated them. My self-indulgent lamentation needed to end. It was one thing to sob alone in a streetcar and a different matter entirely to cry right next to a stranger.

"Are you all right, miss?" the man asked.

I sensed rather than saw the other people in the streetcar stare at him. His question was most irregular. Strange men did not speak to strange women. Anywhere. For any reason. His was a far worse offense than my weeping.

I shifted my gaze entirely to the window and slid as far away from him as possible. I tried to focus on the gray-smudged office buildings passing by and the bustle of workers — primarily older gentlemen and youth, as most men in their prime were away at war — but the man's presence so close to me made it hard.

The man began speaking to me. "When I was a boy, I worked as a messenger for the telegraph company. The sky was even darker from the mills then than it is today, and on bad days, I couldn't see my hand in front of my face. To deliver my messages in the allotted time, I had to memorize the streets because I couldn't always see where I was going. Sometimes, I'd have to assist deliverymen who'd lost their way by walking along the curb with one hand on their horses. From this experience, I learned that when you've gone astray, a helping hand will always emerge from the darkness."

I had no idea why this man was telling me

this story or, indeed, why he was speaking to me at all. Was he trying to comfort me? Regardless of his motives, his behavior was wholly inappropriate, and I did not want the other passengers to think I'd done anything to elicit it. I moved even closer to the window, clouding the pane with my breath.

"Perhaps another poem by Robert Burns will lift your mood," the man said.

Turning away from the window, I looked at him. I realized that the stranger was the elder Mr. Carnegie.

He continued. "Although, if I recall from my last reading of Mr. Burns, he brought a tear to your eye. Perhaps a different poet will soothe."

I stammered out an excuse for my rudeness in not greeting him and my inappropriate emotional behavior. "M-my apologies, Mr. Carnegie, that I did not recognize you at once. I did not expect to see you on the streetcar. Please forgive me."

"There's nothing to forgive, Miss Kelley." Kindly ignoring my behavioral lapse, he focused on the safer question of transportation. "It's true that I sometimes take the family coach to work. But in truth, I prefer the train or streetcar. I started my career in the railway business — work I continue to this day — and it returns me to my roots to take the train home at the end of a workday."

"What a noble notion, Mr. Carnegie."

"There's nothing noble about me, Miss Kelley. We Carnegies are simple folk from a simple Scottish town."

His candor startled me. Mrs. Carnegie carefully avoided any details of the family's origin, although she was staunchly protective of anything to do with her Scottish homeland in general. I'd suspected that their background was lowborn, of course, given her unfamiliarity with the nuances of Pittsburgh's upper echelons and her malleability to my suggestions. But I'd received no confirmation other than the innuendo of the unpleasant Misses Coyne and Quinn. Now I had it.

Disarmed by his frankness, I spoke freely for the first time since leaving Ireland. "Mr. Carnegie, your life at Fairfield is anything but simple. It is wondrous." Immediately regretting my overreach, I begged his pardon.

"Once again, you ask for forgiveness when you've done nothing wrong, Miss Kelley." Then, changing the subject to Fairfield, he said, "You're right that our home isn't simple. I've worked hard to give my mother

113

the beautiful house that she deserves. Still, I suspect your upbringing was far grander than mine."

Our exchange was so fresh and natural, I nearly laughed and dissuaded him of his false beliefs. Nearly. Then I recalled the Clara Kelley I was meant to be and settled on a vague statement. "I think you overestimate my upbringing, sir. Learning was the mainstay of my youth rather than luxury." This was a true enough statement, given Dad's insistence on the education of his girls.

A triumphant expression passed across his face. "Ah, then I was right. Your heritage was rich indeed."

Hoping to turn the subject away from my background, I returned to the topic of poetry. "Has Robert Burns always been a favorite of yours, Mr. Carnegie?"

"There's none better for a fellow son of Scotland. Do you have a particular favorite of your own?"

Many months had passed since I'd had an intellectual conversation with anyone, so I had no answer at the ready. I considered his question carefully. "Many poets beguile, Mr. Carnegie, but I do have a particular fondness for Mrs. Elizabeth Barrett Browning."

"I've heard the name and read a few of

her works, but I confess to being no scholar of Mrs. Barrett Browning. Is there a poem you especially cherish?"

"That is a difficult choice, Mr. Carnegie. Each of her poems is a treasure. However, if I were pressed to pick one, I'd select *Aurora Leigh,* which is not a traditional poem but more of an epic. It takes up nine books."

"Nine books?" He exclaimed. "Your favorite poem is one that takes up nine books? It must be incomparable."

Laughing behind my hand, I answered, "It is."

"What draws you to *Aurora Leigh?*"

Which of the many controversial social issues raised by Mrs. Barrett Browning in *Aurora Leigh* — chief among them the obstacles women must overcome to be independent in a world dominated by men — would be the safest to choose? I couldn't risk scandalizing Mr. Carnegie. "I suppose it's the strength of the main character, who is a writer named Aurora, and her passion for scholarship."

"I see. Do you identify with Aurora?"

"I suppose I do, in some respects." I didn't want to dive too deep into *Aurora Leigh*'s murky pool of issues, so I turned the conversation back to the poet herself, to a viewpoint she espoused that I knew — from overheard conversations — the Carnegies shared. "I am also moved by Mrs. Barrett Browning's personal beliefs, the abolishment of slavery in particular."

He nodded emphatically. "That's a belief I share as well. President Lincoln's Emancipation Proclamation was an inspiration indeed. It moved me to write an antislavery pamphlet of my own."

"So you are an ardent supporter of the Union Army cause, sir?"

"I am indeed, Miss Kelley." He puffed up a bit. "At the outset of the war, I served Assistant Secretary of War Scott in the War Building in Washington. I was his assistant in charge of the Transportation Department, ensuring that the military railroads and telegraphs were safe and strong."

"That's commendable, Mr. Carnegie. I'm certain that you have helped far more soldiers in that role than on the field."

I meant for my words to serve as a compliment, but he winced. I guessed that his decision not to fight alongside the soldiers on the battlefield wasn't as highly regarded by others.

"It was certainly an honor to assist a country that has done much for me. And that work gave me the opportunity to meet President Lincoln, as he would often come

116

to the office and sit at the desk awaiting replies to his telegrams, which was a great privilege. Of course, I continue helping the Union cause with my endeavors to bolster the iron industry and iron production. Iron is in great demand for the war effort, and my iron businesses help supply it."

The conductor walked through the car, calling out "Homewood Station!"

As Mr. Carnegie and I rose, he said, "This has easily been the swiftest ride from downtown Pittsburgh to my home in Homewood thanks to you, Miss Kelley." He held my elbow as I stepped down onto the platform, as if I were a lady instead of a maid in his home.

When we reached Reynolds Street, I took my place behind him, as I did with Mrs. Carnegie. But unlike his mother, he did not stroll ahead. He slowed his step to match my pace. "Tell me more of this Mrs. Barrett Browning," he said as we walked.

Conversing easily on the topic of poetry the whole length of Reynolds Street, we had very nearly reached Fairfield when a familiar-looking lady approaching us from the other direction slowed her pace and stared at us.

Mr. Carnegie paused and, obviously recognizing the woman, tipped his hat. As it did not seem appropriate to leave my master's side, I stood nearby, my gaze lowered. Then he said, "Good day, Miss Atkinson. It's a pleasure to see you as always."

With the mention of her name, I recalled the woman. She was the unmarried daughter of the Carnegies' neighbor Dr. Atkinson and had been in attendance at one tea and two dinners at my mistress's invitation. Small-boned and delicate of features, the sharp-tongued woman had beautiful, raven-colored hair but was otherwise quite plain. Her marital status had been discussed at several ladies' teas at which she had not been present.

"Why, Mr. Carnegie, I thought that was you, but you had me confused," she replied. I did not lift my gaze to assess her expression, but I heard the sarcasm in her voice along with a wry, flirtatious tone.

Mr. Carnegie answered in his usual genial tone. "My apologies, Miss Atkinson. It pains me to think that I have engaged in some action that might confuse you. Can you share the nature of my behavior so that I might never repeat it?"

"Well, Mr. Carnegie, I do not think I have ever witnessed a Reynolds Street man walking side by side down the boulevard in deep conversation with a maid. I almost didn't recognize you because of it." She giggled, as if the very idea was comically preposterous.

I froze, waiting for Mr. Carnegie's reaction. Perhaps the kindness he showed me on the streetcar and in his home would disappear when faced with the judgment of his social acquaintance. Was his social climbing paramount above all else? It certainly was one of my mistress's primary goals.

The pleasantness in his voice turned cold. "I have no wish to alarm you, Miss Atkinson, but I also will not apologize for enjoying a conversation about Mrs. Elizabeth Barrett Browning with Miss Kelley." He turned toward me. "Miss Atkinson, may I have the honor of introducing you to Miss Kelley?"

I curtsied deeply, keeping my eyes on the ground. My position in the Carnegie home was tenuous — built as it was upon a lie — and I had no wish to jeopardize it by alienating my mistress's social circle, even if her precious son provided the impetus. "Good day, Miss Atkinson," I offered without looking up. I wanted to make certain she had no cause for calling me impertinent.

"Good day, Miss Kelley," she replied, her tone easily as icy as Mr. Carnegie's. "And to you, Mr. Carnegie, as well."

I did not glance up until I heard the clip

119

of her footsteps. Once I did, I locked eyes with Mr. Carnegie. "My sincerest thanks, sir."

"Miss Kelley, you should not have to thank me for treating you humanely in the face of disrespect. I was raised by grandfathers who had a long-abiding disdain for the aristocracy and the inequitable treatment of men and who pursued Chartist political beliefs unpopular with the British rulers that advocated for equal rights for the rich and poor alike. I am not about to stand idly by when a classist remark is doled out here in democratic America." He inhaled deeply. "Now back to Mrs. Browning."

We continued our conversation about poetry until we finally reached Fairfield. There, standing before the two very different entrances to the Carnegie family home, however, we could no longer pretend a divide did not exist between us.

As he approached the main stairs to the Fairfield, I curtsied to him. "Good evening, sir," I said, and before he could respond, I turned to walk behind the house to the servants' entrance.

CHAPTER TWELVE

March 16, 1864
Pittsburgh, Pennsylvania

The ladies erupted in laughter. Even the typically somber-faced Mrs. Carnegie smiled at the comment. I tamped down my own surprise at her reaction — indeed at the abundant merriment so atypical for the Carnegies' receiving room during the ladies' afternoon teas — to maintain my impassive servant's expression.

Mrs. Jones echoed Mrs. Vandevort's remark. "I too am thankful that my status as a matron does not require that I have the nineteen-inch waist demanded from these young girls today."

"Nineteen?" Mrs. Vandevort cackled. "I heard that the girls are whittling down their waists to thirteen inches with these newfangled corsets."

"How on earth do the girls eat in such

constrained conditions?"

"Rarely. And daintily when they do."

The laughter subsided as Mrs. Vandevort asked, "Any word from the war?"

Mrs. Jones responded. "My husband believes that the appointment of Ulysses S. Grant to general-in-chief of the Union Army by President Lincoln will bode well for our forces. General Grant plans on grinding down the Confederates with offenses on many fronts — Eastern, Western, and Mississippi."

"Your husband's views are, of course, well founded, Mrs. Jones. But I cannot help but wonder whether this strategy of multiple fronts won't lead to more casualties," Mrs. Vandevort said.

"So many young men lost already," Mrs. Jones whispered with a slow shake of her head.

None of the ladies in this room had lost sons or husbands, but certainly they knew many people who had. I watched as Mrs. Carnegie's always-erect posture stiffened further. War talk made her uneasy. She felt as though she had to explain the presence of her sons at home instead of on the battlefield, even though no one would ever openly challenge the choices of Andrew and Tom Carnegie.

Mrs. Carnegie interjected, "Andra dined with General Grant here in Pittsburgh when the general was journeying to and from Washington. General Grant, of course, knew Andra from his War Office days when he was in charge of military railroads and telegraph lines."

"How did Mr. Carnegie find General Grant?" Mrs. Vandevort asked politely. I sensed that the ladies understood what Mrs. Carnegie was trying to do.

"During their dinner, the general spoke freely about his war plans. Andra found him to be shrewd and deliberate in his strategizing but without any affectation."

Mrs. Jones sighed. "Perhaps we are in good hands then."

Mrs. Carnegie looked relieved that her contribution was well received. I watched her gaze shift from her visitors to the mantelpiece clock. When she glanced toward me, I knew that I needed to find out why the tea and pastries had yet to be delivered.

As I scuttled through the opulent entryway into the plainer back hallways that led to the kitchen, I thought how, most days, the war didn't touch Fairfield. This luxurious cocoon was well-nigh immune to what was transpiring across the country. The war only impacted the Carnegies on their balance sheet.

"Good afternoon, Mr. Ford." The cook stood before his vast stove, alone in the kitchen, a rarity.

"Good afternoon, Miss Kelley. Let me guess, the mistress is wondering where her tea has gone to." Mr. Ford ambled over to the enormous wooden table commanding the kitchen's center upon which sat a tray of bite-sized cakes. Miraculous how he managed to turn out magnificent foodstuffs with the war rationing.

"You have guessed correctly, Mr. Ford."

"It seems as though our housemaid Hilda has gotten lost at the market. Lord only knows how she can take so long finding some onions," he explained as he began filling the silver tea urn with hot water from the stove.

"I would be happy to take the tea in to the ladies myself, Mr. Ford."

"Are you certain?" He looked surprised. It was outside the purview of the lady's maid to actually carry trays and serve tea to larger groups, but I thought Mr. Ford understood by now that I did whatever was necessary to please Mrs. Carnegie.

"It's no trouble at all."

As he placed the silver sugar bowl and

creamer upon the tray, he asked, "How is the call with Mrs. Jones and Mrs. Vandevort going?"

"The talk has turned to the war."

He shook his head and whistled. Everyone at Fairfield knew the war was not Mrs. Carnegie's favorite topic. "That's got to be a tough subject right now."

"What do you mean, 'right now'?"

"Well, the elder Mr. Carnegie was just drafted into the Union Army."

My stomach lurched. Although I worried about his deployment for the sake of his mother, I'd grown fond of Mr. Carnegie since our exchange on the rail car and didn't want him to risk his life. "You mean he's going to fight in the war?"

"No, Miss Kelley. Things would be a bit easier for the mistress with her society friends if he were. No, he's paying for a replacement to take his place, though it's possible the ladies don't know about it."

"Won't he get in terrible trouble for doing that?"

"No, miss. The government created the Enrollment Act so that rich folk could avoid fighting. Perfectly legal."

"Who on earth would agree to take his place?"

"Plenty of folk who need the money.

125

Heard an Irish fellow right off the boat got $850 to fight for him."

I felt sick. Such an enormous sum of money would be hard for any desperate immigrant to resist. I shuddered thinking of that fate befalling Patrick. How could Mr. Carnegie, who proclaimed to staunchly support the Union cause and equality among all men, lure a desperate immigrant with no stake in America's war to his near-certain death so that he might emerge from the war unscathed?

Lifting the heavy silver tray, I thanked Mr. Ford and walked down the back hallway. As I drew nearer the receiving room, I heard a man's voice among the ladies. I said a silent prayer that it was the younger Mr. Carnegie who'd stopped to chat with the neighborhood women. I didn't know how I'd react to the elder after hearing Mr. Ford's news. Even as I made my wish, I knew it wouldn't be the notoriously shy Tom Carnegie regaling the ladies with stories.

It was indeed Andrew Carnegie, standing in the room's center, captivating the ladies with a tale about how *his* iron reinforced the beam of an unstable bridge minutes before the Union forces crossed it for a battle. He nodded to me as I lowered the silver tray to the sofa table but didn't greet me by name. A personal welcome to a servant would have been most unorthodox, even for the democratically minded Mr. Carnegie.

"There is no coffee on the tray, Miss Kelley," Mrs. Carnegie said in a tone I knew to be condemnatory.

"I am sorry, Mrs. Carnegie. I thought the ladies wanted tea," I answered, blushing at the thought of Mr. Carnegie witnessing this chastisement.

"Mrs. Vandevort is a coffee drinker. You should know that," she said.

"My apologies. I will return to the kitchen straightaway."

Moving as quickly as was appropriate toward the kitchen, I heard the heavy footsteps of a man echoing in the vast entryway behind me. I assumed Mr. Carnegie had taken his leave of the ladies and was heading into his study. Instead, the clop of his shoes followed me into the servants' hallway.

"Miss Kelley, a minute of your time, please," Mr. Carnegie said.

I turned toward him, shuttering my disappointment in him behind a small smile. "Of course, Mr. Carnegie. I am at your disposal."

"I have something for you."

"For me?" Had I left something behind in the receiving room?

Reaching inside his jacket, he slid a wrapped parcel from his inner pocket and handed it to me. It felt surprisingly heavy in my hands. What was this item? And why was he giving me anything at all?

"It's a gift for you."

"A gift?" I was confused as to why the master of the house would be giving a present to a servant. Suspicion grew within me, and I instinctively took a step backward. Old Galway gossip about preyed-upon servant girls loomed in my mind.

"Yes," he said with a broad, innocent grin. He seemed unaware of the possible implications of his gift, but how could he be? He was no neophyte in the world, surely. "I'd be honored if you'd open it."

I didn't know what to do. It was unsuitable for the master of the house to bestow a present upon a maid, particularly the lady's maid who was under the specific control of the lady of the house. But I couldn't very well reject his overture out of hand, improper though it was.

Deciding upon a middle ground, I demurred. "While I'm most honored, Mr. Carnegie, I've done nothing to warrant such generosity."

"Oh, but you have, Miss Kelley. You've opened my eyes to the wonder of Mrs. Barrett Browning's poetry." He pressed the package into my hands. "I found a first edition of *Aurora Leigh,* and I want you to have it for your personal collection."

"No, sir, I am not deserving. Please allow me to return it to you. Perhaps you can place it in the library for the entire family to enjoy."

"It is my intention, Miss Kelley, that this book inhabit your room. You are used to a world larger than the one in which you now serve my mother. I insist that you broaden it, beginning with this gift. As Mrs. Barrett Browning says, 'The world of books is still the world.' "

CHAPTER THIRTEEN

April 18, 1864
Pittsburgh, Pennsylvania

The day of service had been long, and I was weary. Still, I slid my sister's letter out from between the pages of my green, embossed leather copy of *Aurora Leigh* where I placed it for safekeeping. I wanted to reread her strangely stilted words to see if a second reading would leave me with the same unsettled feeling. Her letter was short on personal information and long on questions about our cousin, my situation, anything but home. This was peculiar for Eliza, who knew me as well as she knew herself and would understand how desperately I craved news from Tuam. What was Eliza keeping from me?

When the letter failed to give me comfort, I endeavored to secure answers.

Dearest Eliza,

Your last letter was woefully reticent on details about home, dear Sister, and heavy on the questions about this strange American land. While I know this country holds a natural curiosity for you, I sense a withholding on your part. Am I wrong to intuit this? I will indulge you, but only if you promise to spare nothing on every facet of life at home in your reply, especially Dad's dealings with Lord Martyn.

You ask about the similarity of the American people to our own. They share our language and certain of our customs, but there, the commonalities stop. The American people, all of whose ancestors, of course, hail from elsewhere, save the Indians, are cruder, plainer speaking than our own kind. At first, I found their manner brusque and off-putting, without any of the softness, nuance, and humor of our fellow Irish folk. Once I grew accustomed to it, however, I embraced its rough honesty, its lack of mystery about one's standing. I have also come to appreciate the directness of the American people's ambition. We Irish assume our status is immoveable and therefore bristle at any effort to climb

131

above one's natural-born station. There is no such assumption in America, and in fact, ambition is not only encouraged but rewarded. For men, I mean.

This quality of ambition is abundant in droves in my masters and mistress, about whom you have peppered me with questions. Their ambition to succeed in business is, in fact, so intense that, but for their Scottish accents, I would not be able to distinguish them from the American born. The elder son of my mistress, Mr. Andrew Carnegie, is a natural leader and charismatic in his way, caring for his younger brother in an almost paternal manner. He also bears an innate kindness and sense of justice that I admire, although he was quick to shirk his responsibilities to fight in the American Civil War. He actually paid for some poor Irish immigrant to take his place in battle. Can you imagine Dad or Daniel paying someone to take their place in a war for democratic ideals? What does this say about the man?

I paused in writing. I wanted to share more about Mr. Carnegie with Eliza, the sort of secrets we would share alone at bedtime. But I knew that Mum, Dad, and

Cecelia would be reading this letter as well and stopped myself.

Mrs. Carnegie is fierce and intelligent, nearly her son's business partner in truth, but stingy with her affection. Only the elder Mr. Carnegie receives her unstinting love. She is demanding of my time and skills and demeans me everywhere but her bedchamber, where she solicits my opinions almost gently. I find her confusing, but I respect her. Together with her elder son, she means to change the American business landscape, and she will use this war that the northern part of America conducts with the south for this end.

No, I have not made any friends among the staff. They hold me in strange regard. I am not the first Irish they've encountered, but I am perhaps the only educated Irish they have met. They are used to rural Irish like ourselves working in kitchens and as maids, but they are unaccustomed to domestics with the sort of rigorous education Father gave us. And they are suspicious of the freedom Irish women have to immigrate alone. They cannot understand how our menfolk allow us to travel so far from home unattended. They do not understand that, though we are far from our homeland, the tether binding us to our families and our values remains strong. Our duty never wavers.

Please, in your next letter, tell me of home. Tell me of Mum, Dad, Cecelia, and the farm. Tell me of Daniel and your wedding plans. Tell me all the village gossip, no matter how trivial. Please tell me that your reticence does not mean something is wrong.

Your loving sister,
Clara

CHAPTER FOURTEEN

May 5, 1864
Pittsburgh, Pennsylvania

"Do you think a picnic would be appropriate, Clara? It may be early days, but it seems as though the Union's position is quite strong, and it is well past our turn to host an event." Mrs. Carnegie was staring out the window at the spring-bright morning, fresh with promising magenta and ivory buds.

The verdancy of the day reminded me of early summer mornings in Galway, and with the reminder of home, my mood darkened. The gnawing sensation that something was amiss with my family had grown in the days since I had sent my letter to Eliza.

"Revelry, of course, has been out of the question in recent weeks, but General Grant's leadership of the Union armies seems to have lightened people's spirits," my mistress continued.

She and I were alone. She was always at her softest, most vulnerable, when it was just us two. In public, she preferred wagging an accusatory finger at me for any number of invented violations. My mistress enjoyed wielding her newfound power and flaunting her status, and while I didn't enjoy being the brunt of her displays, it added to my sought-after indispensability. Particularly since, in private, she relied upon my expertise, even though it was pretend.

"I believe so, ma'am," I answered as I turned my thoughts away from home and started brushing her hair the requisite two hundred strokes of the morning. "Not to mention that many would find the Senate's recent approval of the Thirteenth Amendment to be reason enough for conviviality."

Several weeks earlier, I had overheard Mrs. Carnegie and her boys toast to the Senate's decision to pass the constitutional amendment prohibiting slavery and involuntary servitude. That evening, I'd planned my own private celebration for the hour after I'd shepherded my mistress into bed. Once I bade her good night, I'd padded down to the kitchen to make myself a steaming cup of tea to sip on while rereading the moving discourse on slavery in *Au-*

rora Leigh. But the kitchen wasn't empty. To my astonishment, Mr. Ford was sitting at the kitchen worktable — a first for the hardworking cook — and he was crying.

The sight of the enormous man, usually jovial, wracked by emotion shook me. "Are you quite all right, Mr. Ford?"

He smiled through his tears. "I'm better than all right, Miss Kelley. I never thought I'd live to see the day that the federal government would ban slavery."

Relieved that his tears were happy ones, I sat down next to him. "It's wonderful news, isn't it?"

"It's more than wonderful, Miss Kelley. It's miraculous. It means that if the Union wins this war, I might see my wife and daughter again. Walking free down the streets of Pittsburgh, just like me."

His disclosure surprised me. "I didn't know you had a family, Mr. Ford."

"It's too painful to talk about it most days." He wiped his face with the edge of his apron and sighed deeply. "But not to-day."

To encourage him, I placed my hand over his and asked, "Do you mind telling me about your family?"

He didn't answer at first, just stared down at my pale white hand atop his wide, brown one. Keeping his eyes fixed upon our hands, he said, "My wife, Ruth, has golden eyes. Not the usual chocolate brown of my people, but flecked with gold so they sparkle in the sunlight. And my daughter, Mabel . . . Well, she's got those eyes too. On a warm summer evening with the sun setting, you should see the pair of them all lit up." He chuckled.

I smiled. "They sound lovely."

"Lovely, yes, but tough too. Ruth anyway. Mabel was just five back then. Ruth was the one who made the plans and pushed us to run."

"Run?" I didn't understand what he meant.

He looked up from our hands and stared into my eyes. "Run from the plantation, of course."

I felt stupid. How could I have not understood that Mr. Ford had once been a slave? And that his family was still enslaved? It made my worries about my own family pale by comparison.

My eyes welled up with tears. "I'm so sorry. Where are they now?"

He withdrew his hand from mine. "I don't know. The last I saw them was on the underground rail. We were in a tunnel in North Carolina that connected to the basement of a church that took in runaways, and we heard dogs barking overhead. I was the master's cook, and I knew he wouldn't let me go without a chase from his precious hunting dogs. The barking got louder and louder. So loud, we knew the men and the dogs were down in that tunnel with us. I pushed Ruth and Mabel onward — toward the passageway into the church — while I stayed behind to fight off the men and dogs as best I could. I knew it was their only chance. When the dogs came tearing at me, I realized that Ruth and Mabel hadn't gone ahead like I'd told them to, that they'd returned to fight alongside me." He grew quiet. "The next thing I remember is lying under a collapsed section of the tunnel. Ruth and Mabel were nowhere to be found. Believe me, I looked."

Words failed me. But I couldn't let his story go unacknowledged, so I stammered out a few inadequate condolences. "I'm terribly, terribly sorry, Mr. Ford."

The chair creaked as he pushed himself to standing. As he walked toward the stove, he turned back and smiled over at me, the same welcoming, jovial smile he gave me every day. I realized then that the affable, kindly man I believed Mr. Ford to be was simply a mask he wore. That none of us were who we appeared to be.

"We've all left people behind, haven't we?" he whispered and then bent down to tend to the stove fire.

Mrs. Carnegie interrupted my thoughts with more commentary about the picnic, an event that seemed frivolous in light of its tragic backdrop. "True enough, Clara. Most of our acquaintances would welcome a celebration over the Thirteenth Amendment. Mrs. Wilkins excepting, of course," she said.

I understood her reference to her well-heeled neighbor. During one formal dinner where I stood in attendance, I heard Mrs. Wilkins complain that "negroes" were being admitted to West Point. I had to work hard to suppress a victorious smile when, in response, the elder Mr. Carnegie replied, "Imagine! I have heard rumors that some are even admitted to heaven."

"Of course, ma'am," I said, continuing the brushing ritual. The process calmed my mistress, and I sensed agitation over the notion of the picnic. More questions would undoubtedly follow. "I suppose that the specific impetus for the picnic needn't be explained to Mrs. Wilkins."

"True." She paused, and I watched her face as another question formed. "We wouldn't be accused of callousness, would we? In light of losses others have suffered?" Ever cognizant of her position as a recent immigrant without a personal stake in the war, particularly since neither of her sons were fighting, she was wary of appearing unfeeling to her adopted countrymen.

"No one would ever accuse you or your sons of that, ma'am. I believe most of your circle would welcome the opportunity for a bit of merriment. The war years have offered little enough of it."

"As long as Andra approves." She had made her decision but wouldn't send invitations, plan the menu, or issue orders to the staff until her beloved son blessed the undertaking. The younger Mr. Carnegie, Tom, ever in his older brother's gregarious shadow, was never consulted on social matters and only superficially on business ones. Sometimes, he seemed even more invisible than me.

"I'm certain Mr. Carnegie knows best."

The awkwardness I felt over the elder Mr. Carnegie's gift of *Aurora Leigh* had abated in recent weeks. His travel had lessened, and he and I had been in each other's regular company as I stood by Mrs. Carnegie's side at morning calls, during parlor visits, and throughout formal company dinners. He never referenced our exchanges or his inappropriate gift. In fact, he only acknowledged my presence in the most cursory fashion, as was appropriate for the master of the house. While I felt almost as if I'd imagined our conversations, I couldn't forget about his decision to send a poor immigrant to serve in his stead as a soldier.

I studied Mrs. Carnegie's long, silvery-white hair in the mirror and wondered if this was the moment to summon my courage for a suggestion. "I've noticed that the ladies have begun experimenting with a different hairstyle." Mrs. Carnegie's center-parted style topped by a high bun hadn't been fashionable for a decade even in Ireland, and I worried that one of the women in her circle would mention this. The blame would then fall upon me, as the state of the mistress's hair was the purview of her lady's maid. I could not risk this sort of condemnation.

"Is that so?"

Her flat tone revealed nothing of her actual feelings about my suggestion, giving me no avenue but to plow forward. "Yes, ma'am. In the modern style, the hair is drawn back smoothly without a part, and the bun is worn at the nape of the neck rather loosely. Sometimes, a snood or net is

142

used around the bun."

As she considered whether my brash idea was worthy of commendation or punishment, her face took on a pinched appearance. "How would I wear a bonnet with that sort of hairstyle? The front of my hair would look a fright when I removed the bonnet indoors."

"I presume that you might instead sport one of the smaller hats that perches upon the head. Then the style would not be disturbed."

"I'd look a right jaunty fool with one of those caps sitting on my head. No. We will style my hair the same way it's been styled for years, and I will keep to my bonnet. I'd rather look like an old-fashioned matron than embarrass my Andra with tomfoolery. His place comes before all else, because it is on his position that our family rises."

For the first time, I realized how alike my situation was to that of Mr. Carnegie. Although the scale was quite different, the stakes were not. The well-being of both our families rested on our success.

Chapter Fifteen

May 28, 1864
Pittsburgh, Pennsylvania

All the elite of Reynolds Street had accepted the hand-delivered invitations to the picnic. With Mrs. Carnegie leading the charge, Fairfield focused on little else in the two weeks that followed. Since I wouldn't be needed for the service of the meal — Mrs. Stewart, Mr. Holyrod, Hilda, Mary, and the new footman, James, would present the luncheon — I assumed that I'd stay behind, and I relished the thought of a quiet house. But Mrs. Carnegie would hear nothing of it. "You know Mrs. Pitcairn is prone to fainting fits. You will need to come along and bring the chatelaine to revive her with smelling salts if she does." The heavy chatelaine, with its full complement of instruments to tend ladies' hair and attire as well as smelling salts should their corsets induce fainting, an occurrence that happened with surprising frequency, had become my constant companion.

The morning of the picnic, a delicious aroma wafted throughout the house. After I finished readying Mrs. Carnegie for the picnic and she ensconced herself in the parlor with the elder Mr. Carnegie to finalize the seating arrangement, I followed the smell into the kitchen. There, I found the center table filled with plates of fried chicken, beef tenderloin with horseradish sauce, deviled eggs of every imaginable variety, marinated asparagus, and peaches and cream sponge cake. My family had never seen a repast so decadent.

Mr. Ford, Mrs. Stewart, Hilda, and Mary raced around the kitchen preparing the baskets into which the food would be placed. Having already sent the other footman ahead to the picnic site with the tables, chairs, and china on the groundskeeper's cart with precise instructions on how to arrange them, Mr. Holyrod and James paced the kitchen, anxiously waiting for the final food baskets so they could be loaded onto the returning cart.

As I stood by and watched the mad frenzy, I realized that I was without specific instructions for the first time since my arrival at

Fairfield. Given that I was free until I boarded the coach with Mrs. Carnegie, which wouldn't take place until after the staff had already left, I offered my help to Hilda. I knew no one would ask me directly to assist them, her least of all.

Packing the tarragon deviled eggs into the picnic basket, Hilda sniped, "We wouldn't want you to dirty your dress for the carriage ride, now would we?" The staff would take the groundskeeper's carriage to the picnic. I alone of all the servants was permitted to ride in the carriage, albeit on the back. More fuel for Hilda's dislike for me, fodder for her belief that I lorded over her my access to the mistress and her realm.

I backed quietly out of the kitchen, trying to hide the tears that sprung up against my will. I belonged nowhere in this house. Not with the Carnegies. Not with the other servants. Even my own family members who resided in this city felt foreign to me. I was as utterly alone as the first day I landed on the American shore, with only the tether to my own family back home for company.

A rumble shook the sky in the far distance, from the city beyond the pastures. The azure blue of the sky made this sound seem impossible, almost comical. Because a quintessential spring day spread before us, like a brightly iced birthday confection into which the celebrants were about to bite, it seemed that no rain could possibly fall here.

No one else at the picnic seemed to hear the rumble. The conversation continued its gallop around the track with its participants racing to show off their better knowledge. I began to wonder if I'd misheard the sound. I maintained my position standing behind Mrs. Carnegie, chatelaine in hand, ever ready to serve her or any of the ladies at the luncheon.

Would I always live in this nether space of service? Always present but never seen, never engaging, my presence interchangeable with any number of others? I'd overheard Mr. Holyrod lecture the rest of the staff about the dignity of service, but I couldn't see any dignity in invisibility. Where was the dignity in constantly suppressing your own needs, views, and rights for others?

The picnic table was covered with gleaming silver, etched blue porcelain plates, fine Belgian table linens, and crystal bowls filled with cut peonies, even though the field brimmed with sunflowers. The juxtaposition of the finery against the rustic background seemed incongruous. The Carnegies and their guests seemed to be enjoying nature as if behind glass. As if the rustle of the wind and the buzzing flies couldn't penetrate their world.

A rumble sounded again. Louder. And louder again. Until it could not be ignored.

"Do you think that could be thunder?" the ever-nervous Mrs. Pitcairn asked.

Every eye turned to the sky. In the north, the heavens had begun to turn dark. Mrs. Carnegie glanced over at me, a momentary flicker of terror in her eyes. For all her obsessive planning, this possibility had not been anticipated. I found this incredible, given the propensity for Pittsburgh rain.

Ever jovial, Mr. Jones declared, "People, it will pass. Let's turn our attention back to this excellent pudding. Is it a meringue?"

Crystal glasses clinked and silver clanked on porcelain as the group resumed their picnic as if the storm would disappear simply because they were ignoring it. Mr. Carnegie continued talking pleasantly with Miss Atkinson. The ice that had frozen between them that February day seemed to have thawed. I'd overheard the neighborhood ladies say that Miss Atkinson received her education abroad, but given that her comments focused on gossip and clothing advice to Mr. Carnegie, I saw no evidence of higher learning or depth of thought. And

I already knew what he thought of her political views.

A loud giggle from a quip Mr. Carnegie had made escaped from Miss Atkinson's normally pursed lips. She held on to his upper arm as if his joke was so raucous, she needed his arm to balance. Their exchange inexplicably irritated me. Was it because I knew Mr. Carnegie was capable of conversation with more gravitas? Was it because I found Miss Atkinson undeserving of his attentions?

The thunder clapped loudly behind the picnickers, and a jagged bolt of lightning struck a nearby copse of trees. As if awaiting that precise cue, the deluge arrived.

Guiding Mrs. Carnegie by the elbow, I tucked her into the carriage before turning my attention to the rest of the ladies. Tittering with nervous laughter, they clung to me in the downpour as I packed six into a carriage meant for four. Mr. Carnegie squeezed the same number of men into the carriage they'd hired specifically for the occasion. Mr. Holyrod and the rest of the staff clutched at forks and saucer plates and whatever else they could grab until the groundskeeper's cart teetered with service items, furniture, and the bedraggled, wet staff.

The coachmen tried to calm the horses as another lightning bolt struck the ground. They tried to wait for Mr. Carnegie and me to find a place in one of the carriages, but the horses were ready to bolt. And there was no remaining room for us in any event.

As Mr. Carnegie signaled to the coachmen to leave, I heard Mrs. Carnegie yell out the window, "Don't leave without Andra!"

He called back, "We'll take cover. Send a carriage back for us!"

As the horses galloped across the meadow, we scanned the countryside for some shelter. The copse of trees that the lightning had recently illuminated looked like the best prospect. Hands over our heads in a futile effort to ward off the worst of the rain, we ran.

The trees' broad leaves buffeted us from the bulk of the rainstorm, and the semicircular shape of the copse enclosed us in a protective embrace from the mounting winds. Mr. Carnegie took off his jacket and spread it on the ground. He gestured for me to sit upon it.

"I couldn't, sir."

"I insist. I cannot let a lady ruin her gown."

"There's really no need, sir. It's a servant's

uniform, not a fine gown. And while I appreciate the compliment, I am not a lady but simply her maid."

He gestured to his jacket again, leaving me no option other than to sit. Refusal would have been tantamount to refusing an employer's order, deserving of dismissal or, worse, a place on Mrs. Seeley's blacklist. Although Mr. Carnegie didn't seem the sort capable of such actions.

Settling on the damp grass beside me, he said, "You are a lady, Miss Kelley. No other woman of my acquaintance is as graceful in her demeanor or as elegant in her thinking."

His words shocked me, and I knew they should have offended me. Or made me wary, as I'd grown up with too many stories of the Castle Martyn lords preying on their maids to not be at least a little suspicious. Instead, I found his praise oddly moving. While no one had ever called me a lady before and I secretly reveled in the label, I was more flattered by his compliment to my intelligence. Dad always said that my pride in my wit would lead to my downfall, even though he fostered that wit himself.

But instead of speaking aloud my thoughts, I said what was expected of me. "You shouldn't say such things, sir. They are not appropriate."

The gregarious, confident Mr. Andrew Carnegie blushed. A deep pink that spread across his cheeks like wildfire, contrasting with his coppery hair. "I apologize if I was inappropriate, Miss Kelley. I spoke too candidly, without remembering that you come from a world far more genteel than the rough loomers' world of Scotland from whence I came. I am still learning how to operate in this rarefied environment, and it hasn't been easy."

I felt like he was describing me, not himself. How alike we were.

I tried to explain away my remark. "My cautionary words come not from the divide of our upbringings but from the divide of our current stations. The compliments you gave me are more appropriately bestowed upon the ladies of your circle — someone like Miss Atkinson — than a maid who serves in your home."

He seemed to consider my words for a long moment, then said, "I understand your concern, Miss Kelley, but the ladies of my acquaintance are all artifice and no depth. Their learning, in particular, has no profundity or feeling. Miss Atkinson in particular." He paused, and the blush reappeared. "Unlike you."

We grew quiet, unsure how to act around each another in an environment of disclosure, in a setting outside the stratified world in which we normally operated. I had felt so artificial and unlike myself since my arrival in America, it was a relief to act honestly, no matter how partial my candor was.

"I never thanked you properly for the copy of *Aurora Leigh,*" I said, keeping my gaze fixed on a blade of grass twirling between my fingers.

"Another inappropriate act," he said.

I started to apologize for chastising him earlier about the appropriateness of his behavior when I heard him chuckle. Glancing over at him, his face was full of gleeful mischief, and I realized he was teasing me. Shooting him the sort of scolding look I'd give Dad when he was ribbing me, Cecelia, and Eliza, Mr. Carnegie laughed even harder. And I couldn't stop myself from joining in.

Any vestige of discomfort between us dissolved, and I realized that his sincerity about his struggle opened a door between us. For a moment, I felt like I belonged with him.

CHAPTER SIXTEEN

August 8, 1864
Pittsburgh, Pennsylvania

"Loosen the thread, Clara," Mrs. Carnegie ordered.

Unlooping one skein of yarn from my hands, I slackened the line connecting us. My mistress's sharp knitting needles clicked as they scooped up the charcoal woolen threads and seamlessly integrated them into the scarf she was knitting for her beloved Andrew.

"Tell me more about Thomas Miller's recent business dealings," she demanded. Since Mr. Carnegie had entered the library a full hour ago, they had been discussing Cyclops Iron Company. Mr. Miller, a hot-tempered Irishman who was a friend of the elder Mr. Carnegie, had founded the company after he had been bought out of another iron company — called Iron City

Forge — by other founders John Phipps, the Kloman brothers, and the younger Mr. Carnegie, at the elder's behest. The buyout had ruffled Mr. Miller's feathers for a time, but the charming Mr. Carnegie quickly smoothed over relations and helped create the new ownership structure in Iron City Forge and Cyclops Iron as well.

Iron. It was a constant topic of conversation between my mistress and her son. In the wartime climate, even I knew that the hunger for iron was nearly savage — for ironclad warships, for railroad tracks to carry supplies and troops, and for weaponry and ammunition. From snippets of overheard conversations, I understood that the Carnegies wanted to be major players in the industry, and they were taking necessary steps to bring that dream to fruition.

"Ah, Mother, you've known Thomas Miller for years, as long as he's been a close friend. What more can I tell you? And anyway, I cannot remember any more details about his businesses other than his iron venture," he answered good-naturedly.

"Andra," she scolded him, "you could memorize a poem and recite it back to me when you were three. Do you think for a single minute that I believe that you don't have Thomas Miller's entire business history at your fingertips? That you are not privy to the ventures he's only *thinking* about forming? You're just being lazy. Or defensive. Tell me what's going on."

A fiery-red blush spread across his cheeks, and he glanced over at me to see if I'd witnessed his humiliation. I averted my eyes as if the yarn I held mesmerized me. He knew, of course, I was only pretending, but I didn't want to heighten his embarrassment by meeting his gaze.

He reiterated Mr. Miller's history with Iron City Forge as well as some other ventures his friend had dabbled in before forming Cyclops Iron. His mother was correct that he knew even the smallest details of Mr. Miller's business dealings. What was his reason for obfuscation? The relationship between Mrs. Carnegie and her son seemed that of the closest confidantes, and I'd only ever heard him be totally forthcoming with her.

I followed their discourse, trying to connect it to the chart I'd made the evening before about the Carnegies' business interests. Oftentimes, while I helped Mrs. Carnegie as she sewed or knitted, Mr. Carnegie stopped in the library to engage her in business conversations as an adviser. I wanted to be ready should she raise these issues with me one day. Who knew where the discussions might lead?

Mrs. Carnegie continued with her knitting, uncharacteristically quiet, and I allowed my thoughts to drift to the letter I'd received from Eliza earlier in the week. In a brief letter written without Mum and Dad's knowledge, she confessed that the Martyns had been taking away actual acreage from the family farm since spring, not just bits and pieces as they had in the months leading up to my departure. Acre by acre, they had been giving away pieces of the farm to neighboring tenants, citing Dad's political views. My family still had eight acres, land to raise diverse enough crops to survive, but just barely. The wages I had been sending over had been transformed from safeguard to lifeline. I felt sick with helplessness.

The line slackened, and my mistress stopped knitting. From her sharp intake of breath, I knew she was about to bestow an order on her older son, couched as emphatic advice, when the younger Mr. Carnegie entered the library.

The fair-haired, twenty-one-year-old man walked past the bookcases that held not only leather-bound volumes but also pigeonholes for documents and drawers for games and sat down in the empty chair across from his mother. He did not glance at his brother at all. His face normally bore a placid expression, which hid a quiet intelligence and an eager friendliness reserved for his few close mates. But there was nothing placid about his face now.

"Did I hear you talking about Cyclops Iron and Iron City Forge?" he asked my mistress, directing his question only to her.

She shot the elder Mr. Carnegie an almost imperceptible look. "We were just wrapping up, Tom. Minor details only. Nothing to trouble yourself about."

"Mother, I'm surprised to hear you describe my concerns about my rather large stake in Iron City Forge as 'nothing to trouble yourself about.'" His voice was trembling, whether with nerves or anger, I couldn't tell. His demeanor shocked me.

"I don't know what you're talking about," she answered, her voice guarded in a manner I'd never heard before.

"Surely Andrew has told you about his decision to invest in Tom Miller's Cyclops Iron Company? A venture that will *rival* Iron City Forge — *my* company — for all the big iron contracts." The younger Mr. Carnegie was furious, and he nearly knocked over his chair as he stood to pour himself a whiskey from the sideboard.

I couldn't help but think that the younger Mr. Carnegie must be mistaken. One of the qualities I admired in his elder brother was his loyalty to his family, a trait I shared.

Surprise flitted across my mistress's face, but she quickly masked it. Instead, she snapped, "Tom, isn't it a bit early in the day for a drink?"

"Don't change the subject, Mother."

The elder Mr. Carnegie rose from his position on the couch. "Don't you dare speak to Mother that way, Tom."

The younger Mr. Carnegie turned toward his brother for the first time since entering the room. "That's rich, Andrew, taking the high road when your own feet are filthy with the muck of your dirty dealings."

I almost gasped at the strong accusation. I had never witnessed anything but solidarity between the brothers, under the elder Mr. Carnegie's guidance, of course.

"You're talking nonsense, Tom. Maybe that's not your first drink of the day."

The brothers drew closer to one another until they stood face-to-face, highlighting the elder brother's shorter stature. But this disparity did nothing to make the elder Mr. Carnegie back down, even when his younger brother raised himself even taller in order to intimidate. The elder Mr. Carnegie's eyes flashed with an anger I'd never seen in him before, but then, I supposed I'd be furious if one of my family members accused me of deception. Was this hypocritical of me? I had not exactly told my family the entire truth about my own situation.

"Your nasty secret is out. I know about your planned ownership stake in Cyclops Iron," Tom said in a seething tone. "And I know what it will do to my stake in Iron City Forge. As do you."

"*Your* stake in Iron City Forge? Who gave you the money for that stake, Tom?" The elder Mr. Carnegie's face was red again, although now from rage, not from shame.

"No matter where the money came from, the stake is in my name. And it's going to be worth far less once Cyclops Iron competes for the same contracts as Iron City Forge."

Mrs. Carnegie put down her knitting needles and reached out for my hand. She wanted to stand between her two beloved sons and stop their fighting. I helped her to rise, and then stood by, feeling like an intruder in a private moment. But my mistress had not given me leave to exit the room, and in truth, I wanted to see how this battle would be won.

The elder Mr. Carnegie's eyes narrowed.

"Think about it, Tom. Why would I want to harm the stake I funded in Iron City Forge? Isn't it possible that I have a larger plan in mind? One that benefits both Cyclops Iron and Iron City Forge? One that benefits our family?"

Mrs. Carnegie's mouth opened as if she wanted to chime in, but then she clamped it shut. She wanted to see what her younger son's response would be. And so did I. To my surprise, it seemed that the elder Mr. Carnegie had engaged in some dishonesty with his younger brother as well as possible chicanery. Was it defensible because he meant it for the entire family's betterment? Mr. Carnegie seemed to think so.

The younger Mr. Carnegie didn't answer at first, only quaffed down his drink and stared at his brother. "Why should I believe you?"

The elder Mr. Carnegie's face fell with his brother's words, and I swear I saw the glisten of tears in his eyes. Or was this another manipulation? "Why wouldn't you believe me, Tom? Since you were five years old and we arrived in Pittsburgh from Dunfermline, I've been taking care of you. How can you doubt my intentions?"

The younger Mr. Carnegie replied, his eyes flashing with anger. "Have you forgotten that I've been working for this family since I was fourteen? You may have taken care of me when I was a child, and I may have started out as your assistant, Andrew, but I'm a grown man now with a strong reputation as an astute, trustworthy businessman. One who smooths over the feathers you constantly ruffle."

"I am sorry, Tom. Forgive an older brother who sometimes forgets that you are no longer a lad but a man," his elder brother apologized, although I detected a hint of condescension in his tone. Mr. Carnegie wanted something from his younger brother, and he would say what was necessary to get it. I recognized this because it was a quality I shared, especially now with my family's well-being at stake. But I did not think I'd be capable of lying to and exploiting my family to do so, even if it was for their welfare.

After a brief pause, Mr. Carnegie continued, "And you're correct. You have an impeccable reputation, and I rely on you utterly to run aspects of our businesses. I hope my thoughtless words don't turn you away from this plan. I will need you to see it through."

The younger Mr. Carnegie's face softened a bit, but his eyes still bore a suspicious squint. "What is this plan, Andrew?"

A ruthless glee flashed across the elder Mr. Carnegie's face, and I saw the harder, more determined man who lurked beneath his affable exterior. "I am helping Tom Miller to create Cyclops Iron and investing in it only so I can merge it with Iron City Forge to make one massive iron company, one that can service the war's desire for the metal now and supply the massive rebuilding and growth that will undoubtedly follow the war. With the majority stake owned by the Carnegie family. And you at the helm."

The younger Mr. Carnegie's eyes widened at his brother's words. "Don't sell me a dog, Andrew."

Mr. Carnegie guffawed. "I wouldn't lie to you about this, Tom. You are my man inside the Trojan horse at Iron City Forge. When the time is right, you'll spring out, and together, we will take over Iron City and merge it with Cyclops. We will own a single, enormous company that will corner the iron market, engulfing all the small outfits into our behemoth."

But before the younger Mr. Carnegie could say a word — of apology or continued anger — his mother interjected. "See, Tom, Andra always has your best interests at heart." She said not a word about the machinations through which her elder son put the younger to attain those "best interests."

"If that's true, Mother, why didn't he tell me? Why did I have to hear rumors about it from the Kloman brothers?"

From the fleeting look of surprise on her face earlier, I guessed that my mistress knew nothing of this plan and likely had much the same questions. But she would never break ranks with the elder Mr. Carnegie and admit as much. When she didn't answer the question, her elder son interposed, "Because you're so kind, Tom. So good. I didn't want to sully you with the darker side of business and make you tell lies until the deal is done. But I was wrong to keep my plan to myself."

"I'm not a child, Andrew, in need of protection. And you should never lie to your family."

"I'm sorry, Brother. Old habits die hard. The protection I mean, of course. And this will be a long, tricky business involving the deception of old friends. But necessary if we want to control iron." He stretched out his hand for his brother to shake. "Can I be forgiven?"

The younger Mr. Carnegie's hand trembled as he extended it, and the brothers shook hands and then resumed their seats.

An uncomfortable silence filled the room, and in a few seconds, Mrs. Carnegie lowered herself to her seat, and her needles began clicking again. As if nothing had transpired, she asked, "Tom, will you be calling upon Miss Coleman this afternoon?"

The younger Mr. Carnegie stared over at his mother as if he couldn't believe — at this tenuous moment — she would actually ask about his nascent relationship with the daughter of iron-manufacturing magnate William Coleman.

But I wasn't surprised at the directness of my mistress. She was only reminding her younger son about his familial duty to cement a relationship that would serve the Carnegies well in their quest to control iron. She wanted everyone to be very clear about where they ranked and what they were expected to do. In her own way, Mrs. Carnegie was every bit as unrelenting as her eldest son.

The knitting needles stopped clicking as she noticed her younger son's expression. "Why are you looking at me that way, Tom? You cannot leave everything to Andra. We all have our role to play." Her voice was hard and unyielding.

"Clara, tighten up that yarn," she barked

at me, reminding me that I too had my role to play and that I better play it well.

CHAPTER SEVENTEEN

August 8, 1864
Pittsburgh, Pennsylvania

I needed space from the undercurrents of
Fairfield after the scene in the library.
Instead of retiring to Mrs. Stewart's sitting
room to tend to my darning, where I risked
her prickly presence, I snuck past Hilda
cleaning the glass chandeliers in the dining
room and out the servants' door off the
kitchen. Thankfully, Mr. Ford was in the
cellar gathering a basket of vegetables for
the evening's supper, or I wouldn't have
dared. His eyes were kindly but watchful,
and I cared too much about his opinion of
me to have him catch me in a lie or defend
me in one, especially after suffering through
a torrent of untruths from the elder Mr.
Carnegie.

Once outside, I leaned against the back
wall of the Carnegies' home and inhaled.

Did I dare to duck out farther from Mrs. Carnegie's reach? And even longer? I didn't want to jeopardize my position — my family was depending on me now more than ever — but the backyard of the Carnegie mansion wasn't far enough. Not today.

Skirting the perimeter of the Fairfield property, I walked down Reynolds Street, toward the little row of shops that formed the center of Homewood. I could defend my presence on the main thoroughfare as running a necessary errand for Mrs. Carnegie, but I'd have no excuse once I deviated from it. Glancing behind me to be certain no familiar face followed me, I veered off Reynolds Street into the neighborhood park, an outdoor space that was part sculpted gardens and part farmland.

An abundance of trees greeted me once I stepped through the park gates. Sour cherry and apple trees competed with maples, lindens, and elms for my attention. Bordering the trees were flowers in nearly every hue. Cows and goats inhabited a fallow field in the distance beyond the park's manicured lawns, and the noises of the animals reminded me of home. Would I ever see Galway again? What sort of life would I have there if I returned, especially now that Lord Martyn was whittling away the farm? But what sort of life would I have here if I stayed in service to the Carnegies? I felt mournful and adrift.

Farther down the winding gravel path sat a bench, and I gravitated toward it. Peering around the park to make sure there were no witnesses to my lazy moment, I finally sat down. A shaft of sunlight emerged from behind the cloud cover, and I closed my eyes, allowing my posture to slacken as I turned these questions around and around in my mind.

Footsteps registered in the distance, but I paid them no mind until they grew closer. By the time I was about to rise, a man sat down on the park bench next to me. It was the elder Mr. Carnegie. I straightened my bearing, ready to stand, when he motioned for me to remain sitting.

"I see you've discovered my favorite hiding spot, Miss Kelley." His manner was affable, as if the scene in the library had never transpired.

"I apologize if I have intruded upon it, s-sir," I stammered, trying to decide whether I should defend my presence here or fall upon my sword. Once again, Mr. Carnegie had caught me in a place I shouldn't be, and I couldn't keep relying on his discretion. Especially now that I saw the lengths he would go to accomplish his ends.

"I won't tell if you won't, Miss Kelley."

"I'm not certain I understand your meaning, sir."

"Pardon me for being bold, but I think we are both hiding from the same person. My mother."

I sat up straighter. Had Mrs. Carnegie spied me leaving the house and sent her son out here to test me? I may have been brash in sneaking away instead of tending to my chores, but I wasn't foolish enough to fall into the trap of maligning her, if that was their game. "It is my pleasure to serve your mother, sir. I am thankful for my position, and I would never want her to think I was hiding from her."

Mr. Carnegie looked hurt at my response. "I thought we'd reached an accord, Miss Kelley — that in this confusing world we inhabit, we shared a certain honesty."

Honesty? That was a rich remark in light of the stratagems I had just witnessed. While I sensed a certain shared kinship with Mr. Carnegie based on the few encounters we'd had outside Fairfield, he was hardly a banner-carrier of truth, and I'd been anything but fully candid with him. In fact, I'd buried my actual identity and refashioned myself entirely into a different Clara Kelley than the one I'd been born. The only honesty he'd received was the frankness of certain opinions and emotions, not the truthfulness of biography. In any event, true honesty at this moment would mean confessing that I was running not only from his mother, but also from the dishonest machinations to which he'd just subjected his family. The way in which he'd just bamboozled his mother, brother, and close friend astounded me.

I was too wary of him to respond.

He said, "I'm sorry you had to witness that unfortunate exchange with my brother. And see that side of my mother and me for that matter. If you understood more about our history, perhaps you wouldn't judge us — Mother especially — so harshly."

"I don't judge your family harshly, sir," I interjected, although my opinion of Mr. Carnegie was the one under duress at that moment.

"I cannot imagine this afternoon's conversation left anything but bitterness in your mouth. Will you give me leave to explain?"

I nodded. "Of course, sir. Though you have no obligation to do so."

"When we left Dunfermline in 1848, I was twelve and Tom was four, a white-haired child with beautiful, black eyes. We were

destitute. My father had been a weaver —
he made damask, to be precise, which made
him a king among working folk in our town
— but the industrial tide had turned against
his profession, and he couldn't adapt.
Maybe he didn't want to adapt, because any
new position would have been lower than
his high perch. Mother did the best she
could to support us by running a sweet shop
out of our home during the day and taking
in cobbling at night, while my father sat idle
in our cottage, staring at his empty loom. It
wasn't enough to keep us boys in food and
shoes. My aunt had settled in Pittsburgh,
and Mother thought our chances were better here. She scraped together the fare —
leaving a trail of debts in Dunfermline that
we have since repaid — and we made the
journey to the dankest parts of Pittsburgh,
where our relatives lived off work in the
foundries. Father fared no better once we
arrived. In fact, he seemed worse, spending
days staring off in the distance, while
Mother came to the family rescue by taking
in work cobbling shoes again. We would not
have survived if she had not supported our
family. She was our heroine. My father
passed away within the year."

"My condolences, sir," I said.

"Thank you, Miss Kelley. In truth, it felt

as though my father left us long before his actual death. Supporting our family — including Tom — fell to me, although my mother continued bringing in wages as well with her shoemaking in the late-night hours, in addition to all the housework she had to undertake. That's the way it's been ever since, even though Tom does help out at my behest at the different companies in which I've invested. It doesn't excuse the dynamic you witnessed today, but hopefully, it gives some context. Mother is determined that we will never experience poverty again. And so am I. I am ever mindful of my duty to them." He paused, his eyes glazed as if imagining those difficult times.

"That must have been a heavy burden for you."

He shook off his reverie and met my gaze. "No heavier than that shouldered by many others. And anyway, I was lucky. I got work right away as a bobbin boy in a textile factory, and then I became a clerk for a factory tending steam engines."

"You've risen far from those days, sir."

"It was that messenger-boy job I told you about on the train that really gave me unique opportunities. I took advantage of every chance it offered, making sure I would never work on a filthy factory floor again."

His lips involuntarily curled at the memory.

"May I ask what opportunities?"

"I quickly worked my way up from messenger boy to telegraph operator at O'Reilly Telegraph. Once in that spot, I made certain I was the quickest and ablest telegraph operator. Not just for your usual raise or promotion, but so that the most important businessmen in Pittsburgh would ask for me when they had a message to deliver or receive."

"How did you do that?"

"I have already told you about how I memorized the streets, so I was able to hurry along my telegraph delivery no matter the weather. But I always made sure to deliver more than the telegraph. I kept a journal at the telegraph office, where I recorded any interesting business information we received from the telegraphs. I began to piece together an understanding of the Pittsburgh industrial and business community. So along with messages, I would share with the businessmen I met anything I'd heard about their dealings or related businesses. They came to know me, know my intelligence and my work ethic. Soon enough, division superintendent Mr. Thomas Scott of the Pennsylvania Railroad began requesting me. And after Mr. Scott ordered the construction of a telegraph line along the railroad's Philadelphia to Pittsburgh tracks for the railroad's private use — so that he could better juggle eastbound and westbound trains along a single track — he hired me as his personal operator. Within a few months, I became Mr. Scott's secretary and chief assistant. In that role, I learned everything possible about the railroad business and worked harder than anyone else, proving my indispensability to him."

Indispensability. The very quality that I wanted Mrs. Carnegie to see in me. Again, how alike Mr. Carnegie and I were in our desires, although I hoped we did not share our ethical boundaries. He seemed not to comprehend the questionable morality in his youthful sharing of others' personal telegraph information or in his deception of his brother and mother today. As long as he met his objectives and furthered his family's goals, he viewed his behavior favorably. But how could I claim a higher moral ground when I lied about who I was every single day?

A wide, proud grin spread across the flat plane of his face. He seemed to adore telling me about his climb, a tale undoubtedly too coarse to share with his society friends.

Or perhaps too secret. But when he looked into my eyes, he guessed at my thoughts, and the smile quickly disappeared. "I wonder if this all sounds very crass to you. Your background was genteel."

"You seem to have a misguided notion of the gentility of my upbringing, as we've discussed before. I grew up with education aplenty but not much else. And now I must fend for myself, supporting my family at home as best I can. Just like you." He had no idea how alike we were. And how I envied his ascent.

A different smile reappeared, one much harder to read. "You do understand."

A rogue thought appeared in my mind, one that wasn't fully formed and one I suspected would never come to fruition. Especially since I was a woman. But the idea demanded a voice.

Before I could censor myself, before I could think through the moral implications of my request, I asked, "How did you do it? How did you change your fate?"

CHAPTER EIGHTEEN

November 24, 1864
Pittsburgh, Pennsylvania

If I had been expecting a template, he had none to deliver. But my question yielded many afternoons with many answers. Whenever Mr. Carnegie was at Fairfield for the day — instead of his offices downtown or traveling — we met in the park on that same bench during my mistress's afternoon rest. There, in thirty-minute increments, he offered me hope, for myself and my family.

I knew my route would not match his precisely. But if a poor Scottish immigrant could carve out a fresh, successful path for himself, maybe there was some way I could too. I began to believe this, even though I was a woman and the climb from one societal echelon to another had only been accomplished by men. And only very recently at that.

177

I listened. And I learned.

By working harder than anyone else, always at the behest of Mr. Scott, Mr. Carnegie had scaled the hierarchy of the Pennsylvania Railroad to reach his current position of division superintendent, which made him the man in charge of safely moving all rail traffic in western Pennsylvania. A heady height indeed for a small lad from Scotland, as he liked to tell me. But his true success came not from advancing rung by rung up that corporate ladder — a rare enough feat — but by investing in companies, a notion that had been novel to him. And to me.

"What do you mean by investing, Mr. Carnegie? Do you mean handing over money to a company founder? Like a loan?" We had developed an open dialogue in our park afternoons, where Mr. Carnegie tolerated, even encouraged, my many questions about the business world. Plainly, he enjoyed the role of teacher and orator as well as the freedom to share his actual thoughts and advice, not just the carefully crafted opinions he offered his societal and business acquaintances.

"No, Miss Kelley, an investment is not a loan, although banks and individuals certainly do loan money to companies. An investment is the opportunity to purchase ownership shares in a company. It gives you a piece of the company, if you like. When the company does well, the part owner receives a monetary payment called a dividend." He laughed. "Money for doing nothing. It's incredible."

I laughed along with him. Coming from a society where nothing was earned except by the sweat of your own brow, unless you were part of the aristocracy, I understood the disbelief at the idea of money making money without a lick of personal effort. Dad would be shocked at the notion, and I could well envision similar astonishment on Mr. Carnegie's face when, ten years earlier, Mr. Scott offered him a loan to buy two shares in the Adams Express Company, stock which had been made available to all Pennsylvania Railroad executives as quid pro quo for the lucrative contract into which Adams Express and Pennsylvania Railroad had just entered, and then, a mere month later, Mr. Carnegie received his first ten-dollar dividend check.

This dividend check was the first of many, he informed me. Initially, Mr. Carnegie made small investments based on Mr. Scott's recommendations. But then Mr. Carnegie developed his own methodology:

invest not just in companies but in a group of trusted people; only invest in companies he'd examined himself; and invest in companies that deliver goods and services for which the demand was growing. The most important factor in his decision-making, however, was the requirement that he had insider knowledge about the company and its dealings. This notion seemed illegal to me, but when I asked a gentle question about its propriety, Mr. Carnegie assured me of its legality, although neither one of us spoke of its morality.

Once he struck out on his own, he invested in oil companies capturing the crude bubbling beneath the ground throughout western Pennsylvania and in companies with contracts with the railroad companies to supply coal, wood, and iron, to build their bridges, and to manufacture their rails and cars. These were contracts about which he had insider information from his role at the Pennsylvania Railroad. When I pressed him for company names, he scratched his head and listed Pittsburgh Grain Elevator, Western Union, and Citizen's Passenger Railway, claiming that his investments were so numerous, he couldn't remember them all out of hand. I found this difficult to believe. But why would he bother keeping information from me, a harmless maid?

Key to his methodology was diligent research, he said. Mr. Carnegie had previously extolled the virtues of the free access that he — along with other working boys of Pittsburgh — had every Saturday evening to the private library of four hundred volumes owned by Colonel James Anderson, who had made money in the iron business. It was here, he claimed, that a poor Scottish boy was educated about the ways of the American business world. This library, he maintained, made him into a successful man.

"What if you don't have access to the information like that you found in Colonel Anderson's lending library?" I asked Mr. Carnegie. Aside from Colonel Anderson's library, which the working-class men of Pittsburgh could enter freely only on Saturday nights and only with a letter vouchsafing their employment, I had never heard of a library open to the public without a hefty subscription fee.

"I can tell you exactly what I would do if I did not have access to a lending library. When I was a boy, Colonel Anderson's library was only open to those boys and men who did manual labor. This did not include young men like myself, who were messenger boys or employed doing other sorts of lower-class labor not manual in nature. So I wrote a letter to a local newspaper petitioning Colonel Anderson to open his library on Saturday nights to 'working boys' who did not qualify as manual laborers. You can guess what happened."

"You persuaded him."

A broad grin spread across Mr. Carnegie's face. "I did indeed. From that day forward, Colonel Anderson's library opened to other employed young men, giving them — me — the ability to check out a book a week. Each Saturday night, I debated which of the many magnificent books I would take home. Would it be the inspirational Paul Allen's *American Adventure by Land and Sea,* or the practical Robertson Buchanan's *Practical Essays on Mill Work and other Machinery*? Should I pick the sentimental Sir Walter Scott's *History of Scotland,* the useful Joseph Black's *Lectures on the Elements of Chemistry,* or the classic Charles Darwin's *Natural History and Geology*? Or would Alexander Dumas's *Progress of Democracy* be the right selection? I can distinctly remember standing before those bookshelves and feeling inspired and overwhelmed by the opportunities found there. I would carry my book around with me the following week, reading it in breaks snatched from my work."

"What a wonderful story."

"It's much more than a story, Miss Kelley. I cannot describe to you the impact that library had on my life and my success. It quite literally made me who I am today."

"Countless other men undoubtedly shared your experience, Mr. Carnegie, and they have you to thank for it," I congratulated him. Then almost to myself, before I really thought it through, I whispered, "Although your success wouldn't have given me access to Colonel Anderson's."

"You needn't worry about entrée into libraries, Miss Kelley. You know very well you can read whatever we have on our shelves at Fairfield." His barrel-shaped chest puffed up a bit. "I've tried to secure a copy of nearly every book that Colonel Anderson had for our home library."

What about men like my poor cousin Patrick, who had no way to elevate himself. He had not grown up with books and had no current access, as Colonel Anderson's library had been closed since the onset of the Civil War. The impasse of his situation and that of his family troubled me. "How would the average person — man or woman — who wasn't able to secure free passage into one of the rare lending libraries like Colonel Anderson's that give access to the common man rise above his station? You've said that education — and research — were key to your success."

His proud, expansive posture deflated a bit. "I suppose the average man would be at a disadvantage there. Although not all knowledge comes from books. Life presents its own education."

"Not the sort to which you've been referring, Mr. Carnegie," I said rather harshly, the inequity angering me a bit. The barb slipped out before I had a chance to soften it, and I instinctively put a hand to my mouth. I couldn't risk angering him. These meetings, if discovered, would endanger my job, and I walked a very narrow road by continuing them.

He didn't seem to notice my inflection. Perhaps a lifetime of pointed conversations with his mother inured him to hardness. "True, Miss Kelley. And a fair point at that. Perhaps there will be a way to rectify this inequity one day."

I tried a different, softer tact to get my answer, the key to my own ascent. "How did your mother become so knowledgeable? As a woman, she never had access to the library or the business world, and yet I watch you consult her on all your dealings. She appears to be your most trusted business adviser."

He paused. Had I gone too far? A lady's maid, along with every other servant with access to the family, was meant to be oblivious to those they serve.

"Mother was always incredibly bright. While she didn't receive any formal education, my grandfather Morrison, who, as I've mentioned, was a leader in the Chartist movement, which advocated that working men should be able to run for Parliament and make conditions better for the poorer classes, encouraged his daughters to be well read. Once we arrived in America, she devoured every book I brought home from Colonel Anderson's library, studied every newspaper she could get her hands on, and gleaned nuggets of information from any source possible to achieve a deep understanding of our new world. Mother is the quickest study I've ever met, with the truest instincts."

Perhaps the template I should have been following was that of my mistress, not Mr. Carnegie. But without a son to influence, a husband with whom to partner, or money to invest, how would I forge a path like hers either? How could a woman make the near-impossible climb from a lower class?

Distracting me from these practical troubles, Mr. Carnegie explained his larger plan, the manner in which he would knit his investments and ventures together to dominate various metals industries in the years to come. The scope of his vision astonished me, and I longed to play a role in his ambitious undertaking, although I knew it was an impossible inclination. "I see the connection between these businesses, Miss Kelley. I envision the ways in which I can make these industries more effective, more efficient, than anyone else. It was one reason why I elected to have someone serve in the army in my place. I knew I could serve the Union better by increasing production and meeting its demand for iron than fighting in the battlefield."

I doubted that this proffered altruistic motivation fully explained his choice — I knew by now that his ambition played a powerful role in his decisions — but I was glad that a reason other than fear and selfishness was behind his conscription of a poor Irishman into the Union Army.

Church bells began to toll in the distance. "Your mother will be looking for me soon, Mr. Carnegie. I must excuse myself."

He stood up alongside me, and together,

we perambulated down the winding path toward the park gate. The air was heavy with the buzz of insects, awoken from their autumnal slumber by the unusually warm weather, and the only other sound was the crunch of our feet on the gravel path. We didn't speak.

Startling me, he broke the silence between us by quickly turning toward me and saying, "Sometimes, I feel —" He shook his head. "I shouldn't say it."

"Say what, Mr. Carnegie?"

"Sometimes, I feel like you are the only person in the world I can talk to. The only one who knows and understands me, with whom I can have a frank conversation."

I experienced the same feelings in his presence, although I tried to suppress those emotions. I had never met a man with whom I felt such kinship. The men I knew at home were farmers with minimal education and aspirations largely focused on their farms, and the men of my station I'd encountered in this country seemed cut from a similar cloth with a focus on mills or foundries instead of farms. I stared into Mr. Carnegie's blue eyes, seeing the outline of my face reflected back at me. I wondered if I was simply a mirror for him. A place where he could practice telling the story that would become his narrative. Or whether he felt more.

He stepped toward me and reached for my hand. I knew I should be wary, but I allowed him to take my hand in his. Although both of our hands were gloved, his in butter-soft, black leather and mine in rough, brown cotton, a castoff from Mrs. Stewart, I felt the warmth of his palms.

"I think about you all the time, Miss Kelley. I have written you countless letters describing how my feelings for you have grown in these past months of our park meetings, but I have always thrown these letters out. They seemed such an inartful expression of the admiration and, dare I say it, adoration I carry for you. Is there any chance —" He paused.

I was not certain what would happen next, what I even wanted to happen, when I heard a distinctive voice.

"I say, is that you, Mr. Carnegie?"

I immediately recognized the voice as belonging to Miss Atkinson, the very worst person I could envision finding us together, alone, in the park. Pulling my hand away from his, I turned back into the park, walking briskly into a thicket of trees and losing myself in their interlocking branches.

CHAPTER NINETEEN

November 28, 1864
Pittsburgh, Pennsylvania

Three distracted days and three sleepless nights after our encounter in the park, I still had not laid eyes on my mistress's elder son again. As I tended to Mrs. Carnegie in her bedchamber, the parlor, and the library, Mr. Carnegie's statements ran through my mind. Every time someone entered a room or rounded a hallway bend, my heart leaped, whether out of excitement or fear, I could not say. My feelings about Mr. Carnegie vacillated hourly.

On the morning of the fourth day, I brought Mrs. Carnegie's breakfast tray down to the kitchen and bumped into Mrs. Stewart, who was directing Hilda and Mary on their daily cleaning routine. "Apologies," I said with a quick curtsy.

"Ah, Miss Kelley." She looked away from

her maids, who she treated firmly but with more affection than she'd ever shown me. "You have been so busy with your mistress that I have not had the opportunity to find you alone for some time. To deliver this."

Reaching into the depths of her apron pocket, she handed me a letter from my sister. I wondered how long she'd kept it in there, her passive way of reminding me that, even though I was not technically in her control, she still wielded some power over me. But instead of challenging her, an act that could only cause me trouble, I said, "Thank you, Mrs. Stewart."

Mrs. Carnegie would be expecting me in a few minutes, but I could not wait to read my sister's words. Apprehension had been eating away at me in the weeks since Eliza told me of their acreage loss, and I needed to know that she, Mum, Dad, and Cecelia were all right. I walked up the servants' staircase, but instead of entering my mistress's bedchamber directly, I tiptoed into the guest bedroom. Shutting the door behind me as quietly as I could, I lowered myself onto the exquisitely embroidered apple-green coverlet.

Without shears to slit it open, I tore the paper as gently as possible. I did not want to lose a single one of Eliza's words.

My dearest sister,

You have asked why I have not shared news with you but have only asked for yours. You were right to sense that I was holding back. Dad would not want me to write to you of our most recent happenings. Indeed, he forbade it, allowing me only the latitude to tell you we had lost acreage, but you and I have never kept secrets from one another. How can I keep one so grave?

Our family has been struck by dual blows, Clara. Dad's fears have become manifest. Lord Martyn made good on his insinuations to rescind the tenancy completely. Citing the treasonous nature of our father's current Fenian ties, a blatant fabrication, he took back the land. He redistributed many of the acres to our neighbors, even the apathetic Malloys, and entered into a new tenancy with the remaining five. Our land is gone.

Yet this is not the only misadventure, although the second stems from the first. When Daniel learned of the termination of Dad's tenancy, he canceled our engagement. As the younger son, Daniel stands to inherit nothing from his own father, now that gavelkind has ended.

He must marry a girl with land as dowry. And I no longer have any to share.

I understand that Daniel had no choice, Clara. But I will not pretend that my heart is not shattered.

We must leave Tuam for mother's sister's home near Galway City today, after selling most of our family's furnishings for a fraction of their fair price. Aunt Catherine has offered us shelter on the third floor of her already crowded house, and the proximity of her home to the city is a blessing. We will be close enough to the factories to procure jobs if there are any, even though none of us are pleased to be moving to a place rumored to have grime and dirt in such abundance, it rivals your Pittsburgh.

As we move away from the farm, we will be more grateful than you know for the regular money you send us and more thankful than ever of your prosperity in America. Without your work and Aunt Catherine's charity, I am not certain how we would survive this terrible time. Maintaining his usual bullishness in the face of this devastating development, Dad insists that we will prevail in Galway City and return to Tuam to reclaim our land and right ourselves, but I do not share his confidence. We may survive, but how will we thrive?

Please direct your letters to the St. Nicholas Parish Church in Galway City. Aunt Catherine thinks it is the safest way to endure delivery of your mail. Pray for us, dear sister.

Yours,
Eliza

My body trembled with Eliza's news. Even though Dad had sent me to America to hedge against this possibility, I never truly believed that the farm would be lost. The shock of the anticipated catastrophe becoming real was too much to bear.

Sobs wracked my body, but no tears streamed down my face. My eyes remained dry. The dispossession was a tragedy that no mere tears could capture. Unless their fortunes changed in some dramatic and inexplicable way, the fate of my entire family now rested upon me.

CHAPTER TWENTY

December 12, 1864
Pittsburgh, Pennsylvania

It no longer mattered whether coincidence alone dictated my separation from Mr. Carnegie over the following weeks. I could not allow myself to wonder whether Mr. Carnegie was avoiding me by taking trips to iron plants in neighboring states. I knew the iron projects were legitimate enough. A review of the papers scattered across my mistress's escritoire confirmed that Mr. Carnegie was hard at work with Mr. Miller, overseeing the construction of a state-of-the-art iron rolling mill for Cyclops Iron, and his travel focused on inspections of other such mills. But the haste of his departure and its duration were unexpected, as my mistress constantly lamented, particularly since he would miss the holiday dinner the family was hosting that evening. I had to believe that his absence was a blessing for me, because I could not afford to think about him as anything other than an employer, and the specter of Miss Atkinson — what she had or had not seen — loomed large in my mind. The letter from Eliza lodged a new wave of fear within me over losing my job; I could do nothing to jeopardize my position as Mrs. Carnegie's lady's maid.

I stiffened my resolve to work even harder to become whatever this land required of me for my family's sake. This was the unassailable duty I owed to them.

"Pull the corset a bit tighter, Clara. Please."

Mrs. Carnegie only said please when it was just we two. I looped my fingers around the silken threads of the corset and pulled with all my might. Somehow, I managed to tighten it around my mistress's generous waist, slimming it by at least a quarter of an inch. Reaching for the black silk gown purchased for the holiday dinner the Carnegies were hosting, I slipped it over the corset and corset cover. As I cleaned the gown with a brush purchased specifically for this new dress, I examined its many ruffles and ebony crystals, marveling at the cost of a gown that looked almost identical to many black silk frocks in her armoire. The same sum of money would have allowed Patrick's wife to stop taking in needlework for a year, which she did by candlelight after her five children had gone to sleep. It would permit my family to rent a simple house of their own for upward of a year.

After I finished buttoning up the back of her gown, my mistress stood to examine herself in the full-length mirror near her armoire. I stood by her side as she spun her gown around until the crystals sparkled. "It looks well, doesn't it, Clara?" she said, glancing at me in the mirror's reflection. No matter how poorly she treated me in front of others, she sought my affirmation in private.

To my eye, the somber gown looked like all the rest. But to her, the difference of a pleat or a ruffle meant the world. I was careful to keep my face composed as I answered, "It is exquisite, Mrs. Carnegie."

"It's not butter upon bacon, is it?"

I almost laughed to hear Mrs. Carnegie, who was usually so careful to avoid slang in her language, use Mum's phrase that meant overly extravagant. "No, ma'am."

She smiled at herself in the mirror, an awkward grin that I'd seen her practice in the mirror before social engagements. Then she settled back into her dressing-table chair so I could finish buffing her nails and tending to her hair. After I secured the last piece of lace onto her regrettably old-fashioned hairstyle, I took my leave. "Enjoy your evening, Mrs. Carnegie. I will see you at day's end."

"Where do you think you're going, Clara?"

"To await you after your dinner party, ma'am." She had not given me any instructions for the evening, so I assumed I would wait for the dinner to conclude from my bedroom. Piles of worn stockings demanded my attention, and I preferred to do the darning from my room rather than Mrs. Stewart's sitting room, where I was permitted but plainly not wanted.

"I will need you to stand by with the chatelaine. Mrs. Pitcairn is coming to the dinner tonight."

"My apologies, ma'am. I did not see her name on the guest list."

"Earlier this week, she had declined our invitation on the basis of illness, but she seems to have recovered. There must be some bit of gossip she wants to hear if she is willing to put aside one of her many manufactured ailments to join us." Mrs. Carnegie, never bedridden herself, had no sympathy for others' sickness.

197

"Of course, ma'am. I will assemble the chatelaine, and I will be at the ready."

Taking my leave, I trotted up the back staircase to my bedroom, where I kept the chatelaine. After checking to ensure that the scissors, thimbles, thread, combs, powder, brushes, and smelling salts were all in place, I latched the container shut and walked back down the stairs. As I passed through the kitchen on my way to the entryway, Mr. Ford glanced up at me from the table, where he was putting sprigs of rosemary on a lamb dish.

"Mrs. Pitcairn must have accepted the dinner invitation," he said with a smile.

I laughed and lifted up the chatelaine. "How did you guess?"

"Brace yourself. It'll be a long night without the master at dinner."

"What do you mean, Mr. Ford?"

"Have you ever served at a meal where the elder Mr. Carnegie couldn't preside?"

I thought back upon the past formal evenings at Fairfield or houses of the Carnegies' acquaintances where I'd been in attendance and shook my head. Mr. Carnegie had always been present.

"Well, consider who will be sitting at the heads of the table," he said, obliquely referring to Mrs. Carnegie and the quiet, younger Mr. Carnegie. Leaving me with that thought, he returned to his task.

Chatelaine in hand, I passed into the formal area of the house and took my place in the entryway outside the parlor, where Mrs. Carnegie, the younger Mr. Carnegie, and their guests were having aperitifs before dinner. I listened as the talk drifted from the successful Union Shenandoah Valley campaign in the autumn to the recent reelection of President Abraham Lincoln. The conversation, mostly dominated by the gentlemen, was hopeful and light, perhaps because of the ladies' presence. When a lull descended upon the group, Mr. Holyrod stepped into the parlor and announced dinner.

The Carnegies, the Wilkinses, the Pitcairns, the Dallases, and Miss Atkinson and her father, Dr. Atkinson, walked by me in the entryway as they made their way into the dining room. My heart started beating quickly at the sight of Miss Atkinson, who I had not expected at this occasion. She and her father had originally declined the invitation as well.

Even though I kept my eyes downcast as they passed by and so couldn't be certain, I felt Miss Atkinson's eyes on me. I felt heat rise to my cheeks, and I prayed to Mary that

I was wrong. That I was looking for trouble where there was none.

I waited until I heard their chairs finish sliding under the table to take my next place in the back service hallway within earshot of the dining room. The dining room was almost silent as Mr. Holyrod and his footmen served the first course, a savory watercress soup. Silver clanged on porcelain as the guests began sampling Mr. Ford's creation, and the awkward quiet was finally broken by conversation about the excellent first course, which Mrs. Carnegie attributed to Mr. Ford, her cook.

With the mention of Mr. Ford, the group seized upon the topic of servants, relieved to have a ready subject to fill the void. The ladies took the lead as they analyzed their housekeepers, butlers, footmen, and maids in turn, each complimenting the other on their choices. My ears pricked up when I heard Mrs. Wilkins reference her lady's maid. It was only a matter of time before I was mentioned.

"You seem to have done quite well in your choice of Clara, Mrs. Carnegie," Mrs. Pitcairn said.

I held my breath, waiting to see what Mrs. Carnegie would say about me. "She is certainly an improvement on the previous lady's maids Mrs. Seeley sent over to me. Her training in the finer houses in Dublin, of course, gave her a solid footing for this role, although I did have to submit her to a rigorous reeducation to make her suitable for an American household."

"You have done a fine job," Mrs. Pitcairn responded, to which Mrs. Wilkins agreed.

I smiled to myself at Mrs. Carnegie's compliment and the ladies' concurrence. It seemed that at least one hurdle in my strange new life — that of pretending to be Clara Kelley, experienced lady's maid — was succeeding.

Miss Atkinson, never one to hold her tongue, was strangely quiet during this exchange. When the ladies were done congratulating each other on their fine efforts molding their respective staffs, Miss Atkinson spoke into the conversational gap. "Your Clara does seem to be an excellent servant, although I swear I saw her in the park in the middle of the day a few weeks ago. I recall seeing her because it struck me as peculiar that she would be out without her mistress at that time of day."

My fear, nebulous and gnawing, took on sharp and vivid form. Miss Atkinson *had* seen me in the park. She had simply been waiting for this dramatic moment to report it. Would she inform everyone about Mr. Carnegie's presence next?

"The park?" Mrs. Carnegie asked. "That can't be, Miss Atkinson. I keep Clara to a strict schedule, and she spends the afternoons with me or in the housekeeper's room doing her mending."

I could almost hear the smile in Miss Atkinson's voice as she replied, "I am quite certain it was her, Mrs. Carnegie. I've seen her often enough at your side to recognize her and her awful coat. You do not doubt me, do you?"

I knew my mistress wouldn't dare challenge Miss Atkinson directly. Her position in this society was too tenuous for open disagreement with someone as well-established as Miss Atkinson. Only with her sons would she reveal her feisty nature. Instead, Mrs. Carnegie would feel honor-bound to raise Miss Atkinson's charge with me privately and then report back to Miss Atkinson about my punishment. Firing was not out of the question, in light of the public nature of Miss Atkinson's claim.

I heard Mrs. Carnegie's sharp intake of breath as she readied her reply when the sound of a door slamming echoed throughout the dining room.

"Andra, you made it!" my mistress exclaimed with evident relief.

I could imagine her beaming at her son with the first real smile of the evening, made even brighter by the respite he had just granted her from Miss Atkinson. Despite my trepidation at his homecoming, I was grateful for my mistress's distraction from Miss Atkinson and whatever damaging news she would report next.

With the garrulous Mr. Carnegie taking over from his recalcitrant younger brother at the head of the table, the mood grew merry. The talk danced from business to politics to the war to neighborhood gossip without a single delayed beat. I could envision Mr. Carnegie's bright eyes and optimistic outlook infecting the table with ease, and despite my own discomfort, I felt relieved at his return.

Mr. Holyrod and the footmen traipsed back and forth, switching out the watercress soup for scalloped oysters and then bringing out the rosemary lamb and creamed potatoes I'd watched Mr. Ford prepare. The delicious smells wafting by me made my stomach grumble, as only cold ham, pickled cabbage, and apple slices had been on offer for the servants tonight. But I knew movement into the kitchen for any leftover food was out of the question. I would have to await Mr. Ford's generosity after our masters and mistress retired for the night.

Mr. Holyrod and James together began to carry a towering charlotte russe across the threshold when an enormous clatter sounded from the dining room.

"Clara, come here at once!" Mrs. Carnegie called out.

I raced into the dining room to find Mrs. Pitcairn unconscious on the floor, the ladies forming a circle around her while her husband knelt by her side. Her coloring was high and her breath shallow.

Reaching into the chatelaine, I pulled out the smelling salts and held them under Mrs. Pitcairn's nose. The strong scent did nothing to revive her, alarming the ladies. It was common enough for a lady to faint during a social occasion but quite uncommon for the smelling salts not to trigger the lady back to a state of alertness.

I stood up for a moment and whispered into Mrs. Carnegie's ear, "Perhaps Mr. Carnegie could bring the guests into the parlor. I will need to loosen her dress to improve her breathing."

After a quiet word from his mother, Mr. Carnegie led the gentlemen and all the ladies excepting my mistress into the parlor. While Mr. Holyrod sent for the doctor, I undid the buttons on the back of Mrs. Pitcairn's dress and tugged open the corset lacing. Spreading her dress as wide as possible in the circumstances, I waved the smelling salts in front of her face again. No response. I pulled her bodice wide open — far wider than decorum would allow — and held the salts directly under her nose. This time, she gasped and opened her eyes wide.

"Oh, thank the Lord," I heard Mrs. Carnegie whisper.

I leaned Mrs. Pitcairn up against me to facilitate her breathing.

"It isn't the Lord you should thank," Mrs. Pitcairn croaked between breaths, "but your Clara here."

CHAPTER TWENTY-ONE

December 12, 1864
Pittsburgh, Pennsylvania

The last guests had taken their leave. The staff had retired for the night, even Mr. Ford, who often worked until the early hours before dawn as sleep didn't come easily to him. I had finished readying Mrs. Carnegie for bed. To my astonishment, she had muttered not a word about Mrs. Pitcairn or Miss Atkinson. I wondered whether my efforts with Mrs. Pitcairn had absolved me of Miss Atkinson's accusations, but in truth, I doubted it and knew not where I stood with my mistress.

I closed her door behind me and, exhausted, trudged toward the servants' back staircase. The floorboards creaked loudly underfoot, but I thought I heard someone say my name amid their noise. Shaking my head, I disregarded the sound as the effect of a long day. But when I heard "Miss Kelley" again, I couldn't blame it on my tiredness. Turning in the direction of my mistress's chamber, I realized that the voice came not from her room but from the bottom of the main staircase.

Keeping my step light to prevent my mistress's wakening, I walked toward the sound. At the base of the stairs stood the elder Mr. Carnegie. "May I have a word, Miss Kelley?"

Even though every instinct told me to decline — begged me to avoid another encounter that could be viewed as compromising by an observer — how could I say no to my master without causing less trouble than saying yes?

Instead of waiting for me as I descended the stairs, he began walking toward the library. I followed him through the dark and empty front hallway to the book-lined room. The library was dark, lit only by the fire crackling in the marble fireplace and the low gaslights above the mantel.

He closed the doors behind us and said, "You've had a trying day, Miss Kelley. May I pour you a restorative brandy?"

The comfortable rapport we had established during our park afternoons vanished for me once I stepped over the library threshold and he closed the door behind us. Although we'd met many times alone in the park, I felt a deep discomfort in his sole company in this setting. It seemed more fraught with risk to be alone with him behind the closed doors of the family library in the late hours. "I am fine, Mr. Carnegie."

"Please, Miss Kelley. Allow me the honor."

I made no move toward him, but I agreed to the drink. "Yes, sir."

"Miss Kelley, I thought I told you to stop calling me sir," he teased as he poured the drinks.

The amber liquid glowed in the crystal facets of the glass. Once my hand clasped around the brandy, he raised his glass in tribute to me. I nodded and tipped the drink to my lips. It tasted like fire and heaven all at once.

"We are in your debt, Miss Kelley. You saved a guest of this house."

My exhale felt as fiery as that of a dragon. "Nonsense, sir. I mean, Mr. Carnegie. I was only doing my duty to your mother as her lady's maid." I hoped the pointed reference to my position might deflect an untoward conversation. The sort of talk he'd begun in the park, a discussion I half wanted to continue and half dreaded, particularly when I thought of my family.

"I think smelling salts were the limit of your duty, not the full breadth of resuscitation. Dr. Morton said that if you hadn't acted so decisively, Mrs. Pitcairn might never had regained consciousness."

"I'm just glad she has recovered, Mr. Carnegie." I drained my glass, thinking I should leave the room as soon as civility allowed. "Thank you for the drink and appreciation. As you mentioned, it's been a trying day, so I think I shall take my leave now."

After curtsying my farewell, I passed by him on the way to the door.

His hand touched my arm. "Please don't go, Miss Kelley. I-I feel that I owe you an explanation. You have been on my mind constantly since that day in the park"

I stopped walking, but I didn't meet his gaze. I simply waited for him to speak, fearful and hopeful of what words might form on his lips, all the while telling myself that hope could be dangerous for my family. His hand remained on my arm as he spoke.

"Miss Kelley, when we last met in the park, I shared with you the sense of comfort and ease I experience in your presence. I told you about the admiration I feel for you and your intellect. And I confessed my deep feelings for you." He paused, waiting for my

209

acknowledgment.

"Yes."

"I know that I spoke bluntly, perhaps too bluntly, but my sentiments were true. I feel something for you, Miss Kelley, that I've felt for no other lady. I know our circumstances are unusual, but I'm hoping we might reach a time where they might be less so." He paused again.

I did not know how to answer. My feelings required one response while my obligations demanded another.

In the silence, he said, "But I do not want to presume. Might you feel the same way?"

I turned away from the door to face him. Drawing back from him such that his hand slipped away from my arm, I squared my shoulders and rose to my full height, small though that was. "Mr. Carnegie, I do not have the luxury of indulging any feelings I might have. Miss Atkinson saw us together in the park. While she did not mention seeing you at my side, she told your mother tonight that she witnessed me in the park during the middle of the day. An inexcusable act for a diligent lady's maid."

I expected a strong reaction from him, but his face retained its composure. "I will handle Mother, Miss Kelley. Please do not allow Miss Atkinson to upset you. If you share my feelings —"

I interrupted him. "Mr. Carnegie, I do not think you understand. I cannot let anything jeopardize my position here. Accusations by a well-established society lady like Miss Atkinson will ruin me not only with your mother but with any lady anywhere. I cannot lose the livelihood upon which not only I depend but my family does as well."

"Miss Kelley, I cannot believe that a single sighting of you on a daytime stroll through the park would ruin your career forever."

"A single sighting of me in the park on a daytime stroll *with you* would certainly ruin me forever, Mr. Carnegie. And I believe that, if pushed, Miss Atkinson would not hesitate to reveal your presence in the park alongside mine, particularly in light of her earlier sighting of us walking along Reynolds Street."

Concern flickered across his face, but then the resolute expression returned to his eyes. Mr. Carnegie was used to getting precisely what he wanted. "Please allow me to handle this, Miss Kelley. There are many acceptable explanations for our presence together in the park that day. I cannot forgo our afternoons in the park because of Miss Atkinson's pettiness." His black eyes glimmered in the low licks of firelight. "Those hours mean too much to me. *You* mean too much to me."

The warm brandy had softened me, and I almost agreed. I felt a kinship with Mr. Carnegie unlike any I'd ever known. My afternoons with him were the only moments of authenticity in a world brimming with artifice. Minutes where I could build a pathway to hope. But how could I imperil my family? I reminded myself of the narrow precipice between destitution and sustainability upon which they walked — the sole variable being my wages — and I steeled myself.

"Mr. Carnegie, please allow me to explain my situation. May I be as blunt as you have been with me?"

"Of course, Miss Kelley."

"Ten years ago, when the famine raged in Ireland and I was still a young girl, my mother handed me a basket of freshly picked beets from our family garden plot to bring over to our neighbors. Like most of the local families aside from mine, the Flanagans had only a tiny garden, too small to have much crop diversity beyond the potatoes hit by the blight. Mother was worried because we hadn't seen the Flanagans in almost two weeks, and although we could ill afford to part with food, we knew their circumstances were worse than our own. I tromped several acres through the woodland to the Flanagans' small house on the heath. I knocked and knocked, but no one answered. I'd been taught never to open a neighbor's door without permission, but I knew the food would be welcome, and I couldn't risk leaving it outside where someone might steal it. So I pushed open the door."

Tears filled my eyes. Even though the incident happened over ten years ago, the image burned in my mind. And my spirit.

"What did I find behind that door, Mr. Carnegie? The entire Flanagan family — mother, father, four-year-old son, and an infant daughter at her mother's bosom — lay dead on the kitchen floor. Hunger had wasted them away to nothing. Their bones poked through the many layers of clothes they wore to stave off the winter cold made worse by their starvation."

I wiped away the tears trickling down my cheeks. "The potato famine may be gone, but Irish poverty is not, Mr. Carnegie. My family faces it every day. You've explained to me how the memory of poverty motivates you and inspires your strong sense of duty to your family. Well, the same memory haunts me and drives my decisions."

I walked toward the door. Placing my hand upon the handle, I turned and looked back toward him. "So you see, Mr. Carnegie, I cannot entertain any feelings I may or may not have about you. And I cannot continue to endanger my family by meeting with you any longer."

CHAPTER TWENTY-TWO

December 14, 1864
Pittsburgh, Pennsylvania

"Mother, you should not have been going through my papers."

I froze. Knitting bag in hand, I had been heading to the parlor to help Mrs. Carnegie with a new scarf for the younger Mr. Carnegie. But I didn't dare enter the parlor now. I had never heard the elder Mr. Carnegie speak harshly to his mother. Their exchanges took the form either of gentle ribbing or serious business conversations. This anger was unprecedented, and a troubling thought occurred to me. Did he have something in his papers about me?

"Are you accusing me of nosing about where I am not permitted, Andra? Since when am I not allowed access to your business papers?" My mistress was almost yelling at her beloved son.

215

"Those were not business papers, Mother. You read a draft of *personal* correspondence from me to Tom Scott."

Relief coursed through me at hearing that Mr. Scott was the intended recipient of the letter. But I still didn't enter the parlor. I waited in the servants' back hallway instead. I hadn't seen Mr. Carnegie since our encounter in the library two days ago, and I certainly did not want this tumultuous moment to be the first time.

"Personal correspondence?" She snorted. "I would hardly describe as personal a letter to your superior at the Pennsylvania Railroad, a man who has figured in our business discussions for years."

"This particular letter was personal." His voice was low, but his tone was seething.

"Do you consider personal a request to Mr. Scott that he help find you a position as American consul in Glasgow? A position that would leave behind me and Tom to handle the businesses you created, a responsibility for which Tom is not ready. How can something be personal when it affects our entire family?"

He was thinking of leaving for Scotland? Why? Because I pushed him away? Despite my efforts to bury any hope of a connection between us, I felt upset at the thought of this house — this life — without his presence. *Stop,* I told myself. *It is for the best.* Without Mr. Carnegie, there would be no temptation to stray from my duty.

"Mother, I am a successful twenty-eight-year-old man with my own private reasons for my request. A position in Scotland is the only enterprise I can contemplate at the moment. That's all you need to know."

"Andra, you know what they say. Any fool can earn money, but it takes a wise man to keep it. Right now, leaving behind the fortune you've amassed with only your inexperienced brother to tend to it, I'd say you're acting the fool."

"Mother, I don't plan to leave without making certain that all the proper measures are in place, not only to keep the wealth we've made, but to expand it as well. You must trust me."

She began sobbing. "Andra, I simply don't understand. We have always talked through decisions. Why didn't you discuss this with me first? Why won't you talk to me about it now? How can you leave me and Tom?"

Mr. Carnegie did not answer. The man who had a ready quip for every remark was rendered silent by his mother's grief.

Footsteps entered the room, and I heard the younger Mr. Carnegie ask, "What is going on in here? I could hear your voices all the way in my study, and the pair of you look mad as hops."

I wanted to stay for Mr. Carnegie's answer to his brother's question, but I heard the clatter of my mistress's feet on the main staircase. She'd had enough of her son. I raced through the kitchen — past a gawking Mr. Ford and Hilda who had been listening to the heated exchange between our master and mistress — and up the back staircase. I reached Mrs. Carnegie's bedroom door before she arrived. I did not want her to think I'd been privy to the fight downstairs.

"May I help you, ma'am?" I asked as she huffed up the final stair toward the door.

"Yes, Clara," she said, pushing past me into her bedchamber.

I followed her into her bedroom. Reaching for her elbow, I steadied my mistress as she settled back onto her chaise longue. Turning her back to me, she began to quietly weep.

I brought her a freshly ironed handkerchief from her drawer and asked, "Can I bring you something to calm you, ma'am? Your knitting perhaps? A book from the library?"

"I cannot think of a single object that would calm me, Clara."

"Some tea and biscuits then? A small glass

of brandy?"

"The only thing that would console me right now is the allegiance of my eldest son. And I do not think that is something you can deliver."

Of that, I was certain. In fact, I think I had been the one to deliver his disloyalty.

CHAPTER TWENTY-THREE

February 22, 1865
Pittsburgh, Pennsylvania

Dearest Clara,
The factory jobs were not as plentiful as
we had hoped. In fact, Galway City has
a surprising dearth of industry. Given
the amount of water running from
nearby Lough Corrib, the city could
power many mills. But farming still
dominates, leaving us with few opportunities for work. Dad was able to
secure a job at Persse's Distillery, which
sits on Nun's Island, formed by a fork
in the River Corrib, and produces more
whiskey than any other distillery outside
of Dublin. He will be working as one of
the men heating the liquids in the mash
machines, a dangerous position. In fact,
the job only became open because the
man who'd held it previously died from

his burns. Mum refused to allow him to take it at first until she realized that no other job would be forthcoming. And so she relented.

There was nothing for me or Mum, so we will have to contribute by taking in piecework from a local seamstress, but astonishingly, Cecelia found a temporary post also at Persse's Distillery. She will be helping sell the residual mash left over from the distillation process to local farmers who use it for feeding their cattle. When you think about all the convincing farmers need to buy that mash — we've all heard the rumors about how it taints the cows' milk — you can understand why the distillery folk chose Cecelia. With her bronze hair and striking green eyes, she is the picture of innocence, capable of distracting a wary farmer from his hesitations over buying the mash.

The wages are low, and of course, we have to purchase our food as there is no land upon which we can plant seed. We will have money enough to eat and contribute to Aunt Catherine's household, but little left over even for the necessaries. The money you send us is more important now than ever, and we say prayers nightly for your continued success.

I hope your Pittsburgh is cleaner than this outpost that calls itself a city. Even though factories and mills are few, the foul air spewing from them leaves an indelible mark upon the city streets, buildings, and people. I understand now that the fresh air of rural Tuam spoiled me forever. Coughing, from Aunt Catherine's family, from her neighbors, even from Mum, Dad, and Cecelia, especially given our constant, close proximity to one another, is more prevalent now than the chirping of birds once was. Do you despair of a clean breath as well?

Upon reading this letter, I see that I have painted a bleak picture for you. The actuality of our daily life is not as despairing. We have each other, and we have the support of Aunt Catherine and her family. And that is more than many in these hungry days. Worry not.

Please write me, Clara, with more details of your new American life. Tell me tales of your wealthy masters and mistress, until I can imagine a life as grand.

Until then, I am forever yours,
Eliza

I dipped my pen in the inkwell, intending to invent stories for Eliza's entertainment. I even wrote the name "Mr. Carnegie" before my pen stopped. I was unable to pretend anything for Eliza when it came to him.

The details of the Carnegies' lavish life would not be invention, of course, but the ebullience and happiness that she imagined it brought would be. Ever since our encounter in the library and Mr. Carnegie's conversation about Scotland with his mother, Mr. Carnegie's business trips had grown longer, and his presence became more and more uncommon. Without him and his uplifting spirit, a dreariness had settled upon Fairfield, particularly on my mistress. I shuddered to think what the house might be like if he should get his wish of a consular post in Scotland.

The only consolation for me was that as Mrs. Carnegie grew ever more despondent, her dependence upon me grew. Although I loathed the reason behind this, I knew that I'd achieved the indispensability I'd sought. And that it would serve my family well.

CHAPTER TWENTY-FOUR

April 15, 1865
Pittsburgh, Pennsylvania

The Scottish consular position sought by Mr. Carnegie did not come to fruition. My mistress was elated at the news, but only until her son made plain that he intended to leave Pittsburgh regardless. He never explained to her his need to flee, although I understood. And he knew it.

Mr. Carnegie continued to keep busy, away from Fairfield. On those few occasions he could not avoid me, I would feel his eyes on me as I served his mother, and quiet would overcome the previously gregarious Mr. Carnegie. Only on social occasions would he reenter the fray, turning back into the affable, confident industrialist. This transformation, striking in its quickness, often reminded me of a conversation he and I shared in a rare moment alone in the Fairfield parlor.

"What do you see in this room?" he had asked me.

The question had confused me at first. The answer seemed obvious, but I'd learned that nothing about Mr. Carnegie was ever obvious. I'd walked around the room, giving simple answers. "I see fine paintings hung one above another. Louis XV chairs upholstered in red silk fabric with long fringe and short, turned legs. A floor laid in parquet marble and covered with a red, flowered rug. Walls hung in crimson damask with a frieze of full-blooming roses painted above it. A Carrara marble fireplace topped by an onyx mantel clock and candelabra from France and porcelain vases from England. On the center table, a ewer and stand from Austria, a painted tile from Germany, and small ivory figurines from the Orient."

He gawked at me. "That is a mightily impressive recitation, Miss Kelley. How on earth do you know such minute details about this room?"

I smiled, a slightly devilish grin. "I've heard your mother describe it often enough to her guests."

"Of course you have. How silly of me to ask." He laughed. "Would you like to know

225

what other story this room tells?"

"Please."

"This room is actually meant to be read like a book, with each object functioning like a word in a story."

I stared around the parlor, trying to tease out the story in the room. Nothing came to me from the crowded, overstuffed, chaotic space. "I confess to ignorance. Will you read the room to me?"

"It would be my pleasure." He walked over to my side, placing his hand against my elbow as he would to any lady visiting Fairfield. I felt like a guest instead of a servant.

Pointing with his free hand to the center table and the mantel, he said, "The specimens you've so perfectly described tell the 'reader,' or guest, that the family residing in this home is well and widely traveled."

"I see." I didn't mention that the Carnegies had not traveled to the Orient as the figurines might suggest, but I understood how this "word" worked in the room's narrative and how a family might manipulate those "words" to send particular messages to their guests.

Moving his hand from my elbow to my palm, he guided me to the wall most crammed with paintings. "This array of choice artwork demonstrates that the Fairfield inhabitants are steeped in culture."

As he continued describing precisely what each painting would tell the observer about the family, I nodded, but I wasn't truly listening. All I could think about was the warmth of his hand on mine. While I wanted him to clasp my hand more tightly, at the same time, I was more terrified that Hilda might enter the room and witness us in such a compromising position.

Delicately sliding my hand out of his, I asked, "What about the furnishings? And the silk walls? What part do they play in the story?"

"Ah, excellent question. They are sumptuous and expensive but not overdone. This tells Fairfield's guests that its owners are well-to-do but not ostentatious. They are instead dignified and refined." He described the varying fabrics on the walls and furniture of the room, and once again, I wasn't listening. I had been struck by an insight about Mr. Carnegie.

The "book" about Fairfield was like the narrative of his life Mr. Carnegie was crafting. I sat back and watched him wield his "words" like a painter wields his brush, each a masterly stroke in the creation of a seamless whole. Except I was not witnessing the creation of an average painting, I realized. I was watching a masterpiece in progress.

Mrs. Carnegie had arranged a formal dinner for April 15 at Fairfield. The evening was meant as a joint celebration of the Civil War's end, as General Lee had surrendered to General Grant at Appomattox, and the European trip Mr. Carnegie had planned in lieu of his Scottish consular position. The furor that raged over her elder son's decision to leave Pittsburgh for a "grand European tour" with his friends Harry Phipps and John Vandevort at month's end had abated. Once it became clear that he was determined to leave Pittsburgh, my mistress relinquished her resistance and began to enjoy the details of his journey, a "gentlemanly trip," as she referred it to with the ladies of her social acquaintance. These ladies, as of late, did not include Miss Atkinson, to my great relief. Her recent engagement to a gentleman from the East End of Pittsburgh meant that she rarely frequented occasions where Mrs. Carnegie was in attendance. That worry, at least, had abated.

But the celebratory tone of the dinner changed to one of mourning with the assassination of the beloved President Lincoln on April 14. The Carnegies decided not to cancel the event. Instead, they sent servants around to their guests' homes with letters stating that the dinner would observe the rules of mourning and serve as a memorial meal in President Lincoln's honor. The menu was tamped down from its prior extravagance of melons, consommé, salmon, sweetbreads with peas, filet chateaubriand, roast duck, and dessert. All the servants wore black mourning bands around our upper arms, and black curtains were draped around the home. The Carnegies donned funereal clothes, although the change was not terribly noticeable on my mistress, as she always wore black.

The guests were dressed accordingly, and a somber mood prevailed at the beginning of the evening. From my vantage point in the servants' hallway, where I waited with my chatelaine as always, I heard eulogies for President Lincoln. Two gentlemen made various proclamations about the wonders of the late president and how he led the nation to victory.

Then the elder Mr. Carnegie began to speak. "During my time as the head of the telegraph department under then Assistant Secretary of War Scott, I had the great fortune of meeting President Lincoln on several occasions when he awaited information. His eyes and speech bore a plainspoken intelligence I've never since had the honor to encounter. Yet the most striking and admirable quality of the esteemed man was not his intellect or even the bravery of his convictions, but the perfect democracy of his everyday actions. He treated every man and woman he encountered with the same deference and respect, no matter their station. We should all aspire to his great example."

"Here, here," the dinner guests called out, clinking their glasses.

After every remaining gentleman made their tribute, well wishes to Messrs. Carnegie, Phipps, and Vandevort were offered. The clinking of crystal lasted close to an hour, and the mood of the dinner guests lightened with each sound. It seemed strange that they would be celebrating and mourning in the same breath.

A chair's legs scraped across the floorboards, and suddenly Mr. Carnegie was standing before me. His eyes had a glaze I'd never seen in them before, although I recognized it well enough from my occasional visits to Galway pubs with my family. Mr. Carnegie was inebriated, an oddity, since he usually abstained from alcohol.

We were alone in the back hallway. Drawing so near to my face that I could smell the whiskey on his breath, he took my free hand in his. He said, "Forgive me, Miss Kelley, for taking liberties. But given the impending date of my departure, I'm left with little time to speak my mind. And it's been torturous having you near but not being able to talk with you."

Did I dare to speak authentically? I was sick of lies and pretending and burying my feelings, and I wanted to admit the truth. Just once. "For me as well, Mr. Carnegie."

"You do understand that is the reason I'm leaving, don't you? That you have decided we should not share each other's company? And that we should not speak of any mutual affection?"

"I do," I confessed, looking at the floor.

"One word from you, and I will not go." He tilted my chin up so I would meet his gaze. His eyes searched mine, as if he might find the word *stay* there if he couldn't find it on my lips.

I had missed him terribly, and I was sorely tempted to do as he asked. "I wish I could ask you to stay, Mr. Carnegie. I truly do. But I cannot. My duty to my family comes before all else, which means I must earn my wage and send it to them."

231

"I could help with your family. I certainly have the means."

I heard a note of pleading in his voice.

I paused, trying to understand what he was really offering. Was he proposing that we simply continue our covert meetings and that he would help my family financially? I did not hear him offering something more formal. What would happen if he tired of me or his mother finally discovered us and objected? Given his intense loyalty to his own family, I'd likely lose my job along with the hope of securing any other comparable one — Mrs. Carnegie would surely carry a vendetta — and my family would be lost. No, I could not afford to indulge my feelings. I must stay the course, but respectfully, so as not to alienate him.

I could not risk meeting his gaze. I might soften. Keeping my eyes averted from his, I shook my head.

He removed his hand from my chin but kept the other wrapped around my hand. "I understand, and I admire your selfless duty to your family. Will you do me one favor before I leave?"

A knot formed in my stomach. What was he going to ask of me? I had always perceived Mr. Carnegie as above the sorts of antics I'd heard about other masters. Perhaps I had been wrong.

"Please call me Andrew, not Mr. Carnegie. I need to hear you say my name out loud before I go. Grant me that wish at least."

It was a small enough request. "Andrew," I whispered to him, and I felt my resolve soften.

He pulled me closer to him, and as I looked into his eyes, a jarring call sounded out from the dining room. "Andra."

"Andra!" The voice grew louder. "What are you doing near the kitchen?"

It was his mother. My mistress. And whatever chance remained at that moment was lost.

CHAPTER TWENTY-FIVE

November 4, 1865
Pittsburgh, Pennsylvania

I had believed nothing could be bleaker than an Irish winter. Gray skies without a hint of sunlight. Barren tree branches reaching toward the sunless sky. Relentless cold and damp that no amount of fireside warmth could thaw. But I was wrong. Nothing was worse than the onset of the Pittsburgh winter after Mr. Carnegie's departure.

Not that the weather was harsher than the winter I'd previously served at Fairfield. The frigid temperatures and the bitter winds and the snow made dark by the unyielding black smuts drifting from the city to the countryside were all the same. No, the sole difference was Mr. Carnegie. Not until he departed for his trip to Europe did I understand how much hope and lightness he brought me, even when our park afternoons had ended.

Without him, my life became an unending routine of service to an ever-demanding taskmistress, made increasingly difficult with the harsh change of seasons.

Without her beloved Andra to soften her, Mrs. Carnegie oversaw Fairfield and the Carnegie business investments with a domineering fist. Although the elder Mr. Carnegie left behind strict instructions to his younger brother on managing the family affairs, Mrs. Carnegie insisted on ruling alongside him like a co-regent.

Instead of accompanying her to morning calls throughout Homewood and afternoons of whist at neighbors, I began traveling with her to the Carnegies' downtown offices. I stood by her side while she attended meetings with the younger Mr. Carnegie to review the affairs of Cyclops Iron, Iron Forge, Union Telegraph, Lochiel Iron, Keystone Bridge, Central Transportation, Columbia Oil, Pioneer Coal, Adams Express, and a number of other brick, coal, locomotive, and iron ventures. Always quiet during the meetings — she was ever cognizant of reinforcing the impression of the younger Mr. Carnegie's leadership — my mistress's strength and intellect were unleashed behind closed doors with her younger son at home at Fairfield. She came alive in this new role, and I realized how brilliant she was. And I learned about the industrial forces in play in post–Civil War America.

The absence of the elder Mr. Carnegie not only fueled my mistress's tongue, but also freed her younger son from his subservient role to some extent. I watched as he stood up to his mother's edicts in those private business conversations. And while his mother had instigated the younger Mr. Carnegie's pursuit of Miss Lucy Coleman for the family's sake, he now sought out the courtship for his own reasons. The twosome shared a comfortable banter and attraction evident to any bystander, and it pleased me to watch him pursue the young woman for her own sake during the increasingly frequent family dinners between the remaining Carnegies and Colemans.

In truth, Mr. Carnegie was never really absent. Multiple times a week, lengthy letters with exotic stamp marks arrived at Fairfield. My mistress and her son acquired the habit of reading the letters aloud to each other in the hours after dinner. She reveled in his descriptions of the Atlantic crossing on board the newest and quickest ship called the *Scotia;* laughed over his trip home to Dunfermline, Scotland, where he stayed up all night singing Scottish songs with relatives in a town that seemed "miniature" to him after America; and soaked up his accounts of theater, restaurants, concerts, museums, operas, and architecture on the continent. Her son was becoming a gentleman, and while she missed him terribly, she delighted in the status of his well-earned trip, even bragged about it with her friends.

But the letters did not bring me comfort. In fact, they only worsened my mood. To hear of his adventures, accompanied by his friends, with words full of wonder and merriment, made my situation bleaker by comparison because it threw my lingering feelings about him into bold relief.

"Are you listening, Tom?" my mistress barked at her son.

Reluctantly, Tom lowered the newspaper he had been enjoying by the roaring fire and feigned attention. I surmised that his interest in these travel letters was minimal, as he received his own regular missives from his older brother with demands that he send written reports on the state of the family's business interests and that he undertake specific tasks at the different ventures. The younger Mr. Carnegie believed himself to be capable of making decisions on his own and often disagreed with his brother's determination to continually reinvest the capital they made. If the young Mr. Carnegie were in charge, I had heard him complain to his mother, he would operate far more conservatively, putting the money safely away or paying off accumulated debts. But he never disobeyed his elder brother, who insisted this post–Civil War period was the time for aggressive investment as the demand for iron and railroads was sure to rise. For all his blunderbuss, the younger Mr. Carnegie wouldn't dare challenge the elder.

"You have my rapt attention, Mother," Tom answered.

She glanced over at her younger boy, eyes squinting suspiciously as she asked, "Is that sarcasm I hear in your voice, Tom?"

Tom dropped the paper to the floor, folded his hands upon his lap, and said, "Of course not, Mother. I am waiting."

"Excellent," she said with a victorious smile. "Listen up."

Dearest Mother and Tom,

It is a Sunday and therefore, a day of literary labor, as we boys have dubbed it. As you know, my task is to make a record of our travels in the form of long letters to you, and I hope you will indulge me in the finer details of our journeys.

We continue to take the continent by storm. We get along famously here in Dresden, Germany, each of us keeping to our established roles. Vandy is our resident German speaker and jack-of-all-trades; Harry serves as our postmaster by mailing all letters and ensuring the safe travel of our luggage; and I am the consummate planner and chief enthusiast, by which I mean I map out the excursions and spur the boys along. The boys cannot keep up with me, tiring far too easily, but then, no one has ever kept my pace but you, Mother. As usual, Harry and Vandy try to restrain my determination to visit every museum, sight, theater, and restaurant of note, without success.

We arrived in Dresden but two nights ago, greeted by a most exquisite jewel box of a city. Impressive church spires stared out at us out over the winding Elbe River, where all manner of boats sailed. Despite evidence of industry, the skies, the river, and buildings bear none of the dark marks of progress so prevalent in Pittsburgh. Quick study that I am, I am learning the language of Dresden's breathtaking, often fanciful, buildings, especially the baroque and rococo structures that inhabit the center of the city like the Coselpalais. These churches, palaces, and government offices are unlike any of the structures in the New World or Old that I've encountered so far, with artwork to match. I am torn as to whether to name as my favorite the Sophienkirche, the city's sole Gothic church built in early 1200s if legend can be believed, with its massive twin steeples, or the marvelously rococo, eighteenth-century palace the locals simply call the Zwinger. If pressed, I would likely pick the Sophienkirche, because it houses an enormous Silbermann organ where, rumor has it, Bach himself once performed.

Shall I regale you with details of the opera we heard at the famed Semperoper? No, since we have been speaking the language of architecture, I will first describe to you the opera house itself, worthy of visiting even without the exquisite singing that resounds within its hallowed walls. Considered one of the most beautiful opera houses, it boasts of three different architectural styles — renaissance, baroque, and Greek classical revival — a boon for a student like myself who finds the styles much easier to distinguish when studied side by side. Have I impressed you yet, Mother, with my new art terminology?

Vandy's German has been indispensable in this regard. It assists us not only in our study of art and culture, but in our conversations with actual locals, not the guides we usually hire to educate us about the cities we visit. Last evening, after a hearty meal, we sat down to drink bottles of beer like every local German man in the establishment, and after we had quaffed down a few, we engaged in a lively discussion with a local tradesman, with Vandy as translator.

While I enjoy the expansive education I am receiving here, I miss the connection I felt with the local history in Dunfermline. There, aunts, uncles, and cousins were quick to tell tales about our very own ancestors, with descriptions so lively, it seemed as though the ancestors had walked the town streets that very afternoon. Here, we learn impressive histories about peoples with whom we have no connection, and while interesting, I do not feel the same bond I felt in Scotland, with its incomparable history, tradition, and poetry. How fortunate we are in our birthplace.

How does life fare at Fairfield for you and Tom, Mother? Do you still attend and host tea with the Reynolds Street ladies? Does your lady's maid, Clara, continue to meet your high standards? Does she fare well herself?

Mrs. Carnegie stopped reading aloud and looked over at her younger son. "How kind of Andrew to inquire after the staff, Tom. Don't you think? He could have just as easily spared the paper. Such a generous spirit."

I wondered at Mr. Carnegie's question, which I understood he meant for me. How did I fare, in these bleak days without him?

CHAPTER TWENTY-SIX

December 2, 1865
Pittsburgh, Pennsylvania

Mrs. Vandevort held out her teacup for Hilda to refill. The kitchen maid glanced over at me with an unpleasant look visible only to me. It was a familiar expression, one that telegraphed her irritation at having to pour tea when she had piles of work in the kitchen while I was merely standing there doing nothing, chatelaine in hand. If her glowers weren't so commonplace, I might have sympathized with the inequity in our positions.

"It sounds as if the boys' recent time in Germany was particularly well spent," Mrs. Vandevort said to my mistress, Mrs. York, Mrs. Coleman, and her daughter, Lucy. The ladies had gathered around the parlor after dinner for tea and sweets, while the men retired to the library for cigars and port. In the low gaslight, enveloped by the scarlet and golden hues of the parlor walls and furnishings, even the wrinkly Mrs. York appeared softly attractive.

"Indeed. Andra sent us fine accounts of their tour of Dresden. It sounds as if the boys enjoyed their evening at the *Semperoper*," Mrs. Carnegie answered.

I flinched at her botched pronunciation of the Dresden opera house. Although I was no student of German, even I knew her delivery was awful.

"Oh, it did sound wonderful," Mrs. Vandevort concurred, sipping from her teacup.

My mistress placed her cup in its saucer, reached into the generous folds of her black silk gown, and retrieved a letter. I knew this moment would arrive. Due to the frequency of Mr. Carnegie's letters, she usually had the upper hand in terms of information on the boys' travel, and she delighted in wielding it.

"May I share with you a snippet from a letter I just received from Andra?"

Mrs. Vandevort could not suppress a sigh, whether of frustration or resignation, I could not tell. "Of course," she said. "I welcome any news of our sons."

Mrs. Carnegie cleared her throat and said, "I will skip directly to the most interesting part . . . Ah, here it is."

To stand on Mount Vesuvius in the early morning mist, looking down on the once-great city of Pompeii, is to brush against history. The boys and I could almost hear the rumblings of that fatal morning when the eruption began. With the azure ocean on the horizon and the picturesque mountain to our backs, we could envision how the Pompeiian people might have been lulled to complacency even with the first rumble of the volcano. But once we descended from the mount to the city below, we sensed no complacency. Instead, examining the discoveries of the archaeological excavations, we felt the urgency of their ancient plight, almost as though we were reliving that horrific day along with the poor Pompeiian citizens. Because volcanic ash fell from Mount Vesuvius upon the Pompeiians, burying them intact, we can see precisely how the Pompeiians lived and how they died. The House of the Faun with its astonishing mosaics, in particular, provides the most intact, incredible example of the sophistication and erudition of these earlier people. How unexpectedly advanced they were. This visit to Pompeii made us all reflective — history seemed alive and close to us — and the boys were uncharacteristically quiet on the train ride back to Naples. It seems we were all wondering how history would view us.

"A most moving rendering of their visit," Mrs. Vandevort said.

My mistress sat back in her chair, a self-satisfied, almost smug grin forming on her thin lips. "It is, isn't it?"

"I only wish I'd brought *my* latest letter to share with you." Mrs. Vandevort set her teacup down on the table to reach for a cocoa flummery, one of the pastries laid out by Hilda. "What do you make of this 'Committee on Matrimony'?"

Mrs. Carnegie stopped chewing her almond cake midbite. "What matrimony committee?" She attempted to sound nonchalant, but I heard the alarm in her tone.

"Do you mean your Andrew hasn't written to you about it?" Mrs. Vandevort tittered, reveling in her rare superiority of information.

"Of course he has," she bluffed. "I just can't recall the details at the moment."

The word *matrimony* jolted Mrs. Coleman out of her seeming somnolence, perhaps because of the specter of Miss Coleman's marriage to the younger Mr. Carnegie. "Please do tell, Mrs. Vandevort. I am certain Lucy and I would be interested in hearing about this committee," Mrs. Coleman urged, leaning into the conversation.

"It seems that our European travelers have formed themselves into a committee of sorts, making lists of the beauties of Pittsburgh and discussing their qualities as potential brides." Mrs. Vandevort glanced over at Lucy and said, "No doubt you'd be at the top of the list, my dear, except that you are very nearly a married woman."

Miss Coleman's fair skin turned a vivid shade of pink. Even though she'd conducted meetings with a dressmaker to design her bridal gown, she couldn't stop herself from blushing at the thought of what an actual marriage would bring.

Given that the "Committee on Matrimony" did not involve her own daughter's marital plans, Mrs. Coleman's interest faded, and she went back to her usual stillness. The floor returned to Mrs. Carnegie. "It sounds as though young Mr. Vandevort is having a bit of fun with you. I cannot imagine our sons and young Mr. Phipps making lists of eligible brides."

"Oh no, Mrs. Carnegie, the boys are in earnest. In fact, I understand that at least two of the young men have identified serious prospects."

For once in her life, my mistress was shocked into silence. And although I had not consciously thought about Mr. Carnegie in the specific context of marriage, I found very unsettling the idea of him marrying one of the Pittsburgh "beauties" I'd seen at various social functions. The exchange he and I shared during his send-off dinner returned to me, and my cheeks burned. My reaction to this talk of Mr. Carnegie paired with someone else made patent my continued affection.

"Although," Mrs. Vandevort continued, "my son confessed that it is possible that the young ladies they have designated may not be aware of their intentions. And may not agree."

The ladies laughed, and I watched as my mistress attempted to laugh along with them. The talk turned to the travelers' next destination, and much to Mrs. Carnegie's relief, her youngest son strode into the room to call the evening to a close. He had an early morning train to catch, he announced, and he offered his apologies to the group.

As my mistress bid farewell to her guests, I readied her bedchamber for her evening's ablutions. Uncharacteristically quiet when she entered the room, I removed her dress and undergarments in complete silence. She still did not speak as I rubbed her favorite rosewater cream into her face and hands, brushed her hair two hundred licks, and buffed her nails to a sheen with a chamois. If she did not wish to initiate conversation, it was not my place to do so, and in any event, I knew why she was so quiet. I did not wish to speak of it either. My own mind was muddled with the idea of Mr. Carnegie marrying.

As Mrs. Carnegie stared absently into her mirror, I curtsied and turned to leave. I felt her hand on my arm, holding me fast. "You don't really think he'll come home with a bride in mind, do you, Clara?"

I hoped not, but I didn't know. I knew that wasn't what she wanted me to say, so instead, I said, "I cannot imagine he has the time or inclination for anyone or anything but his work or his family."

She met my eye in the mirror. "Truly?"

"Truly."

"What would I do without you, Clara?"

A year ago, those words would have been the fulfillment of my dream. I had become indispensable. But I had changed.

CHAPTER TWENTY-SEVEN

December 26, 1865
Pittsburgh, Pennsylvania

"The Carnegies are really making their mark on you, Clara," Maeve called across the single room that served as the entire first floor of their tiny Rebecca Street home. She was washing the potatoes and carrots I'd brought with me for our belated holiday meal in the water she kept on low boil over the hearth. None of the Slab Town houses had running water, and the well water used by the local families smelled foul without extensive boiling.

"Why do you say that, Maeve? Is it the fancy cut of meat?" I yelled back, a necessity given the noise of the five children and the loud grinding of the mill that served as their backyard. Knowing where I was headed for the single holiday day I'd been granted by the Carnegies for the Christmas season, Mr. Ford wished me a "Happy Christmas" as I walked toward the servants' door to catch my train and slipped a wrapped joint of roast beef inside the basket in which I carried some vegetables and a loaf of bread.

Hands full of scrubbed potatoes and carrots, Maeve marched over to the kitchen table and laid them out for me and her eldest daughter, the almost seven-year-old Mary, to peel.

"No," she said with a laugh. "Although I do appreciate the beef. I can't say that I've ever tasted such a fine cut before, and I cannot wait until Patrick sees it when he comes home from the foundry."

Patrick's employer was not as generous as the Carnegies. He worked not only Christmas Eve and the day after Christmas, which was traditionally a holiday, but also worked Christmas Day too. The mill had a backlog of contracts, making a day off — even Christmas — unfathomable for its employees.

"Then what do you mean that the 'Carnegies have made their mark on me'?" I asked her, scrubbing furiously at the grime covering the kitchen table once Maeve turned her back toward the hearth. While I could not bear to allow the clean potatoes and carrots to touch the black-smut-covered table surface a second longer, I also couldn't bear to embarrass Maeve by washing the table in her line of sight. I never wanted her to think I judged her or her home and found them wanting.

"It's your speech, Clara. You sound so posh. Like some fancy Dubliner instead of a farm girl from Galway," she said with a glance at me. Slender after the birth of her fifth child, who had displaced the fourth one from her hip, Maeve still had the same dark circles under her eyes. If anything, the circles had gotten blacker from the exhaustion of another child. "You even carry yourself like one of them Carnegies."

I'd grown so accustomed to acting the part of Clara Kelley, lady's maid, that I'd almost forgotten how to behave as the real Clara Kelley. "I hadn't realized. I'm sorry."

"No need for apologies, Clara. It's just an observation. Funny, really. Anyway, Patrick tells me that you and your sisters were always a bit different. Your father educated you to think like men, he says."

Maeve's words took me aback. Not that she meant any offense; no, that wasn't her intention at all. Maeve was a plain speaker, and she was just repeating the generally held perception of my family. It seemed that I'd been an outsider for longer than I'd realized.

"We might have to bring out the farm girl again if we're ever to get you a husband," she said with a laugh.

A husband? I stopped scouring the table, praying to Mary that Maeve and Patrick hadn't planned any matchmaking for the evening. But Maeve's eyes were elsewhere. She was busy juggling the baby on her hip and tending to the beef sizzling over the fire. Perhaps she was simply joking.

The front door slammed, sending a shudder throughout the rickety house. Patrick kneeled on the floor so that Mary, Anthony, and John could fly into his arms. As he allowed his children to crawl all over him, Maeve smiled, not seeming to notice or mind that each child's face came away smeared with the filth of the foundry that had seeped into every pore of Patrick's body. Even though he'd washed in the communal neighborhood well before entering his home.

I was relieved that Patrick arrived home alone. After Maeve's remark, I had half expected a fellow foundry worker in tow. I wasn't looking for a potential mate in Slab Town, although I could never say that to Maeve and Patrick.

Patrick stood up, the children clinging to him like flowering jasmine on a vine. He hugged me, leaving a dark smudge on the white cuffs of my servant's gown. "You've been too scarce, Clara."

"I've come when I can. You know how stingy employers are with holidays," I answered with reference to his own over-worked situation.

"True enough. We've had to celebrate the season in fits and starts around here." He sniffed the air. "What's that I smell?"

"Clara's brought us a joint of roast beef for our holiday meal," Maeve said.

Patrick whooped. "I'll have nothing but fine compliments for the Carnegies today, even if they have been withholding you from us."

I did not correct Patrick's belief about the Carnegies' largesse. "They might be stingy with free time but not worldly goods," I echoed Patrick.

"How is your master, Mr. Andrew Carnegie? A regular brick, is he?" He asked the question with a snide tone, expecting the worst. As he did from all employers.

Warmth spread across my cheeks as I answered. "He's not a bad fellow. When he's around. He is still on that long European trip."

"You're blushing, Clara," Maeve accused me.

"I most certainly am not." The protest only made my cheeks feel more fiery. "It's warm in here, Maeve."

Patrick interjected, "There better be no funny business, Clara. You know how those toffs can be."

"He's no toff. He comes from a background like ours."

"Except he's Scottish, not Irish. He's rich now, not poor." Patrick crossed his arms and stared at me. "And he's your master, not your equal."

"It's not like that. We just have the occasional pleasant conversation. Used to, anyway, before he left."

"Sounds to me like it's a good thing he's gone, Clara. Nothing good can come of a 'pleasant conversation' between a master and his housemaid. Not to mention that your father would kill me if I didn't give you a stern talking-to."

"Well, consider your duty done. But you've wasted your breath for no sensible reason."

An awkward quiet descended as I busied myself with peeling the potatoes and carrots, little Mary at my side, and Maeve returned to tending the roast beef. Patrick tickled little John, and as his peals of laughter filled the room, the tension broke.

"What do you hear from home, Clara?" Patrick called over to me from the spindly wooden chair he'd pulled close to the hearth.

I froze. Uncertain of how widely known my family's situation was and keeping in mind how maniacally private Dad was, I lied. "The usual. A rundown of which crops provided the best yield and what they're laying in the cellars for the winter. Some village gossip about a family squabble over some land."

Patrick and Maeve glanced at one another.

"Nothing else?" His voice held a peculiar tone.

I stopped peeling and stared over at him. "What else should I be hearing?"

Patrick, usually so fast with a quip, didn't answer me.

Maeve spoke instead. "She deserves to know."

He sighed. "The Fenians had planned an uprising simultaneously in New York and Ireland. They were backed by arms smuggled in from the United States and by American soldiers who'd just finished with the Civil War and were willing to fight as mercenaries. English authorities caught wind of it, and now they're looking for Fenian leaders." He paused. "Like your father."

"You've got your information wrong, Patrick. Dad's sympathetic to the Fenians but certainly isn't active in the movement, let alone a leader. Sure, he dabbled a bit in the years after the famine, because he was furious with England for its unwillingness to help us when we were starving. The Fenian message of equality and freedom for all people made sense at that time, he told me. But that was years ago, although it is true that rumors of past Fenian sympathy were enough to make the Martyns take away some of the family land recently."

"So you know about the land?"

"I know the Martyns were mistaken."

"Clara, I think your dad told you that to protect you. According to the letters we're getting from home, your dad never really gave up his leadership role with the Fenians. The organization just went underground. And now, even though they've got no proof, the Martyns are under pressure from the Crown to crack down on your father. More than they have in the past."

My hands and voice trembled. "What does that mean?"

"It means the Martyns have rescinded

your family's lease. No more tenancy, no more land, I'm afraid."

"Eliza told me," I confessed. "But she said nothing of Dad's current Fenian sympathies. She said the Martyns canceled the lease on the strength of old rumors."

"It is possible she doesn't know, Clara." He paused, shaking his head. "I know the lease rescission is precisely the sort of practice your father hoped to stop with his Fenian plans. He wanted fixity of leases' tenure and the right for all people to own land, not just lease it. I'm so sorry, Clara. We all are. Your dad is a good man."

"I feel terrible being so far away from them right now." While I felt sick with helplessness, I also felt rage surge within me, that Dad would put the family at risk by leading the Fenians in a dangerous revolt and that his risk meant I had to come to America to provide the family extra income because the farm was in jeopardy. How could he have asked for such sacrifice from his daughter? And family? All for a cause that, though worthy, had such little chance of success.

"There's nothing you could've done, Clara," Patrick said, trying to console me. "In fact, working in America — far away from all the political madness in Ireland —

and sending your wages home is the best thing you can do for your family right now. Where are they living?"

"With my mother's people just outside of Galway City." I started to cry, out of worry and anger. "Why didn't they tell me? Why did they fill their letters with lies instead?" Lies about the farm and why it was taken away. Lies about who Dad was.

Maeve put the baby down on a blanket and wrapped her arms around me. "We all tell tales, Clara. Sometimes for ourselves, and sometimes for others."

CHAPTER TWENTY-EIGHT

December 26, 1865
Pittsburgh, Pennsylvania

Several stops before my Reynolds Street
destination, my streetcar pulled into the
Liberty Street station. The station was dark,
save for the light of the ticket taker's window. Only sparsely populated with waiting
passengers at this late hour, the platform
looked nearly desolate. When I left Patrick's
home half an hour earlier, I had intended to
go directly back to Reynolds Street, but
now, I felt compelled to leave the streetcar.
I thought I might find solace in the Catholic church, Pittsburgh's only one, that was
near the station.

Drawn to the sole illumination on the
platform, I asked the uniformed ticket taker,
"Can you please tell me the way to Seventeenth Street, sir?"

Glancing up from his task of sorting used

tickets, he looked at me askance. "Are you heading to St. Patrick Church?"

"Yes, sir."

"Wouldn't have taken you for a Catholic." He spat out the words.

Shocked at his blatant insult — I knew Catholics weren't exactly revered in Pittsburgh, but I thought tolerance was more prevalent here than at home — I recoiled and turned to walk away. Behind me, he relented and called out, "Head west down Liberty, and in a few blocks, Seventeenth will intersect with it."

Wide enough to accommodate several lanes of traffic, though hardly better lined with cobblestone than a dirt road, Liberty Avenue stretched before me, as busy as if it were noon on a regular workday. Gaslights lined the street, providing just enough brightness for me to observe the ravages of factory smoke on the storefronts and the black snow underfoot. Horses pulled overladen carriages on the street, stopping to unload crates and bins wherever convenient. Delivery boys, merchants closing up shop, and mill workers starting the evening shift pushed past me, not rudely but with purpose.

I almost walked past the place I sought. Not until I saw a circular tower topped by a cross jutting out from behind a warehouse crowded with carriages and workmen on the corner of Liberty and Seventeenth did I crane my neck to look. There, in the midst of the crowded, commercial city block stood St. Patrick Church, a rectangular stone-and-wood building, plain save for another cross over the front door and the stone tower attached to its side. Even though the structure was simple and unobtrusive compared to the Presbyterian houses of worship that populated the streets of Homewood, St. Patrick was far more elaborate than the Catholic churches at home. Because of the governmental prohibitions on practicing Catholicism in Galway, worship had taken place in makeshift, single-room, thatched structures or the open air, as safety would allow. Only in recent years were more permanent and substantial Catholic churches built in Ireland, but even then, they had the dual purpose of serving as the local schools.

Ironically, I had Mrs. Carnegie and the elder Mr. Carnegie to thank for my knowledge of this church, one of only a handful of Catholic churches in the entire Western Pennsylvania region. One evening last winter, during a regular business conversation between my mistress and her elder son,

262

they discussed an earlier iteration of St. Patrick Church that had existed on Fourteenth Street. The Pennsylvania Railroad wanted the Fourteenth Street site for the railroad expansion that Mr. Carnegie anticipated would be necessary after the end of the Civil War, and at his behest, the railroad had purchased a lot on Seventeenth Street and began work on a new St. Patrick, with the goal of tearing down the Fourteenth Street church and building a railroad facility on the site. The St. Patrick Church near where I now stood was finished and dedicated very recently, on December 15, not even two weeks ago.

The newness of the church was evident from the incomplete, rough exterior and the piles of bricks and wood lining the walkway to the front door. Evidently, they'd rushed to finish enough so that it could be used for the Christmas services but would still have to finalize construction. There was nothing unfinished about the front door, however, with its hefty oak material, intricately carved scenes from the life of Christ, and the numerous padlocks.

I suddenly felt nervous. I had not stepped foot in a Catholic church since I had left Ireland. I couldn't. Everyone thought I was Clara Kelley, good Anglo-Irish Protestant, and consequently, I attended the ten o'clock Presbyterian service with the rest of the staff. Would I be struck down, as Mum had so often warned us girls would happen if we skipped mass? I had always dismissed her admonitions as old-fashioned superstitions, but I felt unsettled.

A stack of newspapers sat outside the forbidding front door, and to assuage my anxiety, I picked one up. It was a *Catholic Herald.* Flipping through it as I stepped into the church foyer, I discovered that, while it included a few articles about goings-on in different parishes, the bulk of the publication contained advertisements from Irish Catholics looking for their lost relatives in America.

July 25, 1865

Information Wanted: Of James Larkin, a native of County Cork, Ireland, about eight years since. He was said to have resided principally in this city. Any information concerning him will be thankfully received by a distressed mother, who has lately come to this country in search of him. Address, care of the Editor of the *Catholic Herald.*

September 4, 1865

Information Wanted: Of Brigid McLeary, a girl of fourteen years of age. She left her native place in the County of Donegal, Ireland, about three months ago, with the notion of emigrating to some part of North America, probably Pittsburgh. Any information respecting her will be thankfully received by her mother, Mary Doherty, in the care of Father Reilly, Washington Parish, Pa.

October 22, 1865

Information Wanted: Of Joseph, son of Michael O'Neil, who left his father at the Hoosac Tunnel in the year 1863, then about sixteen years old, and last heard from by his brother James working on the York Canal. He said he was going to Pittsburgh. Any information about him will be thankfully received by Father Condron, Beaver Parish, Pa.

November 11, 1865

Information Wanted: Of Jonathan O'Rourke, lately from County Limerick, Ireland, who came to this city from

Boston about seven weeks ago. His wife and three children are now in this city, without means of subsistence. Any information of him will be thankfully received at No. 57 Beechview Avenue, where they have temporary residence.

I felt heartsick at these messages. Irish wives, children, siblings, and parents searching for their lost loved ones, who had immigrated to this country seeking hope but instead became adrift in the great mass of immigrants that washed up on American shores. Where was Jonathan O'Rourke? Had his wife and children found him, or had they died without his "subsistence"? What about poor fourteen-year-old Brigid? Was she simply hard at work as a domestic in Sewickley, without a spare moment to write, or had she become prey to the unscrupulous runners on the New York docks? If I had not taken the place of the real Clara Kelley, and if she'd had a family back home in Ireland, would they have posted an advertisement like this for her? My fate could have easily matched any of these poor folk. I felt like crying for each and every one of these forlorn souls, but no tears would come.

I pushed open the door to the church

interior. It was dark, lit only by the flicker of votive candles lining the altar and the low gaslight of an enormous brass chandelier dangling high above the church floor. Despite the hour, I saw five parishioners scattered across the wooden pews. My shoes clattered as I walked down the aisle, but none of the other churchgoers looked up. They were deep in their prayers. Anyone here at this hour must have a serious matter about which to pray, I guessed. I certainly did.

I wondered what this church would be like filled with the sort of music that Mr. Carnegie experienced in Europe. His letters contained wondrous descriptions of the music performed at the Pope's choir in Rome, in cathedrals of France and Germany, and at the Crystal Palace in London. The words from his letter detailing the Handel Anniversary celebration at the Crystal Palace had stayed with me: *"I cannot accurately share how the majesty of music surged through me as I listened to nearly four thousand musicians playing the Israel in Egypt oratorio. The vast cast-iron and plate-glass structure built for the Great Exhibition, nearly one million square feet in all and containing more glass than ever used in a building before, felt as though it pulsated with the di-*

vine." I wondered if I could find my own semblance of divine in this church, bereft of music though it was.

Sliding into a pew toward the back of the church, I knelt on the hard stone floor. I whispered a rosary's worth of Our Fathers and Hail Marys before I even allowed myself to think about my personal prayers. Requests for the safety of Mum, Dad, Cecelia, and Eliza flooded in, followed by entreaties for guidance as to how I might best help them. Prayers asking for help in forgiving Dad for putting his family at risk and placing his eldest daughter across the Atlantic, expecting her to thrive in a world different from her home.

The tears came, thinking of Eliza's latest letter to me and her blissful ignorance over the cause of our family's despair.

Dad says our situation is not near as dire as the days of the famine. Then, he says, people were dying in the roads by the hundreds, and bodies were piled up on street corners as there was not room enough in the churchyards for all the dead that needed burying. He points to his and Cecelia's employment and the food we have on the nightly table and claims we are faring just fine. But, Clara, this is not fine. This is survival only. Cecelia and I realize now how idyllic our life on the farm was — even Cecelia reminisces fondly about chores she used to complain about bitterly, like cleaning out the animals' pen — and how dependent we were upon the acreage Dad had amassed. Although I know it is a sin to hate, I loathe the Martyns for the misguided revenge they have exacted on us all. They not only lost us the farm, but they lost me Daniel. We've learned that he's promised to wed the Flanagan girl, whose father has over ten acres. On hearing the news, I felt as though my heart was breaking all over again.

The sole blessing is the money you send us in your regular mail parcels. The foresight Papa had in sending you to America can only be attributed to the Blessed Mary herself. Let nothing hinder your writing to us, save for the work that keeps us all safe, as there is no greater pleasure in these trying days than to receive a letter from you, dear sister. Perhaps one day, we will be able to amass enough by scrimping to pay for a voyage to America ourselves. What great pleasure it would be to see your shining face again.

Anger at Dad began to build in me again, and as I prayed for the Lord's help in delivering me from my rage, illumination poured forth from the altar directly upon me. I wasn't audacious enough to think that the light was some sort of divine sign, and when I squinted my eyes and stared at the altar, I saw its source. A priest, candle in hand, stood at the altar, setting out a paten and flagon, perhaps for a midnight mass.

But the light had sparked an idea. One that might provide a pathway for me and for my family. It made me realize that the way out of despair was not from an external source but an internal one. Perhaps I need only follow Mr. Carnegie's lead.

Weary from the day's events and my own emotions, I shuffled back to the station to hop on the streetcar. Once I arrived at Homewood Station, I hopped onto a milk wagon willing to drop me at Fairfield as part of its delivery route. When I finally arrived at the servants' door of the Carnegies' home, exhausted and half-frozen, I found Mr. Ford sitting at the kitchen's central table. Normally, if he was awake past midnight, he was busily engaged in a preparatory task for the next day. Not tonight.

"Mr. Ford, it's nice to see a friendly face

when coming in on a cold winter's night."

He nodded but did not offer his usual broad smile. He remained stock-still.

"Thank you again for the generous cut of beef. My family doesn't often enjoy meat like that. It was a treat for us all."

Again, the nod. And silence.

"Whatever is wrong, Mr. Ford?"

An envelope sat before him, slit across its top. Without a word, he slid it across the table to me.

"I assume you've read this?" I asked.

"James read it to me. I don't read myself."

"You want me to read it aloud to you again?"

"No, I don't think I could bear it."

Gingerly removing the letter from the envelope, I saw that it was written by an employee of the Freedmen's Bureau, a newly formed federal government agency designed to help former slaves. One of its primary goals was to help former slaves find family members from whom they had become separated during the war. Knowing Mr. Ford's situation, I felt sick.

" 'We are responding to your inquiry into the whereabouts of your wife, Ruth Ford, and daughter, Mabel, who were last seen on the Francis Plantation,' " I read. After several statements about the role of the

Freedmen's Bureau and the scope of its authority, I continued, " 'We regret to inform you that no former slaves by those names or descriptions have been identified at the Francis Plantation.' "

I reached for Mr. Ford's hands and looked into his eyes. The spark usually found there had deadened. Without the hope that had buoyed him for years, he seemed unmoored in tumultuous waters.

"Maybe they have already left the South and are making their way north as we speak?"

"The Francis Plantation records did not show Ruth or Mabel as having *ever* been there. Not that they were once there but are now gone. I don't know where else to look for them."

I felt as heartsick as I had when reading the *Catholic Herald* advertisements. So many souls lost in the tidal waves of this land. "What terrible news, Mr. Ford. But I am certain that all is not lost. There must be other ways than the Freedmen's Bureau to track people down. And I'm sure that the Carnegies would help —"

He put up his hand to stop me. "They're gone, Miss Kelley. I was a fool to hope otherwise. Since I lost them in that tunnel all those years ago, I've known they were gone."

CHAPTER TWENTY-NINE

March 24, 1866
Pittsburgh, Pennsylvania

Hunched by the embers of the dying fire in the otherwise pitch-black library, I tried to make sense of the tiny letters in the Allegheny Business News. As the words became clear, I saw the familiar names of Mr. Carnegie's former superiors at the Pennsylvania Railroad, Messrs. Scott and Thomson, which were linked with the Carnegies in nearly every one of their investments and companies. Clarifying my chart, I added Messrs. Scott and Thomson as partners in another Carnegie venture.

The complicated chart, twelve pages long, began as a simple list of the Carnegies' ventures and controlling interests. As I listened to my mistress, her son, the guests with whom they socialized, and the businessmen with whom they conducted meetings, the list grew into a chart. I then mapped out the relationships between the Carnegies' ventures and the people behind them. The process was not that different from complicated outlines of European history Dad once made me prepare or the pared-down recapitulation of the English laws governing Ireland he had us girls draft. Only the players and the subject matter were different.

Once I had gained an intimate understanding of this web, I plugged the Carnegies' businesses into the commerce of the entire region and then deepened my understanding of the impact the Civil War — its duration and its conclusion — had on the nation. I learned that, while the federal contracts for iron, coal, and goods dried up after the war, the manufacturers' industrial capacity had increased multifold, and they were eager for uses for its expansion. The railroads fueled that industrial growth by consolidating short-haul roads and forming vast east-west and north-south transportation networks capable of shipping goods and people more cheaply, causing a surge in trade. As the railroads grew, so did the demand for iron again, along with engines, wheels, and bridges.

Everything had occurred precisely as Mr.

Carnegie had predicted. I now realized that his resignation from the railroad when he took his European trip would allow him to exploit his intimate knowledge of the railroad business — as well as his relationships with Messrs. Scott and Thomson — to partner with nearly every venture tied to the railroad and its growth. He was poised to be one of the preeminent national businessmen in the railroad, iron, and steel industries, at the very least.

As I worked on my chart, I learned that invisibility had distinct benefits. By playing the part of perfect servant, by definition deaf and blind to the events occurring before me, I was present for the most confidential of conversations. My reward was information to feed my chart and my predictions. Not that I had the money yet to invest, mind. But the loss of the family farm and the harm into which Dad had gotten the family had spurred on a plan. I would squirrel money away a little at a time, month by month, with the goal of investing as Mr. Carnegie had done. Perhaps I'd amass enough to sail my family here to safety. Hadn't Mr. Carnegie assembled vast wealth using this rubric? The idea gave me hope.

A door creaked behind me. Craning my

neck, I looked around the leather chair that blocked my presence. The library door remained tightly shut. Perhaps the wind from the spring storm had caused the house to shift. I returned to my paper.

A creak sounded again. This time, I stood up, newspaper, journal, and an economics book in hand, ready to flee. I couldn't risk Mr. Holyrod or Mrs. Stewart finding me here. They were already on the lookout for faults with me to report back to Mrs. Carnegie.

The library door pushed open, and my opportunity for escape was lost. Before the interloper revealed him or herself, I wracked my mind for a way to explain my presence in the library. I settled on the excuse of fetching a book for Mrs. Carnegie.

But when the culprit stepped into the room, I didn't offer my justification, because I lost the ability to speak. It was Mr. Carnegie.

"Miss Kelley," he said, sounding as breathless as if he'd walked up a flight of stairs. "I didn't expect to find you here."

"Mr. C-Carnegie," I stammered. "I had no idea that you'd returned home from Europe. I apologize for my appearance." I felt naked in my nightdress and robe, hair unbound. I smoothed out my clothes, as if the removal of errant wrinkles could make me more presentable.

"No need for apologies, Miss Kelley. You are perfectly decorous." He smiled. "There is no way you could have expected me. A surprise return was my plan."

"Yes, you have arrived a fair bit earlier than you indicated. Your last letter — from England I believe, from whence you planned on sailing — said that you would 'return by late spring, with the necessary equipment for an elegant archery set to use at Fairfield in hand.' "

"You have recounted my letter almost verbatim."

"It was my pleasure to listen to your mother read them aloud to your brother almost nightly."

"I had hoped you would find some way to read them. Or hear them." His voice dropped to a whisper. "I sometimes spoke to you through them."

Pretending I hadn't heard his last remark, I said, "Your mother will be delighted, Mr. Carnegie. Shall I get her for you?"

"Thank you, but no, Miss Kelley. I had planned on alerting her to my arrival at breakfast. I wanted to see the expression on her face as she walked into the dining room and found me sitting there, reading the newspaper," he said with a chuckle.

I smiled. "You and your mother always know how to make each other laugh."

"It is laughter I hope to provoke, not fright."

"Your presence can only bring joy to your mother. She has missed you terribly."

"Was she the only one?" he asked, his eyes hopeful.

I answered honestly but vaguely. "No. You were missed by everyone at Fairfield."

Formalities aside, a silence descended upon us. The ticking of the mantel clock seemed to grow louder, but I was fearful of breaking the quiet with a question too stately or too comfortable, particularly given the somewhat confessional nature of our last exchange.

Finally, Mr. Carnegie asked, "How have you fared these past ten months, Miss Kelley?"

"I hope I've served your mother well, Mr. Carnegie."

"I did not ask about my mother, Miss Kelley. I asked about you."

His unexpected presence and frankness unnerved me, and I answered without my usual filter. "These months have been hard."

Alarm sounded in his voice. "I hope no one in the Carnegie household has been mistreating you?"

"Oh no," I hastened to reassure him. "Personal matters have made this time challenging."

"I felt quite the same, Miss Kelley."

"I'm astonished. Your letters brimmed with excitement and adventure. I heard no evidence of challenge."

"Those letters were meant to assuage my mother," he said. "The truth would have caused her unnecessary worry."

"I suppose that was a wise decision. After all, the 'Committee on Matrimony' worried her quite enough."

Mr. Carnegie's brows knit in confusion. "The Committee on what?"

"Matrimony," I answered flippantly, as if it hadn't impacted me as well, as if a surge of jealousy hadn't passed through me at the very mention of this "committee." "I believe that your traveling companion Mr. Vandevort mentioned this Committee on Matrimony to his mother in a letter, and she shared it with Mrs. Carnegie."

"Vandy has always been prone to drama." He groaned. "One late night with one silly idea, and he runs off to tell his mother. I suppose I'll have to undo the damage tomorrow morning."

"Indeed, your mother feared that you

might return with a bride in mind." I giggled a little at the memory of one of my mistress's most histrionic displays. "Or worse, with a foreign bride in tow."

He chuckled again and then grew quiet. "On the matter of matrimony, there has been no change."

Keeping my gaze fixed upon the floor, I refused to meet his eyes, although part of me wanted to see what message I might find there. Was it presumptuous of me to interpret his comment favorably? I longed for an answer but knew it could only cause me trouble. My nerves caused me to fiddle with the newspaper and books I'd kept tucked behind my dressing gown.

"What do you have there, Miss Kelley? Some new verse by Elizabeth Barrett Browning, I hope."

"Nothing quite so interesting, I fear. A newspaper, a personal journal, and an informational text." I did not offer the materials to him.

"May I?"

I hesitated. How would he react to my study of *his* holdings? I desired his opinion on one hand but feared it on the other.

Without other options, I handed him both books and the folded newspaper.

"The *Allegheny Business News* I can

281

understand, but *Political Economy* by Alonzo Potter?" He chuffed at the sight of the top volume. "That's heavy reading, Miss Kelley, and certainly not as well written as Mrs. Browning."

"An attempt to learn more about the business world. To finish the education you began." I did not explain why this knowledge was of paramount importance to me, of course.

"Ah. The nuances of the business world are best learned from people, not books."

"My tutor was in Europe," I said with a smile. "Anyway, didn't you receive your education from Colonel Anderson's library?"

"Touché." He smiled back and then, sliding my journal out from underneath *Political Economy,* asked, "May I look through this?"

I nodded.

He flipped through the first few pages rather quickly, but then slowed down to review each page in detail. "This is magnificent, Miss Kelley. How did you arrive at this understanding? You've displayed mastery not only of the Carnegie businesses but the Pittsburgh industrial community and the national railroad and iron companies as well."

"By researching. And listening. Even when perhaps I should not have."

He glanced up from my chart. "That's when you gather the best information, Miss Kelley."

"Your mother and Mrs. Seeley would disagree. A good lady's maid lives only to serve her mistress. She does not eavesdrop on her mistress's conversations."

"A mind such as yours could hardly turn off the chatter around you." He laughed at my protestations. "In any event, you are far more than a lady's maid, Miss Kelley. You see what I see in the world. The links between industry and history, the synergy and efficiencies between businesses. Most businessmen see the world so narrowly. I thought I was alone in this understanding."

My cheeks grew hot, and I was thankful for the low firelight. He knew my weakness — admiration of my intelligence. "You honor me with your compliments, Mr. Carnegie."

"I'm not offering you empty flattery, Miss Kelley. You've thought of business partnerships that I haven't even considered yet. If you were a man, I'd hire you." He paused, and when he spoke again, his voice was softer and more empathetic. "But you are not. So please allow me to help you. And who knows? You might end up helping me."

He tempted me with his offer. Could this work? Together, could we lay gilt on my shimmering web of a chart, making it gleam with precision and luster? Could we fashion prospective investments based on all the inside knowledge we gleaned so that I could raise enough money to save my family? Or would a business relationship become inextricably intertwined with an emotional one again?

CHAPTER THIRTY

May 2, 1866
Pittsburgh, Pennsylvania

"Mr. Scott, you have always been an incorrigible tease," my mistress exclaimed. The almost coy manner she adopted with Mr. Carnegie's once mentor and now business partner always astonished me, for she utilized that demeanor with no one else. But then, there was no one quite like the handsome Scots-Irish Mr. Scott, who had risen through the railroad ranks like her Andra and who had pulled him up alongside himself. Upon him alone, Mrs. Carnegie bestowed her erstwhile charm, and Mr. Scott was polite enough to respond.

"Only because you inspire it in me," Mr. Scott retorted.

After her almost girlish giggles subsided, Mrs. Carnegie rang for after-dinner cordials. Mr. Holyrod arrived with his silver tray, brimming with colored liquors gleaming in their crystal decanters. He poured whiskey for the silver-haired, august Mr. Thomson, the president of the Pennsylvania Railroad, and sherry for Mr. Scott. Mr. Carnegie declined, as usual, but Mrs. Carnegie uncharacteristically took a sherry too.

"A delicious dinner, ma'am," Mr. Thomson said, leaning forward to clink his glass to hers. These words were the most he'd spoken during the evening. When I'd first encountered him, I'd attributed his quiet to a haughty reserve, until Mr. Carnegie explained that the successful businessman was actually quite shy.

"It was *our* pleasure to serve you, sir," Mrs. Carnegie answered gravely. Like Mr. Scott, Mr. Thomson had been instrumental in her Andra's early and continued success, and she always treated him with particular care. No sour glances for him.

"I gather you gentlemen will be discussing Union Iron Mills and Keystone Bridge Company tonight," my mistress said.

Messrs. Scott and Thomson glanced at Mr. Carnegie, assessing whether he approved of his mother taking the lead in their business conversation, particularly when it involved two companies in which they held secret interests. He nodded. One of the qualities I most admired in him was his faith that a woman could match his business savvy. Few fellows held that belief.

"I would not dare intervene except to wish you well in securing the bridge contracts that will be necessary to the success of the ventures," she continued. "Good evening, gentlemen."

As my mistress started up the grand front staircase, the gentlemen retired to the library to enjoy a few cigars. I followed Mrs. Carnegie up the steps to her bedchamber, cognizant of Mr. Carnegie's eyes upon me. Waiting until I reached the top of the stairs, I smiled down on him. As we'd embarked on our new business dealings, I learned that my feelings had not changed, and I guessed that his hadn't either. But we made no mention of them. We conducted conversations almost exclusively on the topic of industry, disregarding the latent emotions we shared.

Whether the effect was from the sherry or Mr. Scott's attention, Mrs. Carnegie hummed while I unlaced her many layers, slipped on her nightdress, brushed her hair two hundred strokes, and rubbed cream into her hands. As she walked over to her bed, she said, "Clara, I've forgotten the book I'd like to read before bed. It is on the credenza in the library. Go fetch it."

"Yes, ma'am."

As I had no wish to disturb the men's conversation, I tiptoed down the servants' staircase, careful to avoid the step that made the loud creak. Padding down the back hallway, I wondered how I could slip the book out of the library with minimal interruption.

A roar sounded out from the library. My instinct prompted me to race down the corridor to make certain no one was injured, but when I heard Mr. Carnegie yelling, I stopped. Were the gentlemen having an argument? I slowed down and listened.

"Do I not own one-half of your allocation in Keystone Bridge?" I recognized the usually smooth voice of Mr. Scott, now simmering with fury.

"Yes, you do. But that does not give you the right to dictate the decisions I make for the company," Mr. Carnegie responded in kind. Aside from the fight I'd witnessed between him and his brother, I had never heard him angry. "Nor does your five percent, Edgar."

"Never said it did," Mr. Thomson said. His voice bore none of the agitation of Messrs. Scott and Carnegie.

"Let me remind you of the deal we struck," Mr. Carnegie said in a seething tone. "Pennsylvania Railroad, under your direction, commissions bridges by entering into contracts with Union Iron Mills and Keystone Bridges. Union Iron Mills supplies iron for the bridges, which Keystone Bridge then constructs. You gentlemen make money on the contract between Pennsylvania Railroad and Keystone Bridge and again when the Keystone Bridge purchases the necessary iron from Union Iron Mills, because you two own interests in both Keystone Bridge and Union Iron Mills. Unknown interests, of course."

"Sounds about right," Mr. Thomson said into the pause, puffing on his cigar. The pungent cloud drifted into the hallway, and I stifled a cough. "As long as it's on the up-and-up."

"It is, Edgar. Nothing illegal about it. Moreover, you two take none of the risk but reap all of the reward. I take the risks by putting together the deals, arranging the financing, ensuring a safe design is rendered, and overseeing construction of the bridge and the railroad that crosses it. All I ask of you two is to approve the commission. And once we expand beyond the Pennsylvania Railroad's reach, you won't even have to do that. Nowhere in our arrangement is there a provision giving you control over the decisions. That is *my* prerogative." His voice was hard and unyielding. I found it particularly shocking to hear him use this tone with two men who, by all rights, were his superiors.

Where was the genial man I knew? Had the man who had become, once again, my patient teacher disappeared? In the six weeks since he had returned, we had decided that the safety of the Fairfield walls provided opportunity aplenty for the occasional fifteen stolen minutes of business discussion, despite the variable presence of his mother, brother, and any number of household staff. It was far safer than the out-of-doors, as Miss Atkinson's discovery of us in the park last year, paired with her disclosure of the encounter to Mrs. Carnegie, proved. Passing in the hallway, he would apprise me of a new business development in iron or steel or the railroads, and I would jot it down in my journal. As I carried his mother's linens up the stairs, we would quietly review a letter he'd received. When dinner guests sauntered out of the dining room in favor of the parlor, he would return to discuss a guest's whisper I'd overheard about a different process for strengthening iron and steel rails for the railroad. I kept my journal tucked in the generous pockets of my servant's gown, ready for conversation whenever a moment might transpire.

Mr. Scott persisted. "The bridge project you're chasing is too large and complicated. Stick to the local ones. The margins may not be as big, but the risks — which you're always lording over us — are smaller."

"I hadn't figured you for a coward, Tom," Mr. Carnegie roared. "If we fail to bid on any of the large bridge commissions soon to be on the market, we can count on a rival securing the contract. And the next one and the next one. I have no intention of losing a single contract, especially the big ones. Do you understand me? I will undertake *any* means necessary for the success of these ventures."

Chair springs squeaked as a man hoisted himself up. "That will be enough, you two. You know I admire your grand ambition, Andrew, but let's not forget that without us railroad men here, many of these schemes won't bear fruit," Mr. Thomson said.

"And let's not forget that without me, none of these schemes would happen at all," Mr. Carnegie responded. He had no intention of backing down from these powerful men or bending to their will.

The ticking of the clock grew louder as the library stilled. Had the men reached a standoff? Had I missed my opportunity to slip away unnoticed? When I heard a rustling noise in the room and the clip of footsteps, I seized my opportunity and started to back away from the main library door. But I bumped directly into someone.

I swung around. It was Mr. Carnegie. He must have left the library by the door next to the fireplace.

"Clara, were you listening?" he whispered.

I jumped back, hitting the wall. Was he angry that I'd been in the hallway? While I heard no spite in his voice, his conversation with Messrs. Scott and Thomson had scared me. I no longer believed I knew the sort of man he was. He seemed as changeable as a *síofra*. Could I really trust my family's future with him?

I made up an excuse. "No, I was retrieving something for your mother. I must be quick. She's waiting for me."

"Did you overhear the conversation I just had with Messrs. Scott and Thomson?"

"No."

"That's a lost opportunity." He sounded disappointed.

"What do you mean?" I could not imagine that he actually wanted me to overhear that damning conversation.

"I had quite the heated debate with Scott

and Thomson about how these Pennsylvania Railroad, Union Iron Mills, and Keystone Bridge contracts must work. I made certain that they understood I will succeed at all costs. I will do whatever it takes, and so must they, if they wish to do business with me."

"I am sorry that I did not overhear your exchange, Mr. Carnegie. Please excuse me. I must go, or your mother will be missing me." I curtsied and raced down the servants' hallway and up the back staircase to the relative safety of my mistress's bedchamber. I would rather risk Mrs. Carnegie's ire over my failure to deliver her book than face the gentlemen in the library.

As I ran up those stairs, I thought about how, in the darkness, in the privacy of my room, after a long day tending to the mercurial Mrs. Carnegie, I had begun to think about Mr. Carnegie as more than a business tutor again. I considered how, when daylight came, I carefully banished those thoughts so that they didn't emerge in his presence. Equilibrium was necessary for the delicate balance of the shifting roles I played daily. Roles, I reminded myself, upon which my family depended for their survival, in truth. But now, with Mr. Carnegie's change-able nature laid bare, I would have to work harder to keep those thoughts at bay. I would have to be more cautious on the tightrope I walked, for it could shift on his whim.

CHAPTER THIRTY-ONE

May 3, 1866
Pittsburgh, Pennsylvania

"Clara, please help the ladies. This weather has played havoc with their grooming," Mrs. Carnegie ordered me as a stream of bedraggled whist-playing ladies entered the foyer for an afternoon of tea and games.

A late-spring storm had deluged the area with sideways-whipping rain. In the brief distance they'd stepped from their carriages to the entrance of Fairfield, the Homewood ladies were drenched.

"Ladies, if you will follow me." I gestured to the main staircase to the second floor, where my mistress kept a luxuriously appointed spare bedroom stocked and ready for this purpose. I began walking upstairs, checking to see if the ladies were in my wake. Behind me, I overheard their lamentations about the weather, through which they had passed only very briefly. I thought about the daily downpours endemic to life in Galway and how very pampered these ladies were.

Mrs. Pitcairn, Mrs. Wilkins, and Mrs. Coleman followed me into the bedroom decorated with apple-green-striped fabric and matching wallpaper. Mrs. Pitcairn leaned back onto the tufted chaise longue to catch her breath after the flight of stairs; she could go no farther in her tight corsets without rest. Mrs. Coleman glanced at herself in the gilded dressing table mirror, adjusting her elaborate coiffure. What she lacked in conversational ability, she made up for in hairstyles. I offered to brush Mrs. Wilkins's lavender dress free of the raindrops, and soon, all the ladies were requesting this service.

Kneeling in front of the ladies, who were lined up for my ministrations, I listened first to the gripes about the weather by Mrs. Wilkins, who, as the wife of Judge William Wilkins, one of the region's wealthiest individuals, and as the daughter of George W. Dallas, a former vice president of the United States, was always Mrs. Carnegie's most respected guest. Once I'd tidied Mrs. Wilkins's dress, it was Mrs. Coleman's turn to speak on her only topic.

She droned on about the summer wedding plans of her daughter, Lucy, to Tom Carnegie, about which not even the minutest detail escaped her attention, even though it was to be held, in part, at Fairfield. Finally, Mrs. Pitcairn, having calmed her breath with a respite on the chaise longue, took her turn. She complained about the weather, her butler, her florist, the church pastor, her health, and, most vehemently, the challenge of communicating with her married daughter who lived in Philadelphia. The other ladies commiserated with all of Mrs. Pitcairn's complaints, well-known to all her acquaintances, but particularly her communication difficulties. Telegraph service, they carped, was notoriously spotty. Even the slightest change in the weather, they claimed, could knock down a telegraph pole, causing disruption in transmitting critical messages about important social events. How could a nation as advanced as the United States, they wondered, have such an abominable telegraph system?

I stopped brushing Mrs. Pitcairn's dress as a thought occurred to me. The Pennsylvania Railroad owned land that stretched across the entire state, and whenever they needed more, they simply bought out the inhabitants, as they had with St. Patrick

Catholic church. And they ran their own personal telegraph lines alongside the railroads. What if a business was formed that ran *public* telegraph lines alongside the railroad lines, with the Pennsylvania Railroad's permission, of course? There would be greater ability to observe the state of the telegraph lines, as trains were constantly passing by, as well as improved capacity to fix telegraph lines downed or impaired by weather, as the rails provided an easy means to bring workers to the scene immediately. I knew precisely who would be able to secure the permission of the Pennsylvania Railroad and form such a telegraph company.

Mrs. Pitcairn chided me to return to the task at hand. "Clara, I think you've missed the left side of my gown." The state of her cerulean-blue silk gown with dove-gray tassels was paramount.

Resuming the brushing, I smiled to myself. It was incredible how, once I understood the business of this land, insight came in unexpected places.

The smile lingered on my lips as I followed the ladies back downstairs, the ever-present chatelaine in hand. I imagined the expression on Mr. Carnegie's face when I shared my idea with him later that day.

"Ah, my grandson has arrived," Mrs. Pitcairn called out.

Grandson? I had heard nothing of Mrs. Pitcairn's beloved grandson — about whom she often spoke, to the boredom of my mistress — making an appearance at the tea, intended for adult ladies. Mrs. Carnegie would not be pleased.

With the parade of ladies on the staircase in front of me, I could not see the landing. When Mrs. Pitcairn swooshed down the final step, I saw a young boy, outfitted in a crisp, white sailor suit, his hand locked with a maid's. From the sour, thin-lipped expression on Mrs. Carnegie's face when she entered the parlor to greet the refreshed ladies, I saw that my prediction was correct.

"Who do we have here?" my mistress asked, although she knew the precise identity of this child. Mrs. Pitcairn had spoken of her grandson incessantly since her son, Robert, had returned to Pittsburgh after a stint in New York City, although she lamented that they chose Sewickley in which to reside instead of Homewood.

Mrs. Pitcairn chimed in, "My sweet, little Robert Jr., of course. When I learned that he would be in the neighborhood, I insisted that his nanny, Miss Quinn, bring him over for a brief visit. I know you ladies have been aching for a peek at him." The ladies made a show of swarming around the lad.

Miss Quinn? I hadn't heard that name since the carriage ride to Pittsburgh from Philadelphia, although I supposed Quinn was a common enough last name. When the ladies scattered, in search of tea and sweets in the parlor, I got a clear glance at a familiar face and an equally familiar dress, wide pagoda sleeves and all.

My stomach lurched at the sight of her, remembering the unkind behavior meted out by Misses Quinn and Coyne on that journey and recalling the state I was in when they first saw me. Could an ill-timed reference to my bedraggled dress and rucksack ruin my status here? I decided that the safest course was to embrace the part of the other Clara Kelley. In truth, wasn't she who I had become?

"Miss Quinn, it has been a long time. What a pleasure," I said in my poshest voice, as if greeting an old bosom friend.

"Miss Kelley?" The sight of me, poised and in command, seemed to daze Miss Quinn. She clung to her young charge's hand like a lifeline.

"Yes, indeed. The same Miss Kelley you first encountered in a carriage in Philadelphia."

"The Carnegie household has treated you

well indeed. You are much transformed, Miss Kelley." She stared at my composed face, updated coiffure, and perfectly pressed black wool dress.

"I will take that as a compliment, Miss Quinn."

"That was my intent," she answered quickly, with a quivering voice. Why was I making her fearful? Did she think I'd exact some sort of retribution for her earlier rudeness? Had I changed that much?

"How have you fared in service? I seem to remember you were assigned to a family in the East End of the city, but I heard Mrs. Pitcairn say you were in from Sewickley. And she mentioned that you were Robert's nanny. I thought you and Miss Coyne came to this country to serve a tutors."

"After my first posting, Mrs. Seeley decided I was better suited as a nanny." She glanced down at Robert Jr.

"That must have smarted." This small barb slipped out from between my lips before I could reel it back in.

"It did, but I realized that I had to adapt or return home. And there's little work as a tutor *or* nanny in Dublin."

"True enough," I concurred. She and I had that in common.

She glanced around. "You landed well,

Miss Kelley. The other nannies I encounter often talk of your Mr. Carnegie."

My cheeks felt hot. "Whatever do you mean?" Why was *my* Mr. Carnegie the subject of conversation among the local domestics? The intensity of my jealousy and possessiveness surprised me. I had thought of my feelings for him as quiet and pensive.

"I hear that Mr. Carnegie is well on his way to becoming a leader in the railroad and iron industries. Some say he will be the richest man in the world one day."

I smiled at her compliment. "The Carnegie home has indeed been an excellent place to serve."

"Miss Kelley," a man's voice called out, followed by the clip of a well-heeled footstep. The broad grin and bright eyes of Mr. Carnegie lit up the foyer. "Ah, there you are. Will you settle a bet between Tom and me about Mrs. Elizabeth Barrett Browning? You are the expert, after all."

Miss Quinn looked over in astonishment at the high regard in which my master, the famed Mr. Carnegie, held me. Curtsying in farewell to her, I grinned at him, thinking that Miss Quinn was correct. I had indeed transformed.

CHAPTER THIRTY-TWO

June 14, 1866
Pittsburgh, Pennsylvania

The guests cheered as the elder Mr. Carnegie held up his crystal goblet for a toast. "To Lucy, the lovely bride of my dear brother, Thomas. We welcome you into the Carnegie family." He glanced over at his mother as he spoke, instead of the rather wan, nervous bride to whom he referred.

My mistress gave him a rare, broad smile. Her long-held aspirations that her youngest son would marry one of Pittsburgh's most eligible society maidens, conveniently also the daughter of an iron scion, had come to fruition. Perhaps even more rewarding to her was that the dreaded "Committee of Matrimony" had been an empty threat, and my mistress still had her Andra at her side.

From the vantage point of my post behind Mrs. Carnegie, I looked at the bride and

303

groom. Wearing an ivory lace wedding gown, the pale color made fashionable by Queen Victoria for her own wedding, the new Mrs. Carnegie made the traditional gown her own by adding a cascade of ruffles on the skirt and swaths of handmade Scottish lace on the bodice. Again adhering to the customs made popular by the English queen, in her brown, upswept hair, the bride wore a wreath made of orange blossoms, which symbolized purity, and myrtle, which represented love and domestic happiness and brought a haze of innocent loveliness to the otherwise rather plain bride. She carried these same flowers in her bouquet, and they filled every silver vase on the expanded dining room table. The intense citrus and herbal aroma of the flowers permeated the room, bringing the warmth of the summer day indoors.

The wedding guests, crowded around the dining table made festive with a pressed linen-and-Belgian-lace tablecloth and a new set of china engraved with the couple's initials in silver, raised their glasses. Sunlight streamed through the clear glass of the dining room windows, turning the crimson cabernet filling the raised goblets into glistening, suspended rubies. The groom leaned toward the bride, her downturned eyes hesitant, and they bestowed upon one another a delicate kiss, perhaps their first.

As the crystal clinked, Mr. Holyrod and the footmen simultaneously set out the first course on the table, scalloped oysters. The guests, nearly all Homewood friends familiar with one another from many occasions together but for two Scottish relatives who had been dressed up for the occasion and tucked into a remote corner of the table, grew merry. I kept my eyes and ears open for interesting tidbits, but the chatter around me centered on the day's ceremony and the lavish feast spread before them.

In between courses, the bride's father cleared his throat and then stood up. Mrs. Carnegie shot a concerned look at her elder son, and I too wondered what Mr. Coleman was doing. He had already given the first toast to the bride and groom, and with that, his responsibilities had ended. It seemed he had a second toast in mind.

Mr. Coleman raised his glass. "It isn't often that you perceive the family your daughter is joining as your own kin, especially if they are from far-flung Scotland" — he paused while the guests laughed — "but Mrs. Coleman and I do. We feel blessed to be joining the Carnegie and Coleman families and would like everyone to raise a glass to our fruitful unions."

Fruitful unions? Even though I knew Mr. Coleman ostensibly referred to another sort of fruitfulness, I almost laughed thinking about how "fruitful" the iron manufacturing and oil drilling union of Mr. Coleman and Mr. Carnegie had been. It was one of Mr. Carnegie's few ventures outside his dealings with Messrs. Scott and Thomson.

Mr. Coleman and the elder Mr. Carnegie raised their goblets to each other, and I realized this toast was not for the newlyweds. My mistress beamed at her older son. In her eyes and those of Mr. Coleman, this day was as much his as it was his younger brother's.

Mr. Holyrod and his team of footmen cleared the oysters, and another course appeared, this time, lobster salad. This parade occurred seven times over the next two hours, delighting the guests with plates of pineapple salad, consommé royale, roast sirloin with horseradish sauce, braised spinach and asparagus, trout quenelles, stuffed eggplant fruit, and roasted partridge with bread sauce. As the guests expressed their incredulity at the lavishness of each course, I couldn't help but view the feast in quite a different way. To me, the sumptuous meal was no different from the decoration of Fairfield itself, as explained to me by Mr. Carnegie, with each course telegraphing to the guests an esteemed quality about their hosts.

The presentation of the wedding cake was meant to follow the final course. But instead, Mr. Holyrod and the footmen laid out silver platters of meringues filled with coffee cream, canapés of caviar, cheese soufflés, and strawberries and cream. This disruption to my mistress's carefully crafted schedule enraged her. I could tell from the tightening of her jaw and the squaring of her shoulders. But she did not want to appear anything other than refined on her son's wedding day, so she continued talking with Mrs. Wilkins to her right as if the silver trays were meant to appear first.

Knowing that my mistress was playing a part, I glanced around the room and wondered at what parts all the guests were playing. The Colemans seemed fat and comfortable on the iron and oil trade, but who were they really? Was Mrs. Coleman as vapid as she appeared and Mr. Coleman as ruthless? Perhaps, behind the closed doors of their own estate, it was quite the reverse. Maybe that was true of every guest. Certainly, it was true of me. My own family would have hardly recognized me.

"Clara," my mistress whispered to me, her face turned away from her guests. Unable to tolerate the disruption of her plan any longer, she asked me to see Mr. Ford about the whereabouts of the wedding cake.

Curtsying to her back as I took my leave, I hurried down the back hallway into the kitchen. The wedding feast was nearing its end, which meant that everyone but Mr. Ford was in the scullery, scrubbing the mountain of china and silver that had been dirtied during the feast's nine courses. The bulk of the work over, a mood of relief had settled upon them, as I could hear from their gentle jibing of one another, a sport in which even Mrs. Stewart partook on this celebratory occasion. It was a camaraderie for which I'd long given up hope.

The wedding cake stood in the middle of the battered kitchen table. It was a delectable confection of three stacked cakes, each one a little smaller than the one beneath. Artfully festooned with white fondant swirls and curlicues, the beautiful cake was plated and ready for presentation. All except for the sugared rose petals that were meant to decorate the top layer, that was. Those lay on a plate beside the cake, and Mr. Ford stood next to it, immobile.

I saw why Mr. Holyrod brought out the

silver trays of delicacies before the cake in violation of Mrs. Carnegie's orders. He had no choice. The cake itself wasn't ready.

"Mr. Ford, are you quite all right? Mrs. Carnegie is wondering where on earth the cake is. It was meant to be brought out before the pastries."

He didn't answer me. He just stood there, eyes glazed, staring at nothing.

"Mr. Ford," I entreated him. Placing my hand on his shoulder, I looked into his eyes. "Mr. Ford, can you hear me?"

His eyes focused somewhat, but he still did not seem clear. "It's you, Clara. I mean, Miss Kelley."

"Mr. Ford, it is young Mr. Carnegie's wedding day, and the guests are waiting on the cake. If you tell me what remains to be done, I can do it for you, and you can go take a rest."

Without answering my questions about the cake, he said, as if continuing a conversation we had been having, "You see, this wedding has put me in mind of my own wife. My Ruth. I can't seem to stop thinking about her just now."

"I am certain Mr. Carnegie's wedding has brought back memories, but —" I stopped myself from admonishing Mr. Ford to ready the cake. Wasn't Mr. Ford's heartbreak more important than the precise timing of the wedding cake? I decided to share with Mr. Ford a matter about which I'd been debating in the hopes it would help him. "Mr. Ford, after we discussed the letter from the Freedmen's Bureau last winter, the one about your wife and daughter, I decided to talk over further measures with the elder Mr. Carnegie. I knew from several conversations that he was acquainted with General Oliver Howard, the man in charge of the Freedmen's Bureau. Mr. Carnegie inquired of General Howard directly as to the whereabouts of your family, and the matter is being investigated again as we speak."

"General Howard?" he said, his voice indistinct and a bit fuzzy. As if I'd awoken him from a sleep.

"Yes. If anyone can help find your daughter and wife, he can."

He began pacing around the kitchen, still deep in his memories. "That's good. That's good."

Mr. Holyrod burst into the kitchen. "Where is the bloody cake? It's well past time for serving it."

I had never heard Mr. Holyrod utter a curse word before, no matter how impatient with the staff he became. For a moment, I was shocked into immobility. I quickly regained my composure and covered for Mr. Ford. "Nearly ready, Mr. Holyrod. Mr. Ford just has a few crystallized rose petals to add to the top layer, and he was about to complete this final task when you walked in."

Mr. Holyrod glanced over at Mr. Ford, who hadn't spoken or hastened over to the table to finalize the cake. Understanding that something was amiss, Mr. Holyrod directed his instructions to me. "We will clear the plates and return for the cake in less than a minute. I expect it to be ready."

"It will be ready, Mr. Holyrod."

Waiting until Mr. Holyrod flew out of the kitchen, I raced to place the sugared rose petals on the top of the cake in some semblance of a design. I didn't bother asking Mr. Ford for guidance, as he was lost in the past.

CHAPTER THIRTY-THREE

June 14, 1866
Pittsburgh, Pennsylvania

Cobalt hues began to illuminate the pitch-black of the nighttime sky as I finally closed the door to Mrs. Carnegie's bedroom. Only the harkening of dawn could cajole the revelers into ending the wedding festivities. The music of a string quartet had followed the protracted dinner, and drinks and more silver trays of delicacies had followed the music, and a boisterous farewell to the bride and groom had followed the final round of confections. Conversation lingered until Mrs. Pitcairn noticed the brightening sky and announced that the wedding guests must take their leave.

I paused in the stairwell. I wanted to check on Mr. Ford's spirits after last evening. Would he have awakened for the morning? It would not be abnormal for him to be preparing the day's bread or organizing the larder at this hour, and given that Mrs. Carnegie had excused the kitchen staff after the dinner concluded, he would have had a normal night's rest. Unlike me. Thankfully, Mrs. Carnegie had surprised me by excusing me from my duties for the following morning. Perhaps she was planning on sleeping until noon herself.

I padded down the back staircase to the kitchen. Even the low gaslights Mr. Ford lit for the early-morning hours were dark. Mr. Ford must have been asleep still. Turning back to the servants' staircase, I bumped straight into Mr. Carnegie.

My heart thumped in my chest so loudly, I thought he could hear it. "You startled me." A few weeks before, he'd asked me to stop calling him Mr. Carnegie and to start calling him Andrew, in private of course, but I couldn't cross the bridge to such familiarity. Instead, I'd taken to omitting any sort of name when speaking to him. In response, he'd taken to doing the same.

He laughed. "I am sorry. I did creep into the kitchen like a thief in the night, didn't I?"

"Yes, though I cannot complain. I was lurking around in the dark myself."

"True enough. What's your reason? I

confess to wanting a few more of the éclairs filled with coffee cream."

"Why didn't you ring for the staff to bring some to you?"

"There has been a frenzy of work for the past two weeks — at my mother's insistence — and they deserve their rest."

"I'd be happy to get the éclairs for you," I said and started to walk toward the larder where Mr. Ford kept them.

He reached for my hand to stop me. "Please don't. I'm perfectly capable of serving myself."

As he heaped the remaining éclairs onto one of the kitchen plates, he said, "You never told me your reason for coming down to the kitchen when, by all rights, you should be collapsed in your bed as well."

"I wanted to check on Mr. Ford."

"Is something wrong?" he asked, sliding the plate of éclairs toward me and gesturing for me to select one.

I shook my head and answered, "The wedding made him rather melancholic about his own family."

"Poor fellow," he said. "Did you tell him about General Howard's investigation?"

"I did. I'm hoping that after he rests, the news will lighten his mood a bit."

"Good. I hope we can help find his family. General Howard has the ability to search the records of most plantations and conduct wide-scale investigations, of course."

The plate of oblong éclairs, each piped with an identical flower of icing, sat between us. Neither of us reached toward the plate, although, after the interminable day, I longed for one.

"You first," he offered.

Normally, I would have resisted, as befitted a maid, but I was too weary. And too desperate to try the confections that I'd been staring at all evening while denied a bite.

"Speaking of news, I have some rather exciting information to share with you," he said.

The delectable coffee cream interior of the éclair filled my mouth, and I couldn't speak.

"Your company is in the works, Miss Kelley."

I dabbed at my mouth with a napkin and asked, "What do you mean?"

"Your telegraph company."

"*My* telegraph company?"

"Yes. It's called Keystone Telegraph Company." His barrel-shaped chest swelled with the excitement of sharing his news. "Your idea to string public telegraph lines along the railroads was the work of genius. I ran the idea by Scott and Thomson, and they wholeheartedly agreed to grant us the necessary rights of way along the Pennsylvania Railroad, in exchange for becoming silent partners, of course. So I formed Keystone Telegraph, and at Thomson's behest, the Pennsylvania Railroad entered into contract with Keystone Telegraph, giving it the right, for an annual fee of four dollars a mile, to string public wires along the Pennsylvania Railroad's poles."

I clapped my hand to my mouth. "I don't believe it."

He grinned at me. "Believe it. And I took the liberty of granting fifty shares in the new company to you. Much as Mr. Scott granted to me over ten years ago when I helped him with the exclusive contract Pennsylvania Railroad entered with Adams Express to transport packages between Philadelphia and Pittsburgh."

"Fifty shares to me?" I felt like giggling. A wildly inappropriate giggle at the idea of me, farm girl Clara Kelley from Galway, owning a piece of a telegraph company. I kept my hand clamped over my mouth to stifle an unseemly act.

"Yes indeed. But I haven't even told you the most brilliant part of my news."

"Mr. Carnegie, I cannot imagine news more marvelous than fifty shares in Keystone Telegraph!"

"Haven't I told you to call me Andrew?"

"Andrew," I said, although the word felt raw, even exposed. I stifled the urge to look around for witnesses to this almost-licentious behavior.

"The Pacific and Atlantic Telegraph Company caught wind of your idea, and they need a telegraphic connection to Philadelphia."

Why was Mr. Carnegie — Andrew — telling me about the aspirations of the Pacific and Atlantic Telegraph? I didn't understand. What did Pacific and Atlantic Telegraph have to do with *my* company, Keystone Telegraph?

"So that they can string lines from Pittsburgh to Philadelphia, along the route that the Pennsylvania Railroad granted to *your* company, Keystone Telegraph, Pacific and Atlantic Telegraph has offered to buy Keystone Telegraph in exchange for six thousand shares of Pacific and Atlantic stock and the contract to string the wires from Pittsburgh to Philadelphia, which one of my companies can handle and for which we will be paid a premium. All before we dig a single hole for a telegraph pole, string even one telegraph line, or spend a single dollar."

"Why would you — we — want to do that?"

"Because Pacific and Atlantic Telegraph is paying us, the owners of the shares of Keystone Telegraph, a huge premium. Each of your Keystone Telegraph shares is now a Pacific and Atlantic Telegraph share worth $25, for a total of $1,250."

I didn't feel my jaw drop at the news that I now had $1,250 — an amount I never expected to earn in my entire lifetime — but it must have. Because Mr. Carnegie — Andrew — stepped closer to me and, with a single finger under my chin, closed it.

"Now it will be a bit of time before you can cash in your stocks, if in fact you even want to do that. But the money will be all yours."

All I could think of was Eliza, Cecelia, Mum, and Dad. This wondrous boon could rescue them. The absurd amount of money was more than enough to save my family from the desperate life they were living in Galway City and bring them here. And until the "bit of time" passed before I could cash in the stock, it could bring them hope. I couldn't wait to write Eliza with the news.

Without thinking of propriety, I hugged him. Whether as an expression of gratitude for what this meant for my family, an outpouring at our enormous good fortune, or something more, I did not know. I simply could not restrain myself. His body was stiff under my arms at first and then slackened as he wrapped his arms around me. I must have shocked him. I had, in fact, shocked myself.

"I told you it was good news, Clara," he whispered. "Now you can really help your family."

We stared into each other's eyes, and I wondered what would happen next. In this moment. In the weeks to come.

And then, Mr. Ford walked into the room.

CHAPTER THIRTY-FOUR

August 8, 1866
Pittsburgh, Pennsylvania

Fairfield echoed emptily in the weeks following the wedding. The younger Mr. Carnegie was a quiet, placid man, and I did not expect the house would grow still without him. But when he and his bride left for their extended European honeymoon, the exhilaration of the wedding planning departed with them, leaving behind a deflated Fairfield.

The frequent business trips taken by Mr. Carnegie, Andrew as I'd been trying to think of him, made Fairfield seem even more desolate. President Johnson had recently authorized the construction of seven bridges across the Mississippi River and down the Missouri River to Kansas City. Given the profit they had made on bridge construction from both Keystone Bridge and Union Iron Mills, Messrs. Thomson and Scott relented to Andrew's ambitions and agreed that Keystone Bridge should compete for those bridges. Knowing about this arrangement, I wasn't surprised when Andrew and his silent partners decided that he should put all of his energies into the pursuit of these contracts. This meant Andrew had to travel to the Midwest, Washington, DC, and New York City to get commitments from railroad companies to build the bridges and to raise capital to pay Union Iron Mills for the iron by selling bridge bonds and stock. He returned to Pittsburgh only to consult with engineers and iron makers over the actual construction of the bridges. In his absence, I worked on business structures and ideas in the evening when I finished with my duties to Mrs. Carnegie, but I felt disconnected from him and the hope I felt with him. And I wondered when the stock money would come in, as Eliza's latest letter described their Galway City situation as "bleak at best." But how could I ask Mr. Carnegie without revealing my real situation?

"Mother, I think a trip to New York City is in order," Andrew announced from behind the *Daily Morning Chronicle,* a Washington, DC, newspaper. A pile of discarded sections of the *New York Times* and *Pittsburgh Daily Gazette* sat at his feet, and the *Daily Morning Chronicle* was the last of his reading material. From the size of the pile, summoning the courage to proclaim this trip must have taken him some time.

My mistress tried to peer around his paper before answering, which left me scrambling to slacken the line of knitting wool that connected us. He refused to lower his *Daily Morning Chronicle* a single inch, so she was forced to talk to the political page, which covered some legislation President Johnson proposed. "That bastion of vice? With Boss Tweed in control of the government and those corrupt financiers Fiske and Gould in control of the money? I am not keen, Andra."

"Keystone Bridge cannot compete in the Mississippi River projects without additional funding, and you know that New York City is where the investors are located," he said, lowering his paper just enough to allow his eyes to peek over the top. He caught not only her eye but mine as well. "And you know that Tom and Lucy need some time alone in the house to make it their own."

Was Andrew planning on handing over the ownership of Fairfield to his younger brother? Perhaps the occasion of his marriage merited a new home for Tom, but did it have to be Fairfield? What would happen to me? Andrew and I rarely talked about any topic other than business and certainly never broached his mother and brother.

She looked startled, and knowing my mistress as I did, I guessed that she'd never really considered that Tom and Lucy would take over Fairfield in any way, although the pattern was not unusual among their acquaintances. Fairfield belonged to her and, to a lesser extent, Andrew. In her mind, Tom and Lucy would simply fall into the existing structure. Or get their own house.

"Why must *we* be supplanted, Andra?"

"It seems to be the way of these wealthy American families. Anyway, I think you and I should experience more than just Pittsburgh. Why don't we stay in New York for the fall season? That should give the newlyweds time to adjust to a new home and schedule, while we enjoy all the culture and entertainment New York has to offer."

I tried to keep my hands still as Mrs. Carnegie continued to pull thread from the skein I held, but they trembled with excitement at the thought of accompanying the Carnegies to New York City. I would have more opportunity to connect with Andrew on our business efforts and more access to information as well. Might I have the opportunity to increase my holdings? I almost chuckled aloud, thinking about how my aspiration had grown to match Andrew's ambitions.

My mistress did not immediately reply. Knots formed in my stomach as I awaited her reaction, and I prayed a silent Hail Mary that she would agree.

"Mother?" Andrew asked impatiently. "Did you hear what I said about traveling to New York for the fall season?"

"Of course I did, Andra. You're talking so loudly, how could I not hear you?" Her knitting needles clicked. "I've been thinking on your proposal, as is a mother's right. New York, giving up the house to Tom and Lucy — you are asking me to make major changes. I deserve the time to think through these matters."

While proclaiming her mother's rights was a favorite tactic of my mistress when she wished to shame her Andra into silence, I would have demanded the same in her shoes.

She continued, "Not to mention we have many social obligations here in Pittsburgh, Andra. We have to introduce Tom and Lucy to society."

"No social obligation would hold back a trip to New York. Imagine, Mother, experiencing the real season among the elite of America, not just Pittsburgh."

The clicking of the knitting needles stopped. He knew precisely how to play to his mother's weaknesses. "I suppose we should give Tom and Lucy the space necessary to make a place for themselves in society. And the Colemans will be on hand for any necessary guidance. The trip to New York would only be for a few months, and we could leave after the party introducing them to society." I noticed that she did not concede to giving the newlyweds the house, only to traveling to New York.

"Excellent decision, Mother," Andrew said, as always allowing her to claim the resolution about the trip as her own, instead of his.

"I need an uplifting tea," she declared. "Clara, tell the kitchen that we would like our tea now instead of the usual time."

As I entered the servants' hallway to the kitchen, I thought about how my mistress adored issuing orders to me. She had a button at her footstep to summon the kitchen staff, but she preferred watching me scurry about on her command.

I expected to see Hilda in the kitchen, but

only Mr. Ford was there, preparing the evening meal. "Sorry to disturb you, Mr. Ford. I know it's a bit early, but the Carnegies are ready for their afternoon tea."

Without a word or his hallmark warm smile, he lumbered over to the battered center table, where he had meringues, apple tartlets, and trout finger sandwiches ready. Reaching for the teapot, he took it over to the fireplace, where he kept hot water boiling throughout the day.

"How is your day going?" I asked him. But he did not respond. He simply shook his head.

I did not know what to say next. Ever since Mr. Ford had caught me and Andrew in the embrace, he would only speak to me when necessary. I had tried to explain that the hug was innocent, an instinctive reaction to good news that Mr. Carnegie had brought me, but Mr. Ford was unmoved. He simply closed himself off to me. Losing his friendship meant losing my only friend in this house, indeed in this city, aside from Andrew, and that relationship was too complicated — fraught with too many stakes — to regard as friendship.

CHAPTER THIRTY-FIVE

September 20, 1866
Pittsburgh, Pennsylvania

Always the requisite two steps behind Mrs. Carnegie, I mounted the steps into the railcar bound for New York City. Following the engineer, we shimmied to the berths that Andrew had indicated down a hallway so narrow, I feared my mistress, wide in build and made wider by her skirts, would not fit. Once she managed to squeeze through the hall, the engineer opened the mahogany-and-etched-glass door and said, "Welcome to the Woodruff Silver Palace car, madam."

In my mistress's wake, I stepped into a railcar berth that looked like the interior of a mansion in miniature. Oriental rugs lined the floor, brass chandeliers hung from the ceiling, two sets of chocolate-brown uphol-stered chairs faced one another, and to my astonishment, a set of twin beds stacked upon each other hid in the rear, nearly obscured by red damask curtains that could be drawn for privacy.

This Silver Palace car was a revelation, and I could not repress a little gasp. The railcars to which I was accustomed were outfitted in hard wooden benches and floors and black-smut-encrusted windows. Or they had no seats at all. Instinctively, I wondered what my family would think of this luxury, and the thought saddened me that they were suffering with so little. I felt guilty at enjoying the Carnegies' largesse.

"It is marvelous, isn't it?" Andrew asked from behind me. Surprised to hear his voice, I turned around. I hadn't realized he had already reached the station from his office.

"It is incredible, sir," I said, adding the *sir* for the benefit of Mrs. Carnegie, who was occupied by the porter but still in earshot.

"This is a very special railcar, called the Woodruff Silver Palace. It usually runs on a different line, but I had it brought here for our journey."

Ears perked at the sound of Andra's voice, Mrs. Carnegie made her way down the berth's narrow aisle to give her son a possessive squeeze. He smiled at me over her head. I knew the Silver Palace was not for my mistress's benefit alone.

"Why are you talking with Clara?" she asked, eyeing me suspiciously.

"I was telling her that this is a Woodruff Silver Palace car. Remember when I first got involved with Woodruff Sleeping Cars, Mother?" he asked as he eased out of her grasp.

She turned to face him directly, so that the conversation would exclude me. "Of course. It was way back in 1858 or 1859, wasn't it?"

He opened the circle to speak with me as well. "Yes, it was. Clara, I was traveling on the Pennsylvania Railroad for work, and I was approached by T. T. Woodruff himself about this notion of sleeping cars. He showed me a model he'd built, which I then shared with Messrs. Scott and Thomson."

Mrs. Carnegie interrupted him, not bothering to change her posture again but speaking only to her son. "And Messrs. Scott and Thomson were so impressed with Woodruff — and with you, Andra — that they offered Woodruff Sleeping Cars a contract to place two of his cars on the Pennsylvania Railroad, and they gave you an interest in Woodruff's company as a way of saying thanks."

I noticed that my mistress did not mention that Messrs. Thomson and Scott also had a partial interest in the Woodruff Sleeping Car Company, which they had insisted upon before signing an agreement with Woodruff. Andrew had shared this private piece with me as I finalized my charts of the Carnegie holdings. Was it possible that his mother was unaware of the role of Messrs. Thomson and Scott in this story Andrew was spinning? Could she possibly be innocent to the fact that using insider information to invest in companies with whom they were about to enter into contracts was common for Thomson and Scott? Indeed, for executives of all sorts of companies, not only the railroads, including her son? I found it implausible that a woman as business savvy as my mistress could be blind to this routine practice, one I'd questioned in the past. Perhaps she simply wanted to elevate the role of her son in the tale.

"Your memory and business acumen are, as always, formidable, Mother." He glanced around the berth, nodding with pride. "We have come a long way since those first two cars, haven't we?"

My mistress ran her fingers along the silk fringe that hung from the end of the arms of the upholstered chairs. "We certainly have, Andra." But then, her eyes narrowed, and her expression hardened. "Now, you've just got to beat that bloody Pullman at this sleeping car game. You will do that, won't you, Andra?"

"Don't I always, Mother?" he answered her with a gaze as hard as her own.

I busied myself with transforming the Silver Palace into an approximation of Mrs. Carnegie's bedchamber, laying out her favorite toiletries, spritzing her perfume in the air, and unpacking her undergarments into the drawers. No one had indicated where I'd be sleeping, and I did not think my mistress would welcome me sharing her bunk beds. The upholstered chairs or even the less luxurious benches I saw in the other railcars would serve me just as well. Certainly, my bed at home in Galway was less plush than either option.

The thought of my bed at home near Tuam stopped me short. Home no longer existed. I would never see the farm with its crooked stream and the emerald hills that rolled like waves, one into the other, or our thatched-roof, white-washed farmhouse again. Had that really registered before? In all my worrying about my family's survival in Galway City, I had not really contemplated the loss of my childhood home. It

331

seemed insignificant when my family was barely surviving and I, by contrast, was inundated by the Carnegies' wealth.

"Clara," Mrs. Carnegie interrupted my unpacking. "Go ask my son when we are scheduled to dine. I need to change before dinner, and I'd like to know the exact time."

"Certainly, ma'am," I said and left the berth.

As I walked the short distance to Andrew's berth, a disquiet nagged at me. I had tried to ignore its source and enjoy the unexpected luxuriousness of the journey, but my parting conversation with Mr. Ford picked away at my ebullience until I could no longer disregard it. Especially now that I would see Andrew in private.

Earlier that day, I'd been alone in the kitchen with Mr. Ford, fetching the basket of food he'd prepared for our journey. I assumed that it would be a silent transfer. Yet when I took the basket from his hands and thanked him, he said, "You shouldn't be goin' on this New York trip, Miss Kelley."

Surprised that he was speaking to me, I was also confused by his statement. "I have to go where my mistress goes, Mr. Ford."

"I think you know what I mean. I don't think you should be traveling with Mr. Carnegie." The judgment and hardness I'd seen in his eyes in the months since young Mr. Carnegie's wedding softened, and I realized that he had not been avoiding me out of anger but because he was worried. And he couldn't tolerate more pain after learning that his long-held hope for his wife and daughter might be dashed, no matter the ongoing investigation.

"Mr. Ford, I care very much for your opinion. But as I explained, there is nothing inappropriate going on between myself and Mr. Carnegie."

"Do you want to tell me how an embrace is appropriate?"

I blushed. "The embrace itself was a mistake, I agree. Although nothing like that has happened before or since, and it was an impulsive reaction to some business news. That's all."

"What business news do you two have that could possibly call for a hug?" Mr. Ford asked me incredulously.

"Mr. Carnegie has been tutoring me in the business world, and in fact, he's rewarded me for the help I've given him."

"Rewarded?" He almost laughed.

"He has repaid me with shares in a company, worth quite a nice amount."

"Has he placed the dollars in your hand? Or the shares, whatever those are?"

"No," I answered quietly. The concern raised by Mr. Ford had been troubling me as well — I'd wondered when I'd actually receive the shares Andrew claimed were my payment — but I would not even consider asking Andrew about the whereabouts of the stock. I worried that appearing greedy for them might jeopardize my ownership of them.

Mr. Ford reached for my hands, holding them tightly in his own. "Listen, Miss Kelley, I've seen this situation before, and I hope you'll take a word of caution from a tired, old man who's seen too many masters and servants crossing the boundaries between them. It never ends well for the servant."

I knocked on Andrew's railcar door, knowing that he would answer it himself. Many men of his stature traveled with butlers or manservants of some sort, but not Andrew. He had grown up simply, he liked to proclaim, and liked to travel through the world simply as well.

Opening the door, he greeted me with his usual disarming grin. "Clara, come in."

Mr. Ford's words were still ringing in my ears, and I chose not to cross the threshold. "I am here to ask a single question on your mother's behalf. She would like to know when you and she are dining tonight."

"Dinner is at six o'clock," he answered. "You can spare a few minutes, Clara. I want to show you a special feature in my berth that I had Woodruff design."

His invitation sounded like precisely the sort of situation Mr. Ford warned me against. "I can see the whole of your berth from the hallway. I don't think it's wise for me to step inside in such close proximity to your mother's berth," I cautioned him.

As giddy as a child, he demonstrated a mahogany desk that he had Woodruff design that folded into the berth wall when the passenger required more space. I watched this display from the hallway.

"It is ingenious, Andrew." I gave him the compliment he sought.

He pushed back into the tufted velvet seat that faced the desk, as if to emphasis its plushness. "When I first pushed the idea of luxury travel with these Woodruff railcars, the war was approaching, and there wasn't much use for them. But now that transcontinental rail is expanding, people will want comfort for long journeys."

"People who can afford it, you mean."

"Yes, it is too expensive for the common man, sadly. And the Pullman cars are even pricier than the Woodruff cars."

"Your mother mentioned Pullman earlier. Who — or what — is that?"

"Pullman is a competitor. Because Woodruff has got eighty-eight cars in service and contracts on the Pennsylvania Railroad and most of the major mid-Atlantic, it has dominated the sleeping car business until now. The Pullman cars have started to take control in an area in which we wanted to expand — the Middle West. And now there are rumors that the Union Pacific Railroad is getting ready to award the sleeping car franchise for its transcontinental trains."

"So you need to put Pullman out of the running for the Union Pacific contract."

"Exactly."

"Tell me more about the Pullman cars and how they differ from the Woodruff cars."

Andrew gave an overview of the engineering behind each car and the differences in structure and size, admitting that the Pullman cars were sturdier, quieter, and even a bit more comfortable. The irony, Andrew said, was that Pullman based his sleeping cars on several of Woodruff's designs.

"It sounds as if Woodruff would be hard-pressed to beat out Pullman. What about aligning with them?"

"I've approached Pullman, even made a

generous proposal to fold Woodruff into Pullman. I thought I'd get him with the financial offer, as I know he needs money for expansion. But he is stubborn. And wary."

"Sounds like a worthy adversary," I joked.

"Too worthy."

An idea occurred to me, one I couldn't believe Andrew had not considered and rejected for some reason. Would he laugh at me if I suggested it? I worried that it was too obvious. "You mentioned that Pullman based his sleeping cars on several of Woodruff's designs?"

"Yes."

"Does Woodruff have a patent on any of those designs?"

Andrew stood up and began pacing around the small berth. "A few."

"What if you file a lawsuit that Pullman violated Woodruff's patents? What's that sort of case called again?"

"Patent infringement. Hmm, interesting."

"Yes. Instead of taking a friendly approach, explain to him that you'll sue him for patent infringement if he will not consolidate his interest with Woodruff's. He won't want to drain his capital defending a lawsuit right now. You might leave him with no choice but to surrender and agree."

I thought I heard my name. When I listened hard, I did not hear it again, so I turned my attention back to Andrew.

He stared at me for a long time, and I feared his reaction. Before he said a single word, a hysterical, body-shaking laughter took hold of him. I didn't know how to react until he finally calmed down enough to say, "Clara, I have at least ten professional advisers working on this Pullman matter, and you — my mother's lady's maid — have arrived at the solution. In less than a minute. You are a genius."

"Clara!" my mistress said, her voice directly behind me. She had walked down the narrow Silver Palace aisle to fetch me from her son's berth, and she was mad.

Pivoting to face her beet-red, livid face, I curtsied and said, "My apologies, ma'am."

"What is taking you so long? I sent you with one question for my son. There is no reason for you two to indulge in a long conversation."

Andrew came to the door of his berth. He had a book in his hand. "It's my fault, Mother. I asked her to wait while I dug this book out of my luggage. I thought it might prove an interesting read for the journey."

She huffed, then said, "All right. Clara, take the book and follow me to my room.

Andrew, when do we need to be ready for dinner?"

He consulted his pocket watch and answered, "Thirty minutes."

"Come along, Clara. You have wasted so much time at my son's door that we will have to race to be dressed for dinner." Of course, she placed the blame on me instead of her precious Andra.

"Yes, ma'am," I answered as I looked down at the book in my hands. It was Andrew's copy of *Aurora Leigh*.

CHAPTER THIRTY-SIX

September 26, 1866
New York, New York

The train slowed as it approached New York City's Thirtieth Street station. Unlike our other stops over the six days it had taken us to get from Pittsburgh to the nation's largest city with over eight hundred thousand people, we were disembarking. Our bags were packed and ready for the porter, and we wore our traveling clothes. Even though I played my usual role of subservient lady's maid, my nerves fluttered at alighting in Manhattan.

From my position at Mrs. Carnegie's side, I craned my neck to witness the train pulling into the maze of rails that made up the back portion of the station. Even through the railcar's window, I saw smothering smoke, soot, and cinders reminiscent of Pittsburgh, a similarity I hadn't anticipated.

I expected that the station would be immaculate and opulent, befitting the city.

When the train chugged into its final destination, I learned that I was wrong. The tracks all led to a nondescript redbrick building that looked like one of the vast warehouses near St. Patrick Church in Pittsburgh. It was smudged inside and out with the indelible mark of industrialization.

"Surprisingly plain for the terminus of the New York Central and Hudson River Railroads," my mistress sniffed in disdain.

"Especially since Commodore Cornelius Vanderbilt is the president of the railroad line and the richest man in America," Andrew retorted. "Mr. Thomson would never allow the hub of the Pennsylvania Railroad to appear so plain."

"I suppose there is no accounting for taste," Mrs. Carnegie pronounced, as if she, a recent immigrant from Scotland who arrived without a penny in her purse and who wore outdated fashions, was the arbiter of taste. I almost laughed aloud at the irony.

As we squeezed down the Silver Palace hallway to the exit doors, Andrew said, "Did you know that President Lincoln's funeral train pulled into this very station when it made its way up the Eastern Seaboard? Imagine his coffin passing through this building."

"That's rather macabre, don't you think?" my mistress said.

"It's not morbid if it's history, Mother," Andrew responded.

Glancing over at him, I wondered how he could make such a statement. History often produced the grisliest of results. Simply because those events were past did not make them any more palatable. I wondered what he would say about the horrific facts Patrick and Maeve told me about the Irish immigrants in New York City for the past decade. What would he think of the fact that my people were living nine people to a room in the Five Points slums and paying four dollars — nearly one week's pay — for the pleasure of a single room with no windows or indoor plumbing but plenty of rats? Would he downplay the fact that my own family was living four to a room in my aunt's damp, candlelit attic with the closest outhouse a quarter mile away?

Had Andrew forgotten who he was and from where he came? He was an immigrant, no different from the thousands of impoverished immigrants inhabiting this country but for his recent success. I chastised myself as soon as the censorious thought entered my conscious. Who was I to criticize? I was in no position to judge him, as I enjoyed the benefits that came from working for and traveling with him. Not to mention I helped him further his business interests and served his family while pretending to be someone I was not. Who was the one who had forgotten him or herself? My dependence on his money caused me to forsake my own immigrant story.

A man in a uniform resplendent with gleaming brass buttons approached us. Hesitantly, he asked, "Sir, are you Mr. Carnegie?"

"I am."

"Then please allow me to show you to your livery."

We exited the station at the corner of Tenth Avenue and Thirtieth Streets, and after the porter loaded the Carnegies' trunks and my paltry bag onto the carriage, we stepped inside. The livery headed south toward the St. Nicholas Hotel, jolting down the uneven cobblestone streets pocked with holes. The city sprawled out before us, and I strained to capture a view of the sights before the livery sped by them. Tall, elegant buildings stood alongside empty lots covered with hardscrabble wooden shacks. Men and women with pushcarts hawking clams and flowers and chestnuts and exotic foodstuffs competed with striped-awning store-fronts displaying the latest in ladies' hats and gloves. Cows and goats roamed in open fields next to elegantly outfitted men and women strolling down the paved sidewalks. The smells wafting in the open livery window were a scintillating mix of perfumes, roasted nuts, factory smoke, and animal dung. I could not wait to send a letter to my family describing the curious mixture that composed New York City. Perhaps it would take their focus off their troubles.

Too soon, we pulled up to the entrance of the St. Nicholas Hotel on Broadway at Broome Street. En route, Andrew had informed his mother that the hotel was so lavish, the first building to cost over one million dollars to construct, that it ended the Astor House's status at the city's leading hotel. I had grown used to his excited hyperbole but soon realized his pronouncement was justified.

After only one step through the white marble facade topped with flying American flags into the hotel's lobby, Mrs. Carnegie and I surmised for ourselves the hotel's opulence. From the white oak staircase leading to the upper floors, to the elaborate crystal chandelier illuminating the first-floor landing, to the Dutch painting presiding over the lobby, to the mahogany-and-walnut inlaid paneling etched with gold paint, the St. Nicholas felt more like a castle than a hotel. What I imagined a modern-day castle to look like anyway.

As a hotel concierge ushered the Carnegies to the front desk to check into their suite, I waited against a Romanesque column with Mrs. Carnegie's personal belongings. The parade of well-heeled hotel guests mesmerized: ladies dressed in striped gowns so fashionable, I didn't know what to call the designs, men with ties and pocket scarves of vivid colors, and children wearing outfits rivaling wedding attire. I was so engrossed that Mrs. Carnegie claimed she had to say my name three times before I heard her call. While she often exaggerated when it came to flaws in my service, I tended to believe her on this occasion.

Hotel porters laden with trunks trailed us as we followed a concierge to the suite, consisting of two parlors, two bedrooms, and two dressing rooms, each with their own bathroom. The black-suited gentleman stepped back to permit our entrance into the rooms with wide windows looking out onto Broadway and framed with gold-trimmed curtains. Modern gaslights and mirrors hung on the walls, and I spied a bathtub cased in walnut in the background. From the call system connecting guests with the front desk to the central heating, every modern convenience was supplied.

For all her pretending to be the jaded sophisticate, when she stepped into the hotel room, my mistress cried out, "Oh, Andra, I wish your father had lived to see this."

The reference to the late Mr. Carnegie startled me. No one ever mentioned him. He was like a specter, at once looming omnisciently and invisibly.

"I wish he could have seen this too, Mother." Andrew reached over to squeeze his mother's hand. "You deserve the best," he said, looking at me as well.

After the porters unloaded the trunks into the designated rooms, one of the men held out my small travel bag and asked, "Where does this belong, madam?"

"That belongs to my lady's maid." Mrs. Carnegie pointed in my direction.

"Where shall we place it, madam?"

"In the servants' quarters."

The porter asked me, "Would you like to follow me there, ma'am? That way, you will know where to find your belongings and your lodgings."

"May I, Mrs. Carnegie?" I asked, curious about the servants' lodgings. Surely, our rooms must be unusually nice, if the luxurious decor of the hotel was any indicator.

"Yes, Clara, but hurry back so you can begin the unpacking."

I curtsied and followed the porter to an unremarkable door at the end of hallway. The dark stairs inside were made of unadorned, simple pine, a far cry from the lobby's grand staircase. They led to the top floor of the hotel, which contained row after row of servants' bedrooms. Clean but sparsely decorated with a single bed each, a washstand, a small, three-drawer dresser, and a narrow armoire, the room resembled my own at Fairfield.

Was this what Andrew meant when he looked at me and said I deserve the best? Not that a lady's maid should expect more, I reminded myself. But the contrast between Andrew's lodgings and my own caused thoughts of Mr. Ford's admonitions about masters and servants to creep into my mind. Even though I kept telling myself that my situation with Andrew was different, that I didn't need to worry, I said a little prayer to Mary that Mr. Ford's prediction about the servant's fate would be untrue. Because if I tumbled, I didn't tumble alone. I took my family down along with me.

CHAPTER THIRTY-SEVEN

October 2, 1866
New York, New York

New York City demanded new gowns, according to my mistress. Andrew arranged for the finest dressmakers to visit the suite at the St. Nicholas, where Mrs. Carnegie and Andrew had ensconced themselves for the season. While Andrew spent his first few days in the city meeting with investors and railroad executives, I passed them in the hotel suite reviewing drawings and fabric samples with my mistress and various dressmakers. The end result of all this fuss was four new dresses that, to my eye, looked substantially the same as her other gowns, except for the odd flounce and slight adjustments to the bustle. I tried not to consider what my family could do with the money constituting the cost of her dresses.

But I knew my mistress would not enter

the New York City society fray without the perfect dress, particularly given that Friday brought with it the prospect of a musical evening at the Academy of Music, which, we had been told, society folk would be attending. We understood that the highest realms of New York society were guarded by the women. Not just any women, mind, but the wives and daughters of a small set of families referred to as the Knickerbockers. These families were the descendants of early Dutch settlers who'd amassed modest fortunes in trade, and their women were eager to keep at bay those made newly wealthy by oil, the railroads, and the stock market — like the Carnegies — particularly if they were immigrants as well. Not that Andrew or his equally ambitious mother would give up before trying.

"How are the dresses coming along, Mother?" Andrew's booming voice traveled all the way into his mother's dressing room, where I was darning. Sometimes, I felt like needlework was all I did.

"Lovely, Andra. I think you'll be well pleased."

"Grand. I want you to look your best for the opera at the Academy of Music."

"It seems such a fuss. In Homewood, we

349

were friends with the best people, and an elegant evening of dinner at someone's home and whist would suffice."

"That's just it, Mother. We can afford the culture and entertainment that New York City has to offer. Why would we want our lives to just 'suffice'?"

My mistress chortled. "Ah, Andra. You never were satisfied."

"The day is lovely. Shall we step out for a stroll? You've been cooped up in this hotel for days meeting with seamstresses and dressmakers and designers on those dresses."

"I'd hardly call spending a day at the St. Nicholas being cooped up. Andra, did you know that the lobby has its own post office, a bookstore, a travel agent, a telegraph office, and four restaurants? Not to mention that there are no fewer than five grand parlors in this hotel. Why, one of them has gold brocade window curtains and bouquets of freshly cut flowers that they replace every day! Imagine the expense." She tsked. "And the waste."

"You don't need to worry about waste any longer, Mother. No scrimping and saving for you." The fabric of the couch rustled, and from my eavesdropping post, I guessed that Andrew had risen to his feet. "Let's take a stroll onto Broadway."

"That would be lovely. I'll summon Clara for my things."

"Why doesn't she come along?" he asked.

My heart skipped at the prospect of venturing into the city streets.

"Why would I want to bring Clara?" Her voice sounded tight.

"I thought it might be helpful."

"I don't think it's necessary, Andra. It's not as if I need her assistance to simply go for a stroll. I will have your arm to steady me if I need it."

"You misunderstand me, Mother. It might be helpful for her to know the location of the pharmacy and various tradespeople, such as hatters, tailors, dressmakers, perfumers, and the like."

"True. Clara will need to know where to go for errands."

A summoning and a coat and I was flung into the madness of Broadway. Instead of irritation at having to keep my mistress in my sights, I was relieved to have an anchor to buoy me. Otherwise, in an instant, I could have been lost amid the clatter of hoofs, the creaking of wagon wheels, the cries of street vendors, and the chatter of a hundred different people.

Periodically, Mr. Carnegie pointed out a

favorite glove maker or a well-stocked pharmacy, but otherwise, we traveled at a good clip until we reached a small but well-tended park with shade from a grove of royal paulownia trees, serpentine walkways, and plenty of benches upon which to rest. We stepped through its wrought-iron gates at Andrew's behest.

"Mother, if you ever need a respite from the indoor wonders of the St. Nicholas, I recommend this park. I often stop here in the late afternoon for a breath of nature before returning to the hotel to see you." He looked at me while making his seemingly innocuous suggestion to his mother. His meaning was clear.

Strains of Vincenzo Bellini's *Norma* wafted through the air. I closed my eyes and let the music wash over me, forgetting that I did not sit in the audience but on a long bench designated for servants outside the auditorium doors. Although the opera was unfamiliar, certain melodies brought back memories of my sisters and I practicing classical compositions at home in Galway. While our neighbors fiddled out Irish ballads, violating the law prohibiting all Gaelic culture, my father pushed us girls to use our instruments for loftier music. It was another reason I was not exactly popular with the lads in Galway.

I had not received a letter from Eliza in weeks. I knew it might take a bit longer to get mail since it had to be rerouted from Pittsburgh, but this was two weeks more than usual. How were they faring? I wondered. I hated having to pretend in my letters that I did not know about Dad's Fenian involvement and to suppress my anger at him for placing the family in danger. Whatever my confusion and misgivings about my situation with the Carnegies, I knew I should count myself lucky to have food, a roof, and salary enough to help my family at home — and maybe more, if the money Andrew made on my behalf actually materialized.

Another lady's maid to my right coughed. I glanced over at her with a ready smile, but she would not meet my eyes. Instead, she turned away and started chatting with the lady's maid to her right. Had I done something to offend her?

The music stopped, and ushers opened the doors to the auditorium. Patrons in elegant gowns and suits began streaming out, heading toward the bar, where aperitifs would be served during the intermission. Many of the ladies seemed to know one another, greeting each other with careful embraces that never mussed their dresses, as did the men, who shook hands.

Andrew and Mrs. Carnegie drifted into the crowd, and I tensed as I watched them. They looked small amid the horde of taller patrons and oddly old-fashioned in their attire, although we had been assured that both Andrew's suit and my mistress's gown reflected the latest fashions. Pretending to sip on a crystal glass of champagne, Andrew attempted conversation with a gentleman standing next to him as I observed nervously.

"Look at those two," I heard the lady's maid with whom I had attempted to establish a connection whisper to the girl to her right. She was staring right at Mrs. Carnegie and Andrew.

"Some nerve those two have coming here among the Knickerbockers," the girl whispered back.

"Like they'd ever be accepted."

"Just look at the length of the lady's sleeves. Bet she got that design out of some ill-informed newspaper society page. Not one of the Knickerbocker women would ever wear a sleeve that touched her hand. It would cover her wrists," she said, aghast at the thought of this secret rule being broken.

"I can only imagine what my mistress, Mrs. Van Rensselaer, is saying about them to her friend Mrs. Morris. Look how they are chatting right next to them and staring."

"Who's going to tell that woman the proper length for sleeves anyway? As my mistress, Mrs. Rhinelander, always says" — the girl raised her voice to a higher pitch and adopted an almost English accent — " 'Our ways should not be widely shared. That would be too democratic, inviting into our society all manner of people who do not belong.' "

The other girl giggled. "My mistress says much the same. I bet Mrs. Van Rensselaer and Mrs. Morris are taking apart that woman's posture. Look how she hunches her shoulders. No swanlike neck for her."

"You cannot blame our mistresses for staring. They hardly venture outside each other's brownstones for entertainment. That mother and son must seem like exotic animals to them."

While the lady's maids laughed at the Carnegies' expense, I prayed a silent Hail Mary that the intermission end soon, taking this painful commentary with it. As if my prayer had been answered, the gong mercifully sounded.

CHAPTER THIRTY-EIGHT

November 24, 1866
New York, New York

"Do you think the evening was a success, Clara?"

My mistress asked the question I dreaded as I brushed her hair. Each morning, after every concert, opera, or dinner at Delmonico's, she inquired as to the success of the previous night.

I knew too much to reply honestly. I had spent too many nights sitting in a row at the Academy of Music or the theater or a restaurant, listening to other servants who gossiped about New York society and mocked the Carnegies' efforts, even when they learned I was their maid. I understood that the Carnegies' evenings at the periphery of New York society — in the only places where the Knickerbockers appeared publicly — were frowned upon by the denizens who guarded the gates. No matter that Andrew's fortune may well have exceeded most of these people's, the Carnegies would never be allowed inside.

So I lied. "Your gown was the loveliest in the entire restaurant, ma'am."

A guarded smile appeared on her face. "Surely, there were younger ladies with lovelier gowns, Clara?"

"Those gowns are too frivolous for my taste, ma'am. I prefer a dress of impeccable quality, solid craftsmanship, and the highest fashion. In that category, yours stood alone."

I was rewarded with a half smile. She observed, "The Delmonico's method of having guests order à la carte instead of table d'hôte takes some getting used to."

"The mistresses I served in Ireland seemed to prefer the individual choice à la carte allows." From overheard conversations, I'd learned that à la carte was modeled after European restaurants. I figured this remark would be safe.

"I wonder when we will be included in evenings with some native New Yorkers. Most of our companions have been railroad executives living at the St. Nicholas or staying here on business. Otherwise, Andra and I have been quite alone." As if she were talking to herself, she said, "It was so much easier in Pittsburgh to meet the right people. We simply moved into the proper neighborhood, and we made friends. Dinners and concerts and games quickly followed."

What could I say? That this would likely be the status quo in New York City? That no old-moneyed Rockefeller or Rhinelander would be inviting them over for tea in their Fourteenth Street brownstone? Was that even the point of this New York City sojourn? When I thought of the serious troubles many faced — inadequate money, food, and housing, troubles that Mrs. Carnegie herself had faced at one time — this pursuit seemed frivolous.

So I said nothing.

"I do want Andra to mingle in the highest society New York has to offer. He deserves it," she said, running her fingers across her coiffure and staring in the mirror.

I wondered if Andrew wanted the same. If I intended to keep my emotional distance from him and focus on business only, his views on New York society should not matter. That the answer was strangely important to me was telling.

I took a chance later that afternoon. Tired after a long morning of shopping for the perfect winter gloves, Mrs. Carnegie took an earlier rest than usual. As soon as the noises in her bedroom quieted, I darted out of the St. Nicholas onto Broadway. If discovered, I planned on using an errand at the pharmacy as explanation.

Even though the hour was earlier than the usual time I met Andrew, I felt certain he would be there. I knew his schedule well — he and his mother reviewed it in my presence every morning — and his meeting with bankers at Atlantic National Bank had ended an hour ago. For the past several weeks, we'd been mapping out the investors amenable to railroad ventures, identifying the key players in a huge, mystifying market. Disagreements between us had arisen — I believed financing might be better acquired from banks local to the bridge construction, while Andrew thought that securing money from national banks would give the projects greater prestige and subsequent funding — but we always reached an amicable resolution, and I was amazed at the respect he gave to my ideas.

A matter other than business plagued me today. Who was this man upon whom I had placed my family's future? What values did he truly hold?

Andrew was already sitting on the shady bench we preferred. Smiling as I approached, he stood up to greet me. After we settled, we spoke freely to each other about his latest meeting, unworried that we would be seen by an acquaintance, since we had so few in this city. I felt a certain freedom with him in New York, a freedom I hadn't felt since I was at home with my family in Galway. Here, in the anonymous bustle of New York, we shared authenticity of spirit and speech, free from prying eyes.

I broached my topic obliquely. "So you are determined to pursue financing through the New York banks?"

"You have raised many excellent objections, but I think backing by the prestigious New York banking community will lend the projects a certain gravitas." He said this with a puff of his cigar.

"Are you certain that you are committed to this method of investment for this 'gravitas' reason only?"

"What do you mean?"

"You're not pursuing the New York banks to help secure a place for you and your family in New York society?"

A fiery redness spread across his cheeks, confirming my suspicion. "Why do you ask, Clara?"

"Your mother seems very determined to find some entrée to the elusive Knickerbocker society. I know you like to please her. Perhaps you think a business relationship is the key?"

"The two pursuits are not mutually exclusive," he answered, his voice guarded.

"Except the one will not guarantee the other."

"You do not know that." A certain combative tone entered his voice, the one I'd overheard in the fight with Messrs. Scott and Thomson. His face changed, almost as though a dark mask had slipped over his normally friendly features, obscuring them from view.

I had forgotten my status as servant to his master, one that hadn't changed despite our unusual relationship and his promises of funds awaiting me. I pulled away from him and said, "My apologies. I have overstepped."

The dark mask disappeared, and the Andrew to whom I'd grown accustomed reemerged. "Clara, there is no 'overstepping' between us. Our relationship is the most honest one in my life, and the honesty makes me treasure it above all else. And if you are telling me that the door to New York society is closed no matter what business arrangements I make with its bankers, then I trust you."

I explained myself. "Servants speak more openly in the company of other servants and make admissions that their masters never would."

"You have overheard something?"

"It's not just what I've overheard. It's what I've gleaned from the servants' comments. These New York City society folk don't have titles like the aristocracy in Europe, so they have to invent ways to distinguish themselves from the rest of the citizenry. Minute, private ways, almost like a secret society of which only its members know the rules."

"What sort of secret ways are you talking about?"

"Things that seem insignificant but outsiders would not notice. The length of sleeves. The cut of a dress or a suit. A particular posture. A turn of phrase. All combined with an invitation by the right person to the right dinner party in the right brownstone. They guard these manners and invitations very tightly so that the wrong people do not slip into their world." I paused, debating whether I should say the next painful words. Should I risk the reaction? His response would tell me much about his true nature.

I breathed deeply and took the plunge. "Andrew, they will likely do business with you but never admit you to their ranks. Commodore Vanderbilt has been trying for years, and he has received constant snubbing for his efforts. And he is the president of the New York and Harlem Railroad, among other things, and he is not a recent immigrant, a fact which can make entrée into society even more challenging. Perhaps you should focus your efforts on Mr. Vanderbilt and his society. An invitation into their ranks might be more achievable."

His eyes squinted in a familiar expression of concentration and determination. The competitive spirit was building within him. "How does one find out these Knickerbocker ways?"

His question startled and disappointed me. I expected him to be as repulsed by this social barricade as I was, with its rejection of the newly arrived. If high society was what he sought, how could he and I ever have a future together? Even though I'd insisted our relationship focus on business, not feelings, my real emotions for him, along with my private dreams, existed beneath the surface. Given that a former lady's maid had no place among the higher echelons, I needed to accept our prospects. "You want to know their secrets so you can be part of their world? Why would you want that?"

His eyes widened in surprise at my question. "Why would I let them conquer me?"

I had never heard him speak so bluntly about his ambitions. My voice rose as I said, "These old New York society people maintain that all people are not equal, that they are superior to all other classes. I thought you believed in freedom and opportunity for all people. That view is the antithesis of what these people espouse."

"I haven't let poverty or lack of education or cultural differences stop my climb so far."

"Why would you want to climb to a station populated by people whose views oppose your own? Who, in fact, oppose you? Their very opposition to you is emblematic of their undemocratic views."

"It is a challenge, Clara."

"Didn't you tell me once that you loved the American ethos of equality and the ability to rise above your born station? These are the very rights your ancestors fought for in the Chartist movement and for which my own father fights too, and you have proven how far one can rise when given those rights. Please carve a different path, Andrew."

He stood up and stared at me. The broad

plane of his face hardened as if chiseled from stone, and his eyes turned flinty. "I am not accustomed to having anyone tell me what to do, Clara. Not Scott and Thomson, as you've seen. Not my mother. And certainly not you."

CHAPTER THIRTY-NINE

December 8, 1866
New York, New York

The uniform-clad nurse softly closed the door to my mistress's room. "Her cough is subsiding, sir, but she will need the breathing treatments regularly."

"Do we let the front desk know when we need you?" Andrew asked, his brows furrowed in concern for his mother.

A few days prior, malaise had overcome my mistress, an uncommon state for one so full of vigor. Yesterday, a dry cough had settled into her chest, which rattled her son but which I recognized as simple exhaustion. New York City, with its late evenings and brisk pace of walking, tired her, and she needed rest. Only illness would give her that permission.

"I will stay with her throughout the evening, sir. Until morning comes, and we can reassess her condition." The nurse slid me a look and said, "I do not believe it is serious, however."

"You are certain?" Visible relief softened Andrew's brow. He was unaccustomed to his strong mother evidencing any weakness, and the sickness, albeit a mild one, had unnerved him.

"Yes, sir," she said. "Would you like to see her before she naps?"

"Indeed." He sighed deeply and entered her bedroom alone.

I felt relieved that he'd left the room. Since our discussion in the park, relations between Andrew and myself had been strained. I recoiled from the harsh side of himself he'd shown, along with his message. He wanted to secure an invitation to join the elite, and no place existed for me there. I needed to halt my residual fantasies, however hard I'd tried to suppress them, that Andrew and I might one day act upon our feelings, and focus on my duty to my family. My continued emotional tie to Andrew jeopardized that, and I was not certain that I could separate our business relationship from it. I needed to be satisfied with my salary and the generous present of shares Andrew had bestowed upon me. Very kindly, so that he would have no reason to retaliate through termination or the rescinding of my stock, I kept my distance and sidestepped his persistent efforts at private conversation.

The nurse and I were alone in the parlor. Staring at her crisp, white uniform and marveling at her efficient, direct manner, I wondered at her position. "Have you been a nurse for long?"

"As a girl, I was inspired by the newspaper accounts of Florence Nightingale. Are you familiar with her?"

"Yes. As a girl in Ireland, I heard stories about her work in the Crimean War."

She smiled. "Such dangerous, inspiring nursing she did there. As a young woman, I searched for opportunities to nurse like Miss Nightingale, but it was religious women who primarily undertook nursing work here in our country. We did not have a formal school to teach nursing like the one Miss Nightingale formed in England. When the Civil War broke out, the Union Army put out the word that it was looking for women to create a corps of nurses, most of whom would receive training in the field hospitals. I volunteered immediately."

"I had no idea that women served in the army."

"I am not surprised. We were volunteers,

and as such, our positions were unofficial. To my knowledge, no newspapers reported on our work."

Impressed by her initiative and bravery, I said, "Thank you for your service in the war, Miss . . . ?" I realized that I did not know her name.

"Carlyle is my surname."

I curtsied and introduced myself. "Miss Kelley. It is a pleasure and an honor to meet you, Miss Carlyle."

Stitch after stitch, I darned holes in Mrs. Carnegie's black silk stockings. I shifted position on my narrow bed, uncomfortable at doing this work on my bed in the dark, windowless servant's chamber instead of a comfortable chair in my mistress's dressing chamber with bright daylight and gaslight to illuminate my needlework. But I was without choice, as my mistress had released me to my room when Miss Carlyle took over her care for the rest of the day. The reprieve gave me time to think about the nurse's profession. I had never considered that professions for women existed outside service or marriage, if one considered marriage a profession. What other positions might there be? I knew that Andrew had hired women to serve as telegraph operators, one of the rare other opportunities.

A knock sounded on my door. I hesitated before answering it, as no one had ever contacted me here before. In the hallway, I passed the other servants, all women as the men had their own wing, with a cordial nod, but no one had made efforts at friendliness, as everyone's time here was fleeting.

"Miss Kelley," a female voice called to me. "A delivery boy has a package for you."

For me? Who in the name of Mary would be sending packages to me? Certainly not my family, and no one else even wrote letters to me. I took the large package from the matron who cleaned and supervised the female servants' floor, and after closing the door behind me, I laid the long, rectangular box, nearly as tall as myself, on my thin blue coverlet. The box was tied with a satin, rose-pink ribbon and smelled of a lavender sachet.

I pulled the ribbon's end and watched as the knot undid itself. Hooking my fingers under the lid, I gingerly lifted off the top. A sleek, cerulean-blue gown sat within the box, the silken layers of its skirt and bustle tucked carefully inside. A wide velvet ribbon of a darker blue encircled the waist and crisscrossed the bodice until it reached the neckline. There, tiny azure crystals trimmed the gown, giving the illusion of a sapphire necklace.

This exquisite formal gown, appropriate for a ball or an evening at the Academy of Music, must have been accidentally delivered to my room. Although how a dressmaker's delivery boy could have made such an obvious and egregious error was unfathomable. Especially when he asked for me specifically.

I began to repack the box and take it down to the front desk when I noticed a small card within the folds of the gown. No name appeared on the envelope, and it was not sealed, so I slid out the note.

For Clara — To help me carve out a different path. Forgive me. Please meet me in the lobby at seven o'clock for an evening at the Academy of Music. Andrew.

Did I dare accept? Did I dare to hope? Or had I already indulged my girlish, innocent fantasies for long enough?

CHAPTER FORTY

December 8, 1866
New York, New York

My footsteps on the grand staircase of the St. Nicholas were small and delicate by necessity. In a gown so glittering and grand, I felt conspicuous, instead of invisible as I was accustomed. Instinctively, I tried to make myself small, an impossibility in a gown designed to draw attention.

Every eye fell upon me, or so I believed. Did they see the Irish farm girl behind the elegant New York lady traipsing down the stairs? Did they recognize me for a fraud? Part of me wanted to turn and run back to my servant's bedroom, where I was only living one lie. I had debated long and hard about accepting his invitation, what it meant about my understanding of who each of us was separately and what we were together. In the end, I understood precisely where I stood, for myself and for my family, and I accepted with that in mind.

From the base of the staircase, Andrew stared as well, making me wonder whether the gown fit properly. I could not check in a mirror, as I only had one small hand mirror on my dresser. Lacing up the dress's elaborate corset, cinching its exceedingly narrow waist, and buttoning the minuscule buttons lining the back presented significant challenges by myself, although the process eradicated any lingering doubts I had about the necessity for lady's maids. I hoped that I'd done justice to the exquisite gown he'd sent me.

When I reached the final step, he did not take me by the elbow as protocol required but continued gaping.

"Is something the matter?" I was prompted to ask.

"Nothing in the world." His cheeks turned pink. "It is simply that — that you look different."

"Unnatural, I suppose?" I asked.

"The exact opposite, Clara. You look more fully yourself. As if the servant's uniform was the costume, and this gown was your natural garb."

It was my turn to blush. "Thank you for the gown, Andrew. I am not certain that it was appropriate to accept such a lavish gift, but as you can see, I decided to put propriety aside. For tonight, at least."

"I am glad you accepted the gown in the spirit I gifted it to you. Forgiveness."

He extended his gloved hand to take my elbow. Together, we walked across the gilt lobby of the St. Nicholas. I tried to glide as other ladies seemed to do, but the evening gown was far tighter and stiffer than the servant's dress to which I was accustomed, and I feared that I appeared rigid rather than elegant. Still, as we crossed the lobby's marble floor, porters bowed, concierges nodded, and doormen swung open doors, acts they never engaged in for the invisible Clara Kelley. It was as if I were crossing the lobby for the first time. I understood why the climb to the highest society realms intoxicated Andrew, although I did not agree with his inclination to attempt the ascent.

We were quiet in the carriage ride from Broadway to Union Square. The landscape between us had changed — the disagreement in the park hovered there, as did my beliefs about what he wanted and what that meant for me — and neither of us knew precisely where to grab a foothold. By the time we pulled up to the Academy of Music,

I decided to inhabit this new role, even if just for tonight. Like I'd inhabited the other Clara Kelley. Then I would accept my destiny.

Smiling at Andrew as we stepped out of the carriage, I entered the candlelit lobby of the academy as if I belonged. An usher guided us to our seats on the auditorium floor. As I settled into the plush, tufted velvet chair, I gazed at the thousands of seats around us. The interior of the academy, lined with red damask, gold-painted molding, a bucolic mural, and a crystal chandelier the size of a carriage, was far more resplendent than I'd imagined from outside on my servants' bench.

Glancing upward, I saw that the academy's five levels soared to an eighty-foot-high dome. It had to be the largest opera venue in the world. Dotted on the different levels were private boxes, each with a gilded balcony of its own and eight seats. "Those are the boxes the lady's maids mentioned," I whispered to myself.

"I am sorry, Clara. I could not hear you."

I whispered a bit louder. "The private boxes reminded me of a conversation I overheard between two lady's maids. The 'upper tens' —"

"Pardon, but what are the 'upper tens'?"

"The 'upper tens' are the most elite of the Knickerbocker families. They raised the initial funds for the Academy of Music, and they reserved the boxes for themselves and their friends. Well-to-do outsiders like the Vanderbilts have been trying to gain access to a private box for years without success. Apparently, rumors have been flying around for years that if the wealthy tradespeople cannot get private boxes, they will build themselves an even grander forum for opera in this city, putting the Academy of Music out of business in the process."

"Interesting," he said, a mischievous grin appearing within his beard. "But, of course, I no longer care about the machinations of New York society except as it pertains to business."

I smiled at him, delighted at his change in opinion. My smile faded when I wondered whether he had really made such a drastic conversion or whether he made his comment to appease me.

The lights dimmed, and the orchestra's strings played a rich chord signaling the beginning of *La Traviata.* Even though I had listened to two other operas and one symphony outside the auditorium doors, nothing prepared me for the visual spectacle that accompanied the music. The crimson curtain drew back, revealing a luxurious Parisian salon where a party was in progress and grandiose characters sung a glorious and tragic tale.

Captivated by the dramatic story of love between Alfredo and Violetta, I lost myself in the connection between the two characters and in Alfredo's desire to woo Violetta away from the baron. Even though I longed for Violetta to recognize Alfredo as her destiny, I related to the conflict between her burgeoning feelings for Alfredo — *È strano . . . Ah, fors'è lui* — and her desire for freedom — *sempre libera.* My own heart broke when, after Violetta finally embraced Alfredo as her love, she agreed to leave him at the urging of Alfredo's father, who could not bear the impact that the couple's relationship had on his family's reputation.

This aspect of the story confused me. I whispered to Andrew, "Why does the relationship between Alberto and Violetta shame his family?"

"Violetta is a courtesan," he whispered back.

My eyes widened at the word. I knew what a courtesan was. I was glad of the auditorium's darkness, as I felt my face flame red.

Nearly weeping at Violetta's bittersweet song at the end of act 2 — *di questo core non puoi comprendere tutto l'amore* — I calmed myself before Andrew and I left the auditorium for a refreshing drink in the lobby. Promenading through the society folk I had watched from the servants' bench only weeks before, the evening did not feel real. This sensation increased when the train of my skirt brushed against the bench upon which sat the monochromatically dressed row of lady's maids.

Once a waiter passed us crystal glasses of claret, I said, "I cannot thank you enough for this evening, Andrew. I never knew the opera would be so moving."

"It is a marvel, isn't it? I confess that the operas I saw during my European trip do not rival those I've seen here at the academy."

"Do you have a favorite?" I asked.

"Before this evening, I might have selected the Giuseppe Verdi operas I had the good fortune to see in Europe. But I admit that tonight, here with you, *La Traviata* speaks to me above all other operas. Perhaps it is the affinity between the characters' dilemma and our own. On my end at least."

A horrified expression must have crossed my face, because Andrew stammered, "E-except for the courtesan bit, of course. Unless I caused you dismay by drawing comparisons to Alfredo and Violetta's situation and our own."

Nervous at Andrew's reference to shared feelings, a matter that simmered beneath the surface but which we had not discussed for many months, I chuckled a bit and said, "It is absolutely the comparison to a courtesan that led to my unease."

We laughed, out of relief or out of apprehension about a conversation to come, I didn't know. Thankfully, the bell rang to signal the return to the auditorium.

I returned to *La Traviata* to see what its final act would bring. I lost myself to the world within a world on the stage where everyone was pretending and no one was what they seemed. Not unlike the Carnegies. And not unlike me.

CHAPTER FORTY-ONE

December 8, 1866
New York, New York

The anticipated conversation sat between us, like a third person in the carriage of whom we were terrified but whom we also desperately wanted to meet. Neither of us wanted to broach the discussion first, but neither wanted to leave the words unsaid.

I remembered my promise to myself aboard the *Envoy,* that I wouldn't wait any longer for my life to begin. I had broken that promise to myself over and over, but I would not again. I dove into the deep, frigid waters. "During the intermission, you mentioned the similarity between our situation and that of Alfredo and Violetta," I said, keeping my eyes fixed on my hands. Summoning my courage to bring up the topic was one thing, but watching the reaction to my bravery was quite another.

"Yes," he said, swallowing hard. I was not accustomed to hesitation in Andrew's speech. "There is a divide between us, not as dramatic as that of Alfredo and Violetta, but a divide nonetheless. Ridiculous though it is, because even though we are now master and servant, we are the same. I arrived in this country a destitute immigrant, in a class below yourself." He took a large breath and then spoke again. "But I hope I'm not wrong in believing that we share feelings for one another. Like Alfredo and Violetta."

I glimpsed up to find him staring at me, his face expectant yet anxious. "You are not wrong."

He clasped my hands in his, asking in a voice quaking with emotion, as if he could not believe my words, "Truly?"

"Truly, even though I know it may be hard to believe because I pushed you away a year ago." His eyes widened with hope, making me hesitate. I pushed myself to say what I must. Voice quivering in fear at his reaction and at the mixed emotions building within me, I said, "Still, in many ways, my feelings are unimportant. You know that I must support my family with my lady's maid position, and I worry that your affection for me complicates that responsibility. The elite would never allow me into their ranks, and you have made clear that you desire to join them. Since I have no place there, you and I have no place together. We have no future, even if you had wished for one, a presumption on my part, I realize. Please understand that I am grateful for all that you have taught me — and your gift of the shares that will help my family immeasurably — but I think we must acknowledge that this is the end of whatever road we have shared."

He stared at me, saying nothing. His silence shook me, for Andrew was never silent. Then he did something even more unexpected. He laughed.

"Oh, Clara, this is yet another reason why I love you. Most women, softened by the opera and dress and my words, would have clung to the idea of our union. But you, you are strong and moral and loyal and, above all, honest. You bear all the qualities I admire. Your rejection of me only makes me more certain."

My brows furrowed in confusion, and my expression must have been almost comical because, glancing over at me, he laughed even harder. "Your pronouncements make me appreciate you more and give me even more faith in our ability to bridge the gap to a permanent union. Clara, if you truly share my feelings, marriage is the bridge I wish to cross."

"I thought fortune and the acceptance into the societal elite were what you sought?" I asked, my voice now trembling.

"You have taught me that I should carve out a different path. Pedigree, an accident of birth, does not give a man the right to public respect. Only good deeds can do that. Consequently, the 'upper tens,' or whatever silly name they call themselves, and their ilk do not matter. You do." He clasped my hands tighter. "Do you wish to cross this bridge with me?"

What should I say? For so long, I had tried to steel myself against him and my own rogue emotions. I knew my family needed me desperately, and I could not fail them. But could there possibly be a way that I could have both — my family's well-being and Andrew? I imagined what he and I could accomplish together and doubted that ever again would I meet a man who recognized my full capabilities and who wanted a strong woman by his side.

"I do, Andrew." Even as I said the words, I wondered whether I'd made the right choice. Could I trust that his whims would not change, that the dark mask would not shift over his face? What if he found out who

I *really* was?

The carriage was dark, save for the passing street gaslights and the odd light streaming from a late-hours pub, but I could hear and feel him draw closer to me. His dark-blue eyes glinted in the low illumination, and I felt his breath on me as he brought his lips to mine.

"We will find a way, Clara. I promise you."

As his soft lips touched mine, I wondered whether he would find success, as he always did. Would my fate indeed resemble the heroine of *Aurora Leigh,* who finally united with her love after surmounting countless barricades?

CHAPTER FORTY-TWO

April 2, 1867
Pittsburgh, Pennsylvania

Stolen moments in the park. Grazing of fingertips in the hallway. Animated business discussions in the servants' hallway. Whispers in the dark parlor after Mrs. Carnegie had retired for the evening. My time in New York consisted of snatched minutes, fleeting but treasured, where we discussed the future in terms of the upcoming months when the path had been paved for Andrew's mother to accept our relationship. I allowed myself to hope that the realization of all my dreams — saving my family and having Andrew — was within my grasp.

But when the season ended and we returned to Pittsburgh, we crossed the threshold into Fairfield and found a very different home from the one we left. The house was now inhabited by the new Mr. and Mrs.

Carnegie, who had made themselves very much at home during the months of our absence. Calling cards were left for the new Mrs. Carnegie instead of my mistress, and the former Miss Lucy Coleman now set the daily menu with the housekeeper. The younger Mr. Carnegie's friends arrived after dinner for rounds of billiards. The newly-weds often played music together in the parlor and read together in the library.

Only the staff remained the same. Mr. Ford continued on with his masterful meals, beaming his affable smile as if his own family was not still among the missing, while Mr. Holyrod, his team of footmen, Mrs. Stewart, Hilda, and the ever-changing cast of housemaids soldiered onward. Running the house quietly in the servants' realm and maintaining Fairfield as if unchanged, they knew better than most how different the house was under its new master and mistress.

Andrew needed to leave. Soon, Mrs. Carnegie would need to leave as well. What would happen to us?

For the next several weeks, until we arrived at a strategy, he said, Andrew decamped to the Union Depot Hotel, a fine hotel that occupied the lot adjacent to Union Station in downtown Pittsburgh.

This location made his lodgings convenient to his office and the train station, from which he traveled often to the Middle West, Washington, DC, and New York City, but inconvenient to visiting Fairfield.

Meetings required creativity, even more so than in the close quarters of the St. Nicholas. I made my errands to my mistress's hatmaker and glove store take an unusual route past Andrew's office on Grant Street, where a tea shop empty in the midday made for a quiet few minutes together. Andrew ensured that he arrived for his visits to his mother, which now required prior appointment, an hour before their designated time, when she was still out at a call or resting, which allowed for a private conversation in the library.

Sometimes, when I engaged in these little subterfuges, I thought of Dad and Mum. What would they think of this life I was leading? When Dad began planning the Fenian revolt and sent me to America to support the family, he knew that this country would call upon me to change in some way. But surely, my many duplicities were not what he intended when he and Mum sent me to America, no matter my *síofra* nature. Would Dad judge me harshly, particularly given the risk to which he'd subjected our family? I contemplated whether the God I once prayed to daily in the white-washed Catholic churches of Galway would judge me harshly too.

Hurrying around the back of the house after one of my subterfuges — my ruse of an errand completed by the pharmacy bag I carried in my hands — I stepped through the servants' door and bumped into Mrs. Stewart.

"My apologies, ma'am."

"It seems you've forgotten your way around Fairfield after your long stay in New York City," she said, straightening her crisp, white collar as if I'd knocked her to the ground instead of barely brushing against her skirts. I knew the staff perceived my trip with the Carnegies as a vacation of sorts, and this was another of her little punishments.

"Just hurrying to get my mistress what she needs, Mrs. Stewart."

"Always the perfect servant," she retorted.

I pretended her snide comment was a compliment. "I do my best."

After hanging my coat on the rack, I crossed the kitchen and began climbing the stairs.

"Oh, wait," Mrs. Stewart called to me. "I

think I have something for you." She fished around in her apron pocket and pulled out a letter.

Almost two months had passed since I'd received a letter from my family, and I practically ran across the kitchen to fetch it. "Thank you, Mrs. Stewart."

I climbed halfway up the servants' stairs and sat on a step. Here, neither the kitchen staff nor the Carnegie family could see me while I read my letter. I ripped it open.

Dearest Clara,

I do not know whether this letter will find you in Pittsburgh or New York City or how long it will take to reach you. I hope its travel across the Atlantic is swift, because I cannot bear this news alone. I know not how to write this except plainly, even though my very being resists writing the words because their memorialization makes the unimaginable real. Cecelia has died.

It started with a cough. A simple cough the sort we have all suffered through before in the relentlessly wet winters. Before, when we still had the farm, Mother would lay warm poultices on our chests, remember? Scented with her dried herbs, specially mixed for whatever ailed us, those poultices smelled like recovery. But we have no herbs now. No poultices. Only a damp, shared attic room in Aunt Catherine's house where we sleep on folded packets of clothes while drafts blow through our hair at night. Dad suffered from the cough as well and still does, but nothing like Cecelia had.

We had been saving most of the money you sent for boat tickets to America. It was meant as a surprise for you. Lucky we had been so thrifty, because we had money enough to summon a doctor when Cecelia worsened. The medicine he prescribed drained the remainder of the savings but kept her cough at bay for some weeks. Still, it was not enough. It was too late.

Our little Cecelia is gone. We are heartbroken, as I am sure you find yourself now as well. Dad says he is well enough, but please pray for him, as work has been impossible. We are existing on our needlework and abject sadness.

Your loving sister,
Eliza

I put my hand over my mouth to stifle my sobs. I could not allow this fate to befall another member of my family. I knew what I had to do to save them.

CHAPTER FORTY-THREE

April 3, 1867
Pittsburgh, Pennsylvania

Steam rose up from the teacup. I lowered my face, allowing the warmth to rise and take the sting from my cheeks. The calendar read April, but spring had yet to reach Pittsburgh.

"Shall I ask the proprietor for cool water for your tea, Clara?" Andrew asked, lightly touching my hand with a gloved finger, his second pair of the day. The first pair blackened with the soot of downtown Pittsburgh by lunchtime and had to be discarded.

I gazed up at his dark-blue, intelligent eyes, the only ones that saw beneath the Clara Kelley I'd become into the Clara Kelley I truly was, even though he was unaware that he'd had to penetrate fabricated outer layers to reach my core. "Thank you, Andrew, but no. The heat feels good," I said quietly.

While the warmth lessened the pain from my cheeks, nothing could soften the suffering of my heart. Poor, lovely Cecelia. I would never see her grow from a girl into a woman. I could not imagine how shattered my parents and Eliza were, having watched the life drain slowly from Cecelia. The powerlessness they must have felt then I was experiencing now. I wanted to board a ship with funds enough to rescue them myself from the Galway City hovel in which they lived and bring them here. But I could share none of this with Andrew. Not my heartbreak over the death of my sister, not the urgency of my family's situation, not the Clara Kelley I'd been when I first arrived in Philadelphia. But how could I save my family and still maintain my facade with Andrew? How would he react when I told him that I bore none of the honesty he prized but in fact had been lying to him and his beloved mother for years? What would he say when I told him that I was nothing but a lowly farmer's daughter whose family was dying in a Galway City slum, and that's why I needed the money he promised me? Yet I could not think of a way to procure the money I needed from him without confessing. I braced myself for the inevitable moment.

"Spring cannot arrive soon enough. Just think, Clara, when the winter thaws, we can meet in parks instead of tea shops and the back hallways of Fairfield."

He spoke of spring, but I could hardly think beyond today, beyond this confessional moment. My stomach lurched with the knowledge of what I must do. My American life sat upon the foundation of my initial deception, and yet I could not see a way to save my family without sacrificing my lies. And sacrificing my future with Andrew along with it.

Andrew pulled two envelopes from the inner pocket of his coat and laid them on the table between us. When I did not reach for them, he asked, "Do you not wonder what is in the envelopes?"

Envelopes did not hold much luster for me after Eliza's letter yesterday. They seemed harbingers of tragedy, not bearers of good tidings. I found myself in no hurry to read the missive.

"I assume business papers for my review. Perhaps a proposal from an investor in the Missouri River bridge contract? I know you've been working hard on that financing," I guessed.

"These documents concern a matter upon which I've been working much harder than the Missouri River bridge. A matter that's been at the forefront of my mind for years, long before President Johnson announced the commission of those seven bridges."

"What could be more important than the Missouri River bridge?" I tried to joke, but my heart contained no joviality.

"Please, Clara." He picked up the smaller envelope and handed it to me. "I want to watch your face when you open it."

I reached for the knife sitting on the table and slit open the envelope. A folded piece of paper sat inside. Sliding it out, I unfolded it and read aloud, " 'In the name of Clara Kelley, in the Bank of Pittsburgh Depository Account Number 24976, the sum of $1,250 is available for withdrawal by Miss Kelley.' "

"Oh, Andrew," I whispered, incredulous. The money I needed now sat in my hand. I had rendered no confession in exchange for it.

"That is the sum you received from selling your shares in Keystone Telegraph, a company you essentially founded with your ingenious idea of stringing public telegraph wires alongside the railroad tracks, to Pacific and Atlantic Telegraph." He grinned.

"Please open the second envelope, Clara. It is compensation for the assistance and insights you gave me with the railcar business."

To what was he referring? We had not discussed the Pullman and Woodruff railcar business since the day we rode to New York City on the Woodruff Silver Palace railcar.

Hands trembling, I slit open the larger envelope. A thick piece of paper drifted out onto the table. The paper bore the distinctive look of a stock certificate. Reading aloud, I said, "Be it known that Clara Kelley is the proprietor of one hundred shares of Woodruff Railcar Company, transferable or cashable only at the offices of said company in person by said stockholder with the surrender of this certificate."

"You no longer need to work as a lady's maid to my mother, Clara. You are now a woman of independent means, a station in life equal to my own."

Tears started trickling down my cheeks, but I could not speak the words of gratitude or affection that bubbled within me. Was it possible that my family could be saved and my relationship too?

Andrew lifted one of his hands from mine and wiped away my tears. "This is not a day for tears, my dearest Clara. It is time to tell my mother."

Chapter Forty-Four

April 6, 1867
Pittsburgh, Pennsylvania

Muck and refuse still clogged the dirt roads of Slab Town. Filthy, fatherless children still ruled the alleyways, while unemployed men gambled on street corners. Fire still sparked from the mills and foundries, dangerously close to the shanties hastily constructed up and down Rebecca Street. The smell of rotting food and human waste still permeated the air. But Slab Town could not touch me today. Andrew and I had agreed that he would speak to his mother in one week's time, and I had written to my family to let them know their boat tickets would come soon. Only one week until my life would change.

Could this be my last visit to my cousins while employed by the Carnegies? The thought distracted me while I sidestepped piles of horse dung and dodged laundry swinging in the wind. I considered the different ways I might rescue the Lambs from this hellhole with Andrew's resources at our shared disposal. I still hadn't decided how I'd handle the arrival of my family with Andrew. Would I confess about my real background or embroil myself in another lie? That, I decided, was a bridge I could cross — to use one of Andrew's favorite comparisons — once my family arrived safely. Their well-being was paramount.

Hurrying down Rebecca Street to the familiar lean-tos, I reached the rough frame of my cousins' house. The thin door to the Lambs' home rattled when I knocked. No one answered, even on repeated banging.

Where were they?

To my surprise, Patrick rounded the bend of Rebecca Street. "I was hoping I'd catch you, Clara."

I was confused. "Have I come at the wrong time? Or the wrong day?"

"No, no, you're spot on."

"Where is everyone, then?"

"It's just that" — he shifted his gaze to the ground, kicking at a stone — "we aren't living here anymore."

I wanted to ask him what happened, but I reminded myself of his pride in providing a single-family home, plentiful food, and hard-soled shoes for his family. He was obviously uncomfortable, and my inquiry might be too injurious to Patrick's dignity. Instead, I asked, "Where are you living?"

"Follow me. I'll take you there. Maeve and the children are waiting for you."

We crossed Rebecca Street to the opposite side, and after walking for five city blocks, we came to a ramshackle house not unlike the Lambs' previous house.

"Here we are." Patrick pointed.

As we walked the remaining distance, I wondered why Patrick moved his family from one lean-to into another, essentially across the street from each other. He pushed open the thin wood door, and I expected to see Maeve and the children inside. Instead, a chestnut-haired mother with three tow-headed children scampering around her feet nodded at us. An entirely different family inhabited the first floor of the house.

Our footsteps echoed as we tromped up the flimsy wooden staircase to the second floor. Once there, Maeve opened the door with her usual warm embrace. "Welcome, Clara."

The children gathered around my legs, stumbling over each other as they hugged them. I knelt down to return their embrace, and from my pocket, I pulled a bag of cakes that Mr. Ford had slipped me before I left. As the children fought over who should get the largest cake in the bag, I stood back up and handed Maeve a basket brimming with three loaves of bread, a salted ham, baking potatoes, a side of beef, early asparagus, and apples. Maeve peeked under the cloth keeping the food safe from the dirt and soot endemic to the train travel to Allegheny City and squealed, "Clara, you shouldn't have brought all this! This will keep us in meals for a week. What did you do, rob the Carnegies?"

Patrick chimed in. "She's blushing again, Maeve. Will you look at that? Didn't we warn her about having eyes for her employer?"

While I understood they were only joking, I felt unusually sensitive about the comments about the Carnegies, even protective of them. "It's nothing like that. Mr. Ford, the Carnegies' cook, knew I was coming to visit you, and he stocked the basket."

Maeve sensed my unease and interjected, "Of course, we understand. Please thank Mr. Ford for us."

As Patrick took my coat and placed it on a shipping box turned upside down to form a table, the only surface not crowded with drying clothes and Maeve's needlework, and Maeve returned to her cooking, I got my first look at their new lodgings, a single room. Cots stacked upon each other in one corner, like the beds in the steerage of a boat crossing the Atlantic, and the room contained no other furniture save the shipping box and a single chair, which Patrick occupied. The windowless room stank of unwashed bodies, fire, refuse, and charred food, as the room had no fireplace or ventilation. Maeve cooked on a small brazier in the center of the space, with no choice but to disregard the danger of the flames. Trunks containing the remainder of their belongings were stacked in another corner, but from the filthy state of Patrick, Maeve, and the children's clothes, the trunks had not been opened since they moved. A greasy layer of black smuts covered every surface and every person.

I was speechless at their circumstances. Was this how my family was living? Perceiving my discomfiture, Maeve offered a conversational topic. "Good to have you back from New York. We're all looking forward to hearing stories about the big city. We are in need of some entertainment around here, Clara."

In an attempt to avoid my obvious questions, Maeve and Patrick busied themselves with the meal and children, respectively, while I talked. When I couldn't stand their obfuscation any longer, I asked, "Are you two going to tell me what's going on?"

Patrick would not — or could not, perhaps — meet my gaze.

Maeve spoke for him. "Patrick lost his job in the mill."

I was shocked. "What? Last I heard, the mill was so busy that you had to work double shifts. What happened?"

I directed my question to Patrick, but Maeve answered for him again. "You know Patrick worked as an iron founder with Iron City Forge?" she asked.

Although I knew the title of Patrick's job, I never realized that he'd worked for Iron City Forge, one of the iron companies with which Andrew and his younger brother once had some dealings. Still, because I assumed that detail was peripheral, I nodded yes.

"About a year ago, Iron City Forge merged with a rival iron company called Cyclops Iron, forming a new company called Union Iron. This merger happened at the end of the Civil War, just as the demand for iron dropped." Maeve continued to explain, but I began to worry about how this part of the saga — a merger of which I was familiar

403

and knew that Andrew had orchestrated — impacted Patrick. "It seemed a change in name only at first. The mill continued at the breakneck pace to which it had grown accustomed for some months. But then, when iron prices plummeted, Union Iron decided that physical consolidation of its two parts — Iron City and Cyclops — was necessary. This meant they had too many men doing the same job. Some of the iron founders had to go, and Patrick was one of those men fired from his position."

Perhaps this loss of employment was only temporary. Grasping at this possibility, I asked, "Surely there is work for iron founders in other mills?"

Maeve answered in her usual matter-of-fact way. "There's no work for iron founders anywhere in Pittsburgh. The consolidation put loads of iron workers of all types out of work. We are living off savings and my needlework for now. We had to give up the house and move in with the Connors downstairs, another family that's in the same situation, to share expenses. If Patrick doesn't find work soon, I don't know how we will manage."

I felt sick with worry and guilt. "What about going home?" I clutched at prospects.

Patrick finally piped into our exchange,

his voice angry. "Home? What work is there for me in Galway, Clara? Farming? My dad lost his tenancy in the famine, and my brothers have been living hand-to-mouth themselves. There's no work in Ireland, as you yourself surely know."

"Another city?"

"We don't have the money for the tickets, even if there was a guarantee of a job. No, Clara, I have to find work here in Pittsburgh. Or we will be lost."

CHAPTER FORTY-FIVE

April 6, 1867
Pittsburgh, Pennsylvania

My shoes echoed throughout Fairfield as I marched from the servants' hall to the library. I didn't care if the other servants, the new Mr. and Mrs. Carnegie, my mistress, or Andrew could hear me. There would be no more stealthy creeping behind the scenes for me.

I was done with being invisible. I was done with waiting. And I was angry.

Flinging open the door to the library, I found Andrew reclining on one of the leather chairs, smoking a cigar, and reading from his beloved Burns. He smiled at me and patted the matching chair next to him. "Come sit with me. Mother will not be home for over an hour, so we have time."

"I think I'll stand, Andrew."

"What's wrong, Clara?"

406

"I spent today with a distant relative of mine from Ireland on Rebecca Street —"

Andrew interrupted me. "That's where we first lived when we came to Pittsburgh."

I could not allow the unfathomable idea of Andrew and his family living in the slums of Rebecca Street to deter me. Returning to my purpose, I said, "My cousin used to work as an iron founder. Do you know what that is?"

"Of course. An iron founder works with the molten ferrous metal and supervises other men. It's one of the more senior roles on the iron foundry floor."

"My cousin Patrick *used* to work as an iron founder at Iron City Forge," I emphasized.

"Ah, the company Tom once ran."

"Yes, Tom ran Iron City before it was merged with Cyclops, the company you founded to compete with Iron Forge, to form Union Iron Company. I believe you orchestrated that merger?"

"Yes, I did. Excellent memory, Clara," he said approvingly. "Although sadly, you had to learn about that plan by witnessing a rather unfortunate conversation with my brother."

"Yes, this is all rather unfortunate," I said, not bothering to hide my irritation. "Did

407

you know that the merger that formed Union Iron led to the firing of hundreds of iron workers?"

He puffed on his pipe, seemingly oblivious to my anger. Was I not displaying it as clearly as I felt it? Perhaps my years as a placid servant had blunted my ability to show emotion. My anger mounted as I saw no evidence on his face of concern.

"Actually, Union Iron Mills itself was very recently reorganized into the venture of Carnegie, Kloman and Company, when one of our partners, Tom Miller, could not reach an accord with the other Union partners. I had been meaning to tell you so that you could update your chart. So to answer your question, technically, Carnegie, Kloman and Company fired hundreds of iron workers. A certain amount of redundancy in positions existed after the various mergers, necessitating the terminations." He said these words matter-of-factly.

His calm only made me more furious.

"You do realize that those 'terminations' will devastate hundreds of families? They will lead directly to their homelessness and the starvation of their children. I thought you espoused equality and opportunity for all people, beliefs that you yourself benefitted from when you arrived in this country,"

I yelled.

Andrew stood up. "Don't you think you are being a bit dramatic, Clara?"

"Is it dramatic to watch your family members worry what will happen in four weeks when they can no longer afford living in a single room on the second floor of a shared ramshackle house? Is it dramatic to show concern about what will happen to your family when their money runs out in six weeks and they still cannot find jobs because they have no access to libraries or education to retrain themselves for some other sort of work?"

"I've never heard you talk about family in Pittsburgh before, Clara. Who are they? Why have you never mentioned them before? I would have liked to have met them." He was changing the subject intentionally.

I almost blurted out the entire truth. *Not only have I been hiding my family, but I have been hiding my real identity.* Instead, I played his game and ignored his attempt at diversion. I asked, "Aren't you troubled by the fact that, by undertaking all those iron company machinations to further your control and your income, you are hurting actual people? Immigrants like yourself. I thought you came from a Chartist family who cared about equality and who understood how the poorer folk are harmed when those in control — whether in business or in government — unwittingly alter the world around them."

"Clara, in business, sometimes hard decisions have to be made. You know that. And unfortunately, sometimes people bear the brunt of those decisions. Anyway, you know we can help your cousin. I wouldn't let family suffer."

He hoped to placate me with an offer of help to my family. Once, his reference to my family as his own family would have elated me, but it didn't now.

"Where is the concern, Andrew? The remorse? Not only for my cousin but for the other lives damaged by the 'terminations of Carnegie, Kloman, and Company' and for the human beings impacted by the stratagems you inflicted upon Keystone Telegraph, Keystone Bridge, Coleman Oil, Piper and Schiffler, and Woodruff Sleeping Car Company? I could go on and on. Don't you want to find out how the people affected are faring? Offer them assistance, food, housing, money, training, anything? Don't you want to find out how that poor Irish immigrant who took your place in the Civil War for a few hundred dollars is doing? Whether he survived? I bet that the

Andrew who first came to this country would have done all those things. I feel like you've forgotten they are people, that they are you." I paused and asked, "Have you forgotten who you are?"

We squared off against each other in a situation reminiscent of his fight with his younger brother about Cyclops Iron and Iron City Forge. Andrew's face turned an angry shade of purple, and his fists clenched. His mouth opened, and his eyes narrowed, but before he could speak, a sound emanated from the entryway.

"Andra, is that you I hear?" The voice of his mother carried into the library.

We froze, midsentence and midgesture. The sound of my mistress's footsteps grew louder, and before either of us spoke again, I turned away and walked toward the closed door. Swinging the door open wide, I almost ran directly into Mrs. Carnegie. Instead of curtsying in deference or apologizing for the collision, I marched straight past her, up the stairs, and into my tiny servant's bedroom.

CHAPTER FORTY-SIX

April 7, 1867
Pittsburgh, Pennsylvania

I should have been glad for the respite. Mrs. Carnegie left Fairfield by carriage directly after she shared breakfast with the new Mr. and Mrs. Carnegie in the breakfast room, gifting me with an expanse of time for the smaller tasks of a lady's maid — sewing, darning, and mending. But I wasn't glad. I was worried.

My mistress had been unusually quiet and rigid during her evening rituals last night and her daytime preparation this morning. I was not privy to the justification Andrew had offered for our presence alone in the library or to his explanation for my obvious upset. I had not seen him since I stormed out. Because I did not know what he proffered, and because I had no understanding of what might transpire next, I matched

412

Mrs. Carnegie's quietude as I served her.

This silence alone would have provided fodder for concern, but her sudden departure without informing me of her plans was very troubling. She kept me abreast of every aspect of her schedule so that I could tailor my time accordingly, and indeed, I accompanied her on most of her calls. Where had she gone?

After an anxious hour in her bedchamber organizing her gowns, gathering mending, and looking for evidence of her whereabouts, I walked down to the kitchen. The staff was in a flurry, readying a luncheon for the new Mrs. Carnegie to share with her friends, some of the younger set from Homewood. I wondered if this displacement caused my mistress's exodus. Maybe her departure had nothing to do with me and Andrew.

"Will my mistress be back for the luncheon?" I asked Mr. Ford as he arranged tea sandwiches on a silver tray.

Hilda tittered in the background as Mr. Ford answered, "She hasn't told you?"

Mock whispering to the new scullery maid, Anne, Hilda said for my benefit, "Isn't the lady's maid meant to know her mistress's schedule?"

"No." I spoke directly to Mr. Ford. "Our

paths crossed this morning before we could review today's calendar."

"I can't be sure, but I think I heard her say to the younger Mrs. Carnegie that she had an appointment downtown."

An appointment downtown? She hadn't mentioned it to me, and I usually accompanied her on those outings. Part of me longed to send a message to Andrew to inquire — about his mother, about us — but another part of me sensed danger. What in the name of Mary was happening? What did I want to happen now, after my quarrel with Andrew? Had I jeopardized my family?

The housekeeper's parlor was mercifully empty of Mrs. Stewart, who was busy taking inventory of the linen cabinets. Without her negative chatter and gossip, I could better hear the goings-on of the house. I listened to Hilda and Anne dust the parlor, Mr. Ford hum while chopping vegetables for the day's soup, Mr. Holyrod instruct James in the proper way of polishing silver, and the new Mr. and Mrs. Carnegie sneak a kiss outside the door to the breakfast room.

I heard everything but my mistress.

Finally, at four o'clock, six hours after her departure, her distinctive footsteps crossed the entryway. Dropping my mending, I raced up the back staircase so I could meet her at her bedroom door. No matter what had transpired with Mrs. Carnegie yesterday, no matter what had passed between myself and Andrew, I needed to know where I stood.

Assuming a stance of service, I greeted her. "I hope your appointment downtown was satisfactory, ma'am."

She grinned at me. Not a pleasant, welcoming smile but a malignant smirk. If the corners of her mouth hadn't turned upward, I might have considered the expression a scowl. "Clara, precisely the person I wanted to see."

On her heels, I walked into her bedchamber. "May I help ready you for dinner, ma'am?"

She stared at me, her face a strange mix of disgust, triumph, and betrayal. The horrible smile had disappeared. "What a perfect servant you are, Clara. Always anticipating my needs. Always handy with the brush, the needle, the buffer."

"Yes, ma'am. I try my best," I answered hesitantly. Somehow her words did not sound like a compliment, not only because her commendations were so rare. Her voice contained an off note.

"Always ready with advice about the proper dress, appropriate behavior, correct language. All based on your vast experience as a European lady's maid, am I correct?"

"Yes, ma'am."

"Except this is your first position as a lady's maid, isn't it, Clara?"

My heart started racing, and my breath became shallow. *She knew.*

"Do you know where I had an appointment today?"

I shook my head, not trusting myself to speak.

Mrs. Carnegie began pacing around the room. "I met with Mrs. Seeley. You remember her, don't you? The woman who paid for your ticket here? Arranged for transportation from Philadelphia to Pittsburgh? Placed you in this position?"

"Yes, ma'am."

"I had her undertake a little investigation for me. On a hunch based on months of watching you and Andra. Much to her astonishment, she learned that the Clara Kelley she hired for me died on the Atlantic crossing. It seemed that she left behind a fellow named Thomas, nearly a fiancé, who had become keen to make contact with her and with whom she'd exchanged a few letters. At my prodding, Mrs. Seeley got in

416

touch with this Thomas, as Clara had no family of which to speak, and after reviewing the records of the *Envoy,* the boat Clara boarded from Dublin, Mrs. Seeley pieced together what happened. Somehow, someway, you — whoever you are — took the real Clara Kelley's place." Her voice rose, and spittle spewed from her mouth. "When I think of all the trust I placed in you . . ."

I backed away from her. "I will leave Fairfield right away, ma'am."

She advanced toward me. "You will do more than leave Fairfield — and this city — immediately. You will foreswear contact with my son forever. It was the hint of a relationship brewing between you two that prompted my inquiries. I would have never let my precious Andra marry a lady's maid, but I would die before allowing him to consort with a liar and an impostor."

Stepping away from me, she inhaled deeply, patted down her hair, and said, "If you try to make contact with Andra in any way, I will inform him that you are a pretender and a fraud of the worst sort. One who usurped a dead girl's identity for her own gain. If you leave now and never speak to him again, I will allow him to believe that the lovers' spat I interrupted yesterday drove you away."

Drawing toward me again, she poked one buffed fingernail deep into my chest. "Don't you dare think I'm offering you this option out of mercy for you. I am doing it for my son. That way, he can move toward his destiny without suffering the humiliation of your deception."

What choice had Mrs. Carnegie left me? What choice had I left myself? If Andrew found out who I was, if he discovered that I'd been lying to him for years, wouldn't he leave me himself? Not to mention, if he learned of my deceit, would he exact revenge upon me and, through me, my family? Would he somehow interfere at the bank so I could not withdraw money from the account that my family so desperately needed? I had witnessed a dark side of Andrew emerge, and I could not take that risk to my family. Even if some minuscule chance existed that Andrew might forgive my lies and marry me regardless, I could never gamble away my family's welfare. Andrew could never discover who I really was, and disappearing forever was the only way.

"Goodbye, Mrs. Carnegie," I said softly, closing the door — and my future with Andrew — behind me.

Sobbing quietly as I walked up the staircase to the servants' floor, I tried to console myself. If Andrew still believed that I was the Anglo-Irish tradesman's daughter Clara Kelley — the woman who had inspired him in business and affection and who challenged him to carve a different, better path than the one driven solely by avarice — the chance existed that my influence might remain. Even though I would be gone.

CHAPTER FORTY-SEVEN

April 7, 1867
Pittsburgh, Pennsylvania

Packing my small traveling bag took mere minutes. Changing into the black second-hand gown that I'd purchased from Mrs. Seeley over two years ago as I wiped away the tears streaming down my face, I left behind my servant's uniforms and the cerulean-blue gown that I'd worn to the Academy of Music. I had no need of them where I was going. I had traveled lightly into this world of the false Clara Kelley, and I would travel lightly as I left it behind.

Only my copy of *Aurora Leigh* and my envelopes from Andrew with the stock certificates and bank account information would journey along with me. Symbols of a love forgone and a new future for my family embraced.

Treading quietly down the servants' hall, I

crept down the back staircase to the kitchen. I had no wish to call attention to my departure and planned on passing through the kitchen to the servants' door as inconspicuously as possible. But Mr. Ford was not going to let that happen.

Spotting me as I landed on the final step, he pulled me into the larder and closed the door behind us in a clear attempt to avoid the prying eyes of Hilda and Anne, who were working in the scullery. "Where do you think you're going with that traveling bag, Miss Kelley?" he whispered.

"You were right, Mr. Ford. It always ends badly for the servants."

Folding my hands into his, he sighed. "The masters are all cut from the same cloth, slaver or not."

"Mr. Carnegie is not to blame. In fact, I am in his debt. I brought this situation upon myself by pretending to be someone I am not."

"If that was a crime, we'd all be in jail, Miss Kelley. We are all pretending in this life. One way or another."

A loud thud sounded throughout the kitchen. Assuming it was Hilda or Anne dropping a platter or bowl upon the floor, we grew even quieter. I willed my breath to still.

"Is she in the kitchen, Mother?" a male voice yelled.

It was not Hilda or Anne making all the noise in the kitchen. It was Andrew.

The recognizable footfall of Mrs. Carnegie clattered on the pine floorboards. She was following Andrew into the kitchen. "I told you she was gone, Andra. You can look in the kitchen, in the servants' quarters, in the library, in any nook or cranny of this house, and you will not find her. She gave her notice, and she left." My mistress was trying to sound matter-of-fact, but she could not keep the self-satisfied tone out of her voice.

"Clara wouldn't just leave, Mother."

"Maybe you don't know Clara as well as you think you do," she taunted him.

Was she going to reveal my secret? Please no, I prayed, not before I got the money out of the account. My heart started beating louder, and I began to feel nauseated. I mouthed a silent Hail Mary that Mrs. Carnegie would keep her word that if I left without notifying Andrew, she would not tell him the truth about me.

"It's you who doesn't know Clara. She wouldn't leave without saying goodbye. In fact, she wouldn't leave at all." He took three deliberate-sounding steps. I imagined he was drawing closer to his mother. "What did you do to her?"

"Why would I bother to do anything to her, Andra? She's just a lady's maid. One I can easily replace. As can you." Ever crafty, Mrs. Carnegie was offering Andrew a path out of his tirade by reminding him of my status. It was an honorable way to walk away from me. "Anyway, why do you care so much?"

"Clara means a great deal to me, Mother, whether you like it or not. We had plans, she and I." Hearing Andrew say those words, hearing him defy his mother for me, I was tempted to step out of the larder and reveal myself to him. But what would become of those feelings when his mother divulged my true identity? What retribution might he exact? The tiny chance that he might still love me when faced with the truth was not worth the damage he might inflict on my family. I had to leave him.

Andrew took one step more, and his voice grew even louder. "I will look in every corner of this house, interview every servant, locate her family, even visit rail stations and carriage stops to track her down. Make no mistake, Mother. I will find her."

The sound of their footsteps leaving the kitchen echoed in the larder where Mr. Ford and I were hiding. I started crying, and he hugged me tightly. Sinking into the warm folds of his generous build, I was consoled for a moment. "You've been a good friend to me, Mr. Ford. My only one in this house," I whispered, choking back more tears.

"You've been a good friend to me too, Miss Kelley. The only one who ever covered for me with a master or mistress. And the only one who ever helped me with my family," he whispered back.

"I wish you all the luck in the world finding them. General Howard is still searching."

I spotted Mrs. Stewart's inventory of the larder hanging on the wall, with a slate pencil on the shelf nearby. Hurriedly, I tore off a corner of the inventory and scribbled down the Lambs' address. Handing it to Mr. Ford, I said, "This is for you alone. Please let me know when you find your family."

"Thank you. But you better get going, unless you want to be found."

I slipped out of Mr. Ford's embrace, and he stepped out of the larder to make sure no one was in the hallway. I heard the rising chatter of Hilda and Anne, who'd grown silent during the confrontation between

Andrew and his mother, and prayed they'd stay put for at least another minute so I could sneak out the servants' door.

Mr. Ford stuck his head back into the larder. "Come on," he said, guiding me to leave.

With a final squeeze of his hand, I stepped through the servants' door out into the night. The moon swelled in the sky, lighting my way to Reynolds Street. Clear and crisp, the air felt refreshing. My lungs expanded, and I breathed more deeply than I had in some time.

I had played at so many roles in the years since landing in America, I had lost myself. Sacrificed myself to one set of ideals and then another — American and Irish, commercial and altruistic, Fenian and Chartist and Democratic, Andrew's and my own, new and old — until I no longer knew my own mind. No more.

I stepped out into the night, onto my own fresh path.

EPILOGUE

October 14, 1900
Pittsburgh, Pennsylvania

I unfolded the letter, spreading it out over the walnut surface of the study desk. The paper on which it was written, over thirty years old now, was nearly translucent with wear. I'd read and reread the words until I had them memorized, but still I carried the letter with me every day since I received it. It had become almost like a talisman for me, a reminder of the righteousness of the path I chose. Before I stepped through the doors of his building today, I needed to read it one last time.

The script on the first sheaf was written by a man I did not know, at the behest of a man I once knew very well. It was dated January 1869.

Dear Clara,

I don't know what became of you when you walked out that door in 1867, but I hope this letter reaches you somehow and finds you well. I know how you struggled with your choice that April day, and I wanted you to know it wasn't for nothing. You did the right thing. You'll see that when you read this paper I found crumpled up in the master's study.

Every time I look into the eyes of my Ruth and my Mabel, I see your eyes. I have you to thank for getting me back my family.

John Ford

Sliding Mr. Ford's letter to the right, I stared down at the undated, second sheaf of paper. It contained handwriting very familiar to me, not only because I'd studied the words. I knew the script intimately before the letter was ever written. It belonged to Andrew.

Dearest Clara,

You found me just before I was beyond all hope of recovery. Your morals, your convictions, and your honesty brought me back from the brink, away from the idolatry of money and self. You reminded me of who I really am, who I was meant to be, and who I can help. For that, I will be forever grateful.

I do not know why you left me. Knowing the goodness of your heart, I can only assume you had reasons of the utmost importance. You have left me utterly heartbroken and inexorably changed. And although I forgive you, I will never forget you.

I have searched for you for well over a year. I have hired detectives and bounty hunters and I have employed my own security men as well. They have looked in Pittsburgh, Philadelphia, New York, Boston, and pretty much everywhere in between. Even the staunchest of private detectives found not a trace of you after you left the bank in Pittsburgh. It was as if you never existed. But you did exist, Clara. You stamped your mark upon me, and I will stamp your mark upon the world to prove your existence and remind myself to stay your course. As you would have desired, any fortune I amass will be dedicated for the betterment of mankind, particularly the education and improvement of the poorer and immigrant classes by the establishment of free libraries. I only wish —

I always wondered how he planned on ending the letter. As I was smoothing the letter out over the desk surface — it was still crumpled after all these years — a little girl wandered into the study.

"Are you ready yet, Great-Auntie?" Maeve called me Great-Auntie due to my age, even though I was technically a cousin of sorts. She was the little granddaughter of my beloved cousins Patrick and Maeve, for whom she was named.

Was I ready to see what I had wrought? I nodded, and together, we donned our coats and stepped out of the Lambs' home.

One harrowing carriage ride later, over the uneven cobblestones of Forbes Avenue, Maeve and I stepped out to examine Andrew's building. She gripped my hand as we climbed the steep steps to the three arched bronze doors guarding the entrance. Occasionally, we would stop, giggle, and catch our breath. The stairs were a challenging climb for us both, although we were equally determined to reach the top.

I wondered what patrons of the building would make of us if they happened to glance out the window. Would they wonder at the relationship between the auburn-haired girl and the petite woman with gray hair streaked red who held the girl's hand? Would they simply assume I was her grandmother, or would they guess at our more complicated stories?

On the first landing, Maeve looked up at the letters carved into the granite facade above the doors. "What does that say, Great-Auntie?"

"Free to the People," I answered with the lilt I hadn't managed to shake in the thirty years I'd lived in America. I lived among too many fellow Irish folk in Boston, the city where I'd settled after fleeing Pittsburgh, to do anything but reinforce my accent, particularly since the patients I served in my nursing practice were invariably Irish. Not to mention I'd been successful in shipping my family to Boston with some of the funds Andrew gave me, so I was greeted with their Galway lilt most days.

"What does that mean?" Maeve asked.

"It means that this marvelous library with all its books and treasures inside is free for all people to use. It is a wondrous gift that allows all people to become educated, even when they cannot afford school."

"Like you, Great-Auntie Clara? You're a nurse, and you need a special school for that." The proud way she said *nurse* made me smile. Perhaps one day, I'd inspire Maeve to pursue a career. It almost made worthwhile the sacrifice I'd made to forge my independent path — a family of my own. Women, who only recently could climb above their born stations, could not have both. In the end, I do not think I would have wanted marriage or a family with anyone but Andrew. I guessed he felt much the same way, as it had taken him twenty years after I left to finally marry.

Continuing our ascent after stopping for another breath, we scaled the next set of stairs to the second and final landing. I reached for one of the bronze doors, but before I pulled it open, Maeve said, "There are more letters, Great-Auntie." She pointed to a granite expanse above the columns that sat atop the doors. "What does that say?"

"It says Carnegie Library."

"What's a Carnegie?"

I laughed. Andrew had grown so famous in the years since I left him, it was hard to imagine that even one as young as Maeve would not know him. "A Carnegie is a 'who,' not a 'what.' In this case, Carnegie refers to Andrew Carnegie, who is the man who built this free library and thousands more libraries with his own money. A man who gave the gift of books and education to every person, regardless of how much money they had." A small, private smile crossed my lips as I thought on the role I played in planting the seed for these libraries — for his vast charitable works, actually — in Andrew's mind.

"Did he give the people any other gifts?"

From the way Maeve's eyes sparkled, I knew she was imagining the sorts of gifts she received at Christmas, china dolls and sugary confections. "Oh yes, Maeve. Not only has Mr. Carnegie established hundreds of libraries around the world, maybe thousands one day, but he has also created educational institutions, museums, and performance halls, and there's talk that he will be forming institutes for peace, teaching, and the recognition of heroes."

Maeve's eyes widened, and she said, "He must have a lot of money."

"By all accounts, he is the richest man in the world. Richer than any man who has come before him or will likely follow." Knowing Andrew's intellect and nature as I did, his status did not surprise me, nor did his continued ruthlessness — as evidenced by the hard line he'd taken against steelworkers in the Homestead Strike — which he undoubtedly justified to himself as helping to raise money for his causes. Only rarely did I feel remorse at not sharing that ascent with him, at sacrificing the chance at love for my family. I regularly consoled myself with the role I played in inspiring Andrew's philanthropy, the scope of which would better the lives of thousands, if not millions, of people. Who knew if I would have had the same impact if I'd stayed by his side? Perhaps his memory of me was my strongest legacy. "And the rumor is that he plans to give it all away."

"Did you ever meet him, Great-Auntie Clara? You know a lot about him."

I laughed again. "I did, little Maeve. I did. In fact, I knew him well. When I lived in Pittsburgh, long ago, I was his maid."

AUTHOR'S NOTE

Carnegie's Maid, with its auspicious story of immigrants and the genesis of philanthropy, was over one hundred years in the making. Unlike my other books for which I can pinpoint a particular historical document or relic that gave rise to the story, the initial spark behind *Carnegie's Maid* did not come from a single artifact or piece of artwork. The idea began with my own family over a hundred years ago, when my Irish immigrant ancestors, deprived of schooling and opportunities, used the first Carnegie library in Pittsburgh to educate themselves and their families. Utilizing the resources of the Carnegie libraries — the vast array of books and the programming — they transformed their families from impoverished mill and steel workers to highly educated lawyers, doctors, and professors, some of whom attended Ivy League universities. Andrew Carnegie has loomed large in my

435

family lore for generations, and I always wondered why the tycoon, long-rumored to be heartless, became the world's first true philanthropist.

After I learned that the impetus for Carnegie's vast philanthropy began not later in life when he was established as the world's richest man but in December 1868 when, at the age of thirty-three, he wrote a letter to himself pledging to focus on the education and "improvement of the poorer classes," I became intrigued by his metamorphosis from success-focused industrialist. After all, his transformation led directly to the transformation of my own family. And when I discovered that historians had long debated the origin of Carnegie's change and this mysterious letter he kept for the rest of his life, I began my investigation and tried to answer that long-standing historical question with a research-based fictional story. I followed him as he traveled across the United States, including a nascent New York City, and throughout Europe during his "Grand Tour" in my efforts to understand why he changed into the man who would, ultimately, become the author of *The Gospel of Wealth,* a book that sparked wide-scale philanthropy, and give away the bulk of his enormous fortune.

Given that some historians had theorized that a personal relationship might have altered Carnegie, but could find no definitive evidence as to who that person might have been, I began to fill in the gaps with my own ancestry. My own female ancestors had served as domestics in the mansions of nineteenth-century industrialists. Why couldn't an Irish immigrant woman like my ancestors, intelligent but without access to formal education, have inspired Andrew Carnegie to change and impact the lives of thousands of others through the formation of the first free libraries and other education-based organizations? After all, Andrew Carnegie himself started out as an impoverished immigrant, who was bright but had no access to education. So, in their honor, I created Clara Kelley and placed her into the very real historical tale of Andrew Carnegie — to give voice to the otherwise silent stories of the thousands of immigrants who built our country. Then and now.

READING GROUP GUIDE

1. *Carnegie's Maid* opens with Clara Kelley's experience immigrating to America from Ireland in the 1860s. Do any aspects of Clara's immigration surprise you, such as the ship voyage or the arrival inspection? If you were in Clara's shoes, how would you feel going through the immigration process? Does Clara's experience mirror that of you or someone in your own family?

2. How does Clara's identity as an Irish Catholic immigrant affect her in America? If immigrating today, what similar or different challenges would Clara face?

3. Andrew Carnegie's history has been described as the greatest rags-to-riches American story, and in some ways, Clara's story mirrors his. Did you find her rise — though not as meteoric as Andrew's due

439

to gender constrictions — believable? If not, would you find it more believable if she'd been a man? If the story were set in today's world, how would Andrew's and Clara's stories change? Would Clara still face the same challenges?

4. Compare and contrast Andrew and Clara. How are they similar? How are they different? Who do you relate to more?

5. While Clara inhabits and works in a traditional nineteenth-century women's realm, she aspires to achievements that would have been perceived as exclusively male. Discuss the spheres available to women at that time and the ways both Clara and Margaret Carnegie operated outside those spheres. Did anything about their allotted domains surprise you? What do you think about the capacity for change in the women's realm? Do you think there is still an opportunity and need for change today?

6. The novel takes place in a unique moment in American history — just as the Civil War ends and the Gilded Age begins, showcasing a world on the cusp of tremendous change industrially, politically, eco-

nomically, and socially. How does this historical setting affect the characters? What role, if any, does it play in shaping their lives? Does it provide them with opportunities they would not otherwise have?

7. What is something you learned about this time period or Andrew Carnegie that fascinated you? If you could live during the Gilded Age, would you? What would your life be like?

8. Commitment and duty to her family in Ireland influence Clara tremendously. How does this sense of duty motivate her decisions and actions? How does it affect her ability to stay on the path she's carved for herself? Is Andrew prompted by the same responsibilities, or does he have different drives? If you were in Clara's shoes, what would drive you forward?

9. Andrew and Clara's master-servant relationship changes during the course of the book. How does this evolution happen? What do you think it was that drew them together? Do you think their relationship could have lasted longer under different circumstances? How did you feel

about the outcome of their relationship?

10. The title of the novel is subject to several interpretations. What meanings can you glean from the title, and how did your understanding of the meaning of *Carnegie's Maid* change from the beginning to the end of the novel, if at all?

11. Andrew Carnegie is a well-known industrialist who was the richest man in the world in his day and the founder of modern philanthropy. What was your understanding of him before you read this novel, and how did your understanding change, if it all? Did you know about his philanthropy and role in the formation of the modern library system? If you had the fortune of Carnegie, what cause would you devote yourself to?

12. While the world of *Carnegie's Maid* is grounded in facts, Clara Kelley herself is a fictional character, although her immigrant experience and her lady's maid role are founded upon historical research. Would the story be different for you if Clara were entirely nonfiction?

A CONVERSATION
WITH THE AUTHOR

What inspired you to write *Carnegie's Maid*? Did something particular draw you to Andrew Carnegie's story?

Growing up, I was surrounded by Irish grandmothers and great-aunts who told tales of our immigrant ancestors who, after enduring arduous journeys to this country and working in mills, mines, and as domestics, elevated themselves through the first Carnegie Library in Pittsburgh, among other institutions. Utilizing those resources, they spurred on their families to become educated professionals. So, you can imagine that Andrew Carnegie has always been a topic of conversation and reverence in my family (despite some of the negative publicity he generated), and I was always insatiably curious about him and his drive to become the world's first philanthropist. *Carnegie's Maid* was born from that curiosity.

Andrew Carnegie is a well-known historical figure who many may feel they already know. What challenges did you face when writing Carnegie as a more well-rounded character? What preconceptions did you have to overcome?

Many people are familiar with Andrew Carnegie's reputation as a ruthless businessman, especially the role he may have played in the Homestead Strike of 1892, which grew out of a conflict between the Carnegie Steel Company and the iron and steel workers' union. And while that reputation is certainly deserved and I do delve into the questionable practices behind the astonishing growth of his businesses — his insider trading in particular — I hope I fleshed out other aspects of the man behind the icon: his relationship with his mother and brother, the singular nature of his intellect and ascent, the kindnesses of which he could be capable, and, importantly for my story, the sense of obligation he developed to immigrants less fortunate than himself.

Carnegie's Maid relies on an extensive amount of research. What does your research process look like? What usually comes first, your idea for the story

or your research of a topic?

Because I write historical fiction that aims to uncover hidden women's stories, the idea for my story and the research process generally occur simultaneously. As I'm reading about a particular time period I find intriguing, I will come across an event, and I'll wonder about the women, who are rarely mentioned in historical accounts. What were they doing at the time? What was their perspective of or involvement in the event? As I envision the women, a story will reveal itself to me. Then I really dig into the research — original source material when I can get it — excavating whatever details are necessary from the past to craft the world and the women. While I began *Carnegie's Maid* with a preexisting interest in Andrew Carnegie, the story did not begin to form until I began the research and saw Clara's story there, and then my usual process took hold.

Clara's story is, at its core, a tale of a young female immigrant forging a path for herself in America. How did you bring to life Clara's immigration story? What experiences did you draw on?

Well, as I mentioned, I grew up with plentiful family tales — tall and otherwise

— about my immigrant heritage upon which I could draw. For example, Clara's story of mistaken identity — when she steps off the boat from Ireland to hear her name being called from the docks for a position that belongs to *another* Clara Kelley — supposedly happened to one of my ancestors. And my great-aunts shared stories about their mothers and aunts who'd served as maids in the "big houses," so that served as an incredible, authentic resource. But when the personal familial well ran dry, or when I needed more details, context, and information to really enliven the narrative, I relied on accounts of other immigrants who endured similar things. The newspaper ads of immigrants searching for family members, who'd traveled ahead of them and then became lost, were particularly moving. I was also amazingly fortunate to have nearby the Frick Pittsburgh, which is a perfectly preserved late nineteenth-century house museum of Andrew Carnegie's colleague Henry Clay Frick. The curators there not only gave me access to material, but also gave me personal tours of the parts of the house that maids would have used, which allowed me to envision the life of a lady's maid in great detail.

Which character did you connect with more, Carnegie or Clara? Which was the greater challenge to write?

I definitely connected more with Clara, particularly because I felt like I knew women like her. Those grandmothers and great-aunts that I've mentioned were all intelligent and outside-the-box thinkers, determined to advance themselves and their families by any means necessary. Scrappy, just like Clara. Carnegie was more of a challenge because I'd always thought of him in his guise as an older, esteemed industrialist, not as a young man. I enjoyed digging his younger self out of the past and trying to discover what made him into the unique person he was — finding the man instead of the myth.

How would you describe Carnegie and Clara's relationship?

I envisioned Clara as a female version of Andrew, in some ways. Like Andrew, she is a very bright but uneducated immigrant who is searching for ways to climb above her allocated station at a particular moment in American history when such ascent is possible. This similarity attracts them to each other, but ultimately, it is the differences in their drives — avarice and greed for its own sake (and his mother and brother) motivates him as a young man, while she is propelled by her duty toward the family she left behind in Ireland — that creates a wedge between them.

Andrew Carnegie has left behind a legacy of philanthropy and a devotion to libraries and other causes that aim to help the underprivileged and marginalized. If you had the means of Carnegie, what causes would you support?

That's a tough question, because there are so many worthy causes, so many needy people. But, if I had Carnegie's means, I would certainly support two of his primary causes: (1) libraries and education, particularly for the underprivileged, and (2) the bolstering of immigrants to this country. These two core beliefs underpin the formation of our country and the elevation of my own family. After that, I'd likely follow Bill and Melinda Gates's example. I like their philanthropic philosophy of seeing equal value in all lives and making the broadest possible impact in improving everyone's basic quality of life.

ACKNOWLEDGMENTS

How can I possibly list all the people to whom I'm indebted for *Carnegie's Maid* when they include a long line of ancestors who braved the journey to this country and managed to elevate my family such that I received the education necessary to write this book? Since I cannot, as some of their names have been lost to time, I must simply express my endless gratitude to them, for all their unimaginable sacrifices.

As to those I can name, as always, I must begin with my champion, my brilliant agent, Laura Dail, who guides and supports me in countless ways. I am so fortunate to have the enthusiasm and tireless backing of the phenomenal Sourcebooks team, particularly my wonderful and talented editor, Shana Drehs; the amazing Dominque Raccah; not to mention the fantastic Valerie Pierce, Heidi Weiland, Heather Moore, Lathea Williams, Heather Hall, Stephanie Graham,

Margaret Coffee, Sean Murray, Beth Oleniczak, Tiffany Schultz, Adrienne Krogh, Heather Morris, Danielle McNaughton, and Travis Hasenour. And I am incredibly appreciative of all the remarkable booksellers and librarians who have been supportive of me and my work, including the staff of the Carnegie Libraries of Pittsburgh and the Frick Pittsburgh, whose resources and knowledge were indispensable to *Carnegie's Maid*.

My extended family and friends have been essential to this process, especially my Sewickley crew, Illana Raia, Kelly Close, and Ponny Conomos Jahn. Yet, it is my boys, Jim, Jack, and Ben, to whom I owe the greatest thanks, for they make *everything* all worthwhile.

ABOUT THE AUTHOR

Marie Benedict is a lawyer with more than ten years' experience as a litigator at two of the country's premier law firms and for Fortune 500 companies. She is a magna cum laude graduate of Boston College, with a focus in history and art history, and a cum laude graduate of the Boston University School of Law. She is also the author of *The Other Einstein* and a forthcoming novel about World War II. She lives in Pittsburgh with her family.

The employees of Thorndike Press hope you have enjoyed this Large Print book. All our Thorndike, Wheeler, and Kennebec Large Print titles are designed for easy reading, and all our books are made to last. Other Thorndike Press Large Print books are available at your library, through selected bookstores, or directly from us.

For information about titles, please call:
(800) 223-1244

or visit our website at:
gale.com/thorndike

To share your comments, please write:

Publisher
Thorndike Press
10 Water St., Suite 310
Waterville, ME 04901